MacLain's Wife

JILLIAN HART

Copyright © 2013 By Jillian Hart

First Published 2000
By Zebra Books Kensington Publishing Corp.

Cover art by Kimberly Killion, Hot Damn Designs

E-book formatted by Jessica Lewis
http://www.Author'sLifeSaver.com

All rights reserved.

ISBN: 1482697580
ISBN-13: 978-1482697582

CHAPTER ONE

"Pa, is today the day the stage is comin'?" Emily MacLain flipped twin ponytails behind her thin shoulders and ignored her steaming plate of pancakes.

Ben set the tin of maple syrup on the table. His heart warmed as always at the sight of his daughter's happy anticipation. Her eyes sparkled. A broad grin lit her face. How Emily was looking forward to meeting her new mother. "Yes, today is the day."

"*Finally*. It's taken *forever* to get here." Emily sighed with deliberate drama, then stabbed her fork directly into the pancake pile.

"Miss Curtis only agreed to our proposal last month." Ben grabbed the blue enamel pot and grimaced. He'd over-boiled the coffee again.

Looked like he wasn't the only one who would be happy with a woman in this house. Maybe, if he could cook worth a darn, he wouldn't have to get married. But he couldn't cook anything but pancakes, bacon and eggs—and those not very well. His stomach hardened at the sight of the fried eggs congealed at the bottom of the blackened frying pan.

Yes, it was a good thing Pauline Curtis arrived today. He couldn't take one more meal of his own cooking.

"I hope Miss Curtis is nice. And laughs a lot just like Adella's ma." Emily took a big sip of fresh milk. "And I hope she knows lots of songs and sings all the time."

"I hope so, too." *Please, be all that Emily needs.* Ben hoped Pauline Curtis was a kind woman, not dour and sour. Little Emily deserved a mother who would love her, a mother who would stay.

Polly Brown rolled her eyes at the skinny stick of a woman dressed in ruffles and frippery. Not that she usually spent time in the company of such people, but crammed in the confines of the stagecoach, she had little choice. She sneezed again at Pauline Curtis's sweet, high-scented perfume that hung in the air like fog. Even though she tried not to watch, her gaze kept straying back to the young woman who dabbed at huge, continuous tears with her expensive lace handkerchief.

What on earth did a woman like that have to cry about?

Polly knew darn well that she was being uncharitable. Heck, maybe she was even a little bit envious. After all, she wore only a pair of men's trousers and a cotton shirt, rolled up at the sleeves. Her boots were worn and scuffed. And her hair, well, there just wasn't much she could do with her shoulder-length brown locks.

She wasn't a golden blonde or a striking ebony-haired beauty. Nor would she ever be. She was just plain Polly Brown, the daughter of an outlaw, who could outshoot nearly every man she'd ever met. She was not in the same class as delicate Pauline Curtis.

"Roland said he wasn't ready to get married,"

Pauline sniffled into her handkerchief. "And I loved him so."

"Well, with the babe in your belly, you'll need a husband soon," the old matron beside her whispered. "Be grateful your father knows of a decent man who will take on a woman, sight unseen. He's desperate, he is. Says there's not a marriageable woman in the whole of Montana Territory. And him with a little daughter to care for."

"I just wish Roland would marry me." Pauline burst into sobbing tears. "I don't want to be with a rough, uneducated sheriff."

Polly pushed her hat over her eyes and sank back into the seat. All that heartbreak made it too noisy to take a nap. Good thing she made up her mind a long time ago never to bother with love and marriage. Look at all the tears it required.

No, she was content with the choices she'd made, content that her only companion was a six-shooter strapped to her right thigh. If only she wasn't running for her life, everything would be perfect.

Gunfire popped outside the stage. Polly snapped open her eyes and sat up. Across the aisle, proper Miss Pauline Curtis let out a shriek.

"Road agents! Indians!"

What use was a female who got scared at every little thing? Polly had been handling ruthless robbers and rampaging Indians for as long as she could remember. All it required was a six-shooter and a little bit of attitude.

"We never should have come," Pauline whined.

Really. Maybe Miss Curtis didn't have everything after all. She could use a bit of backbone and some common sense.

Polly always kept her gun loaded, so all she had to do was unsnap her holster and wrap her hand around the comforting walnut handle. "Keep quiet," she advised the others.

"Nana, she's got a gun!" Privileged Pauline gasped in horror, her eyes widening as if she'd seen a two-headed serpent.

Polly kicked open the stage door and cocked her

revolver. She saw three saddled horses tied to a low pine bough. None of the horses were breathing hard nor sweating, so they had not been ridden hard. She heard men's voices up ahead and climbed out of the coach, keeping careful watch.

"It's just a fellow talking with the driver." She released the hammer but kept the gun in hand in case there was some trouble. Maybe the man just needed a ride to the next town, but maybe he wanted something else.

"Women carrying guns. What's next?" Pauline sniffed as she climbed out of the cramped stage, lifting her nose as she passed.

Polly bowed her chin. Fine, she wasn't a high society lady, not even a pretty, normal kind of woman. How could she be? Her ma had died when she was just a child. And Pa had been busy with his work. He was a rough man and hadn't known anything about little girls—and hadn't wanted to.

Well, if she had been raised right and could wear pretty dresses, she would not be mean like Miss Pauline Curtis.

"Roland! It's you!" In a flurry of ribbons and ruffles, Polly watched Miss Curtis grab up her skirts and run toward the newcomer. They entwined in a tangle of arms and apologies and what sounded like wet kisses.

It just went to show how little sense a woman like that had. Men were nothing but trouble. Polly had learned long ago that men only wanted two things. One involved getting what they wanted—money, revenge, prestige— with their revolvers. And the other involved getting what they wanted with, well, a body part she was too embarrassed to think about.

"Praise be!" The old nana tossed her thanks toward the heavens. "Forget Sheriff MacLain. Pauline will have her prince."

Personally, Polly would be thankful if the stage could get a move on. She had Bad Bart Dixon tailing her with a loaded gun and a grudge. A real big grudge. The problem with Dixon was simple—he was the one man she couldn't outshoot, and he was a gunfighter who wouldn't take no for an answer.

Yes, it would be just fine with her if Pauline's prince would hurry up with whatever it was he wanted.

"Roland has asked me to marry him instead of going to that awful old sheriff." Pauline burst into sight. "He brought horses so we can start heading home right away."

"How wonderful. After all, Roland is a banker's son." The old nana embraced her charge with great enthusiasm. "Let's hurry."

Polly holstered her revolver. It didn't look like she was going to need it. Now the stage was empty. It might be a lonely ride, but at least she wouldn't have to keep breathing in Pauline's nose-stinging perfume.

"What about my baggage?" the pampered princess whined.

"Leave it." Roland, a strong-shouldered man wearing a bowler hat and the nicest black suit Polly had ever seen, strode back into view. "The driver is angry because I've made him late. And I didn't bring a pack-horse to carry your trunks. I'll buy you anything you want once we reach a civilized town."

"Oh, Roland." Pauline threw herself into his strong arms once again.

Polly strode back to the stage, shaking her head. If Pauline knew what was good for her, she'd give that slick-looking Roland a kick in the shins and make her own way in the world.

"Hey, you." Pauline's sharp voice sliced through the air thick with chalk-dry Montana dust. "You, gun-toting girl."

Polly spun around, spine stiff, half in and half out of the coach.

"You might as well have my things. Looks like you could use them. And a bath."

Pauline flounced off. Polly bit her lip. A bath? She was dusty, not dirty. And there was nothing wrong with her perfectly good trousers and shirt.

But as she dropped into her seat and the stagecoach lumbered into motion, her heart felt heavy. It wasn't just Pauline's words, but her attitude as well.

What Polly wouldn't give to be a fine young woman with her hair all twisted up in a knot and those frilly little curls falling all around her face. And a real dress that flounced when she walked.

Then no one would make fun of her when she rode into town. Or look down at her and say what a pity it was when women tried to be like men.

She just didn't know any other way. How could she? She never had a woman around to show her womanly ways. She'd never had anyone to help her. She was alone. Alone, making her way in a world not always kind to females.

As the morning sun rose higher in the sky, Polly started thinking about the things Pauline Curtis had left behind. There was a satchel stashed under the seat, forgotten in the hurry to be with broad-shouldered Roland. Should she look inside it?

Half of it was curiosity over what a proper sort of woman carried in a satchel. The other part was the knowledge that maybe it was something she wanted. After all, Pauline said she could have her things.

Heck, taking a peek wouldn't hurt. She knelt down and tugged the satchel out by one strap. She pulled open the unsnapped top and peered inside, then withdrew two pairs of white gloves, both spotless and brand-new looking. Another lace handkerchief. And a folded piece of paper. Now that was interesting.

Polly smoothed the parchment and studied the letters written there. She had some schooling, not much, but enough to recognize a few of the words. Why, it looked as if Miss Pauline Curtis was going to work for a sheriff in Indian Trails, the next stage stop. She was going to cook and clean for them. And a little girl was mentioned.

Hmm. Polly considered that piece of information. The sheriff of Indian Trails wouldn't know his housekeeper wasn't coming. And there was no way that sheriff knew what Pauline Curtis looked like.

Hmm. Polly leaned back in the seat. She found more beautiful things in the satchel. Pretty-smelling soap. A silver mirror and brush set. A bonnet the color of a Montana summer sky. Why, it was an awfully pretty bonnet. All blue, her favorite color.

In a snap she tossed off her Stetson. The bonnet fit right on her head, despite the lump of her ponytail. A blue feather plumed over her left ear and tickled just a little. She caught hold of the velvet ribbons and tied them in a big bow beneath her chin.

Why, she'd never worn a woman's garment in her whole life. She probably didn't look very good in it. Pa had always been honest in his comments about her appearance over the years. She knew she was no beauty.

But curiosity got the best of her and she grabbed that engraved, silver-framed hand mirror. A woman she didn't recognize gazed back at her in the beveled surface. She saw her own blue eyes, and yes, that was her face, but she looked completely different. Almost fancy, the way a real lady did.

She thought of the clothes up in those three trunks. Pauline Curds had been just about her size. And those trunks were now hers. Suddenly she knew what she would do with all those frilly garments that were probably stuffed inside.

Even Bad Bart Dixon wouldn't recognize her dressed up in a city woman's finery.

CHAPTER TWO

"There she is, Pa!" Emily bounded up from the table. The water glasses sloshed and her chair scraped against the floor, startling the serenity of the nearly empty diner. Ice cream forgotten, the little girl raced toward the door, braids and skirts flying.

"I guess we'll be right back, Martha."

"I'll keep your table for you," the matronly woman called from the back room.

His piece of apple pie could wait. In fact, he had planned all along to take Miss Curtis straight away to the diner and treat her to dinner and dessert, but the stage was late. Emily's disappointment had touched his heart and he had hoped a bowl of vanilla ice cream would help pass the time while they waited for her new mother and his new bride.

Bride. He had to admit, it was damn strange. But marrying her was the only way. The other five domestics he'd hired had never arrived. Each one of them received marriage proposals before they ever stepped foot off the stage in Indian Trails. If he wanted someone to take care of Emily, then he was just going to have to marry her.

As long as she showed up. Ben's guts twisted. Emily

was counting on this so much. She'd talked of nothing else.

Just don't disappoint my daughter, Miss Curtis, and I will forgive any flaw, and be the best husband to you I can be. Just show up.

And she had. The way Ben figured it, he owed Pauline Curtis the world.

He stepped out onto the dusty street just as the stagecoach's door popped open. Emily was already standing before it expectantly, chin up, wind snapping her drooping blue skirts.

Maybe Miss Pauline knew how to iron, too. Cook and clean and do laundry and sing songs. Yes, that would be mighty fine indeed. He missed a woman's touch in his home, her gentleness in his life.

A delicate ankle displayed itself, encased in shining black shoes. He saw blue skirts edged with ruffles and lace, fluttering to hide any farther view of that ankle. A woman, young, slender and finely made emerged from the shadowed coach and into the sunlit afternoon.

Jerrod Mitchell, whose family owned the hotel, dashed up to offer his hand to the beautiful eastern lady. A fresh-faced angel descended from that stage. She was all brown curls, pure blue eyes and grace.

That was Miss Pauline Curtis? Ben's knees gave out. He couldn't believe his luck. She was beautiful. She looked kind. And she smiled. A great big dazzling, friendly smile that made Jerrod Mitchell sputter as he helped her to the ground and eased every last one of Ben's worries.

This was the woman they had been praying for.

In all her twenty-two years, Polly had never been helped down from a stagecoach by any man, let alone the eager-eyed businessman who dashed toward her as if she were a fine-blooded horse up for grabs.

Well, it only went to show how well appearances could deceive. Beneath the satin dress and scratchy petticoats, she was still plain old Polly Brown.

Her foot hadn't even touched the ground when a little girl dashed up to her. Head tipped back, blue eyes shining, brown curls rapidly escaping loosely plaited braids, the girl gazed up at her as if she were a princess. "Are you Miss Pauline?"

"Well, uh . . ."

"I'm Emily. Did you get my last letter? I've been waiting for you forever. How come the stage takes so long? How come horses don't go faster?"

"Uh . . ." Goodness. She couldn't think of a single word to say to this adorable little girl, talking with her head cocked to one side, hardly breaking for breath.

"I'm just glad you're here. Wanna know something?"

"Sure."

"My pa is sure glad you're here, too. He wrecks his coffee every morning and swears and swears. Do you know how to make something besides pancakes?"

Polly's heart warmed. Well, she certainly remembered the letter that she'd tried to decipher—the one she'd found in Pauline's satchel about the housework and the child. But she had no idea the little girl mentioned would be meeting the stage. Or be so cute and charming and sweet. And such a talker!

"I get awful tired of pancakes. Pa can't make anything else but pancakes and eggs. And I hate eggs. They're all slimy."

"Especially the white part." Polly wasn't fond of eggs either.

"Miss?" A man's deep voice interrupted.

Polly's knees weakened. Goodness! She would recognize that voice anywhere. And the distinctive clink of spurs as Bad Bart Dixon strolled closer with his slight limp. The limp she had given him. She looked up and there he was. Dressed all in black from his rumpled, sweat-stained hat to his scuffed, sharp-toed boots.

Her dreams of simply walking unrecognized and

unnoticed off the stage fell like spit in the wind. She couldn't very well admit she was Polly Brown, sometime bounty hunter and gunslinger, the very female who had shot him in the . . . well, in a very private place.

"Is there another woman on that stage?" Bart asked politely, suddenly a gentleman.

Polly glanced over her shoulder. There was no one there. Bart was speaking to her! Why, he didn't recognize her. Relief blended with a strange dizziness as she realized what she'd narrowly escaped. She had been mistakenly thinking Bart was trailing her, when he had been waiting for her at this stop all along.

His eager hands twitched above his double holsters, one strapped to each thigh. He was ready to shoot. Polly thought of her own guns, safely tucked away in the satchel. Fear crept along her spine, gathering like little droplets of sweat. She was unarmed, and that meant she was defenseless against this man, who'd sworn to kill her.

Please, don't let him recognize me. She would be a goner for sure. Polly dipped her chin, then changed her voice so it sounded a little higher. "There's no one in the stage, sir."

"Dangnabbit!" the outlaw cursed. "I guess I got to backtrack and hunt that hellcat down."

He strode away, muttering about women who needed to be taught a lesson.

Thank goodness. Polly shivered. She couldn't believe she'd gotten out of that one. Even if her revolvers had been cocked and ready, Bart could have still outshot her. And right in front of this little girl!

Thank heavens for Pauline Curtis, Roland's undying love, and Pauline's impatience that made her leave her trunks behind.

"My pa ought to chase that bad man off," Emily declared, fisting both hands over her hips. "My pa is the sheriff. And he's a darn good one. He just got shot last week."

"Shot? Goodness." Now that Bart was out of earshot,

there was no sense in letting this sweet little girl think she'd found her new housekeeper. "Where's your pa now?"

"He's right there." Emily pointed across the street at a strong, handsome man striding toward them, hands in fists, broad shoulders set.

"The one right there. Just in front of the livery?"

"Yep." Emily beamed. "Ain't he handsome?"

Handsome? Polly's gaze swept over his magnificent body, from broad shoulders to lean, powerful legs. He walked with authority, and his face gave the overall impression of dignity and high standards. The air wedged sideways in Polly's chest. Her heart forgot to beat, just looking at him.

Goodness. This was the type of upstanding, decent and very handsome man who despised her the most. The type that never stepped foot inside saloons, and expected a woman to wear these silly petticoats and bat their eyelids and faint a lot. The type of man who always had harsh words to say to her when she rode into town.

But he was even worse than that, Polly realized. A silver star twinkled on his broad chest, catching the afternoon light. He was a sheriff. And she was, well, a gunslinger. A woman who earned her living as a hired gun. Sheriffs generally disliked those of her profession, especially when they also happened to be wanted by the law.

Heavens, what a mess she'd made of things. Well, the sheriff wasn't close enough to recognize her. Yet. Now was the perfect time to leave before that handsome lawman arrested her. And then she could save Bart the trouble of hunting her down.

Now, don't panic. Just walk slow and dignified. She took a sweeping step, skirts whispering, and nearly tripped. Darn these petticoats! Who invented such silly clothing? How on earth did anyone manage to walk around in these things?

"Miss Pauline?" There was that little girl again, dashing

after her, kicking up dust with each beat of her foot against the ground. "What's wrong? Do you think my pa is ugly? Don't you like me?"

Aw, now that wasn't fair at all. "Why, I like you just fine. I'm—" She twisted around to look over her shoulder to watch the sheriff's approach.

Heavens, he was getting closer. And worse, there was Bart exchanging words with the stagecoach driver. Gol' darn it. The driver knew she'd taken Pauline's clothes. What if he told Bart? That's when Polly realized she was a dead woman for sure.

"But you're running away from us!" Emily sounded like she was ready to cry.

How did this day go from bad to worse? And so fast? "Dear Emily, don't cry. I just need to—" *Hide from the law. Run from a man I shot in the left testicle.* Now, how was she going to explain that to a small child?

"Do you like ice cream?" The little girl trotted beside her, determined to keep up.

"Sure I do."

"Pa said he would buy you some."

Polly skidded to a stop. Dust powdered the air, and she squinted against the harsh summer sun. "Emily, I don't think I have time for ice cream."

"Why not? The diner's just over there. Didn't you come here just for me? Isn't that what you said in your letter?" Emily's pixie face twisted. Tears silvered those big sad eyes.

Polly's heart fell. She wished she was Pauline Curtis. She wished she was the kind of woman who could be someone special to this wonderful little girl.

"Miss Curtis? I'm Ben MacLain." He towered above her, tall, broad and substantial. She couldn't help but notice how his hard muscles shaped his white shirt in a most breathtaking way. "I paid a boy to run your trunks to the hotel."

"You did?" She bowed her chin, certain that if he got a

good look at her face he would recognize her from her wanted poster. "How kind of you." *As long as you don't arrest me.*

The little girl caught hold of her hand and held tight. So much hope glittered there, blue like the sky, sweet like dreams. "You're really pretty, Miss Pauline."

"And I think you're a beautiful little girl, Emily." Ah, heck. Now what did she do?

To make matters worse, the sheriff kept staring at her. Lord, he was going to recognize her any minute. Weakness gathered in her stomach.

"Come with me." His deep baritone voice rumbled through the air, vibrating over her with the sound of impending doom.

It was over. All over. But with the little girl at her side, she didn't want a fight. Or a fuss. She would go to jail peacefully. "Anything you say, Sheriff."

"That's the attitude I like." His smile softened the serious lines crinkled in the corners of his dark eyes. "This way."

Her knees knocked together. She'd never been arrested before. Thank goodness he was a courteous sheriff, walking slow to accommodate her difficulty with the petticoats, staying calm and offering her a pleasant grin.

And my, what a pleasant grin. Sheriff Ben MacLain looked rock hard from his jaw down to his toes. So well-formed he could make a woman lose control of her senses. He laid his hand on her forearm, escorting her up a set of steps. Heat sizzled where he touched her. He moved away, and a tingling handprint remained.

"Do you like vanilla or strawberry?" the girl asked as she skipped into the building and toward a waiting table. A table where a plate of half-eaten pie waited and a bowl of ice cream melted in the heat. "I think vanilla is the best."

"So do I." Polly glanced around. Why, this wasn't a jail after all, but a diner. And the sheriff wasn't arresting her. He was ordering a dish of ice cream.

Her knees wobbled and she sat down, a little amazed. She wasn't going to jail after all. Yet.

"We eat here a lot," Emily confessed as she scooped up a spoonful of her melting vanilla dessert. "On account of Pa not being able to cook."

"We're regular customers." Ben loomed above her, dependable looking and so strong. Goodness, she'd never before understood how a woman could feel safe in the presence of a man. Until now. "Martha is going to go broke because you're here to do the cooking for us."

Polly stammered. Now was the time to tell him there was a misunderstanding. She could simply explain she wasn't Pauline Curtis. That she wasn't going to cook for them. That she was sorry.

But a movement out of the corner of her eye caught her attention. A bell jingled as the diner's door swung open. Bart Dixon filled the threshold, his small, hard gaze searching the room.

Polly cringed. She could feel him undressing her with those eyes. But could he see who she was? Had he come back to get a closer look at her? What had the stage driver told him?

"Can I help you?" Ben stood, his guns strapped to his solid thighs, his demeanor tough and unflinching.

Polly's heart skipped. Goodness, but he was a powerful man. Strong enough to take her breath away. And what a dangerous reaction indeed.

She knew what happened to women who were blinded by love. She'd seen it all too often. Next thing a woman knew, she was being treated like a servant instead of a human being. She might not have the best life, she might be wanted by the law, she might not be able to afford beautiful clothes, but she had her independence. Polly Brown was not going to be any man's slave.

"Just lookin' for a meal." Bart bowed his head, trying to keep from looking directly at the sheriff.

Bart was probably wanted by the law for some crime,

too.

Martha appeared and took the gunslinger's order. Bart took a table in the far corner where he could watch the town's main street from the window.

Did he recognize her or not? Polly couldn't tell. Maybe he was just waiting until she wasn't in the company of the sheriff.

"I'll make sure he moves on," handsome Ben MacLain said, as if to reassure her. "I don't tolerate gunfighters in my town."

How about at your table? Troubled, she took a bite of ice cream. But the sweetness soured her mouth and curdled in her stomach.

What was she doing? She was plain old Polly Brown and not terribly ingenious. A man as smart-looking as the sheriff wouldn't be fooled for long. No, sir. After polishing off his pie, he was probably going to throw her in jail, right beside Bart Dixon.

"See something interesting?" he asked.

Her hand shook. A slice of ice cream plopped back into the dish. "It's sure a nice town you've got here."

"And I aim to keep it that way." He was proud of his work here, proud of this town. "I never told you much about the house."

"The house?" She set down her spoon, her angel's gaze focusing on him.

"My log cabin. Where we all will be living." Ben polished off the last bite of apple pie. "I thought you might like to see it. Before you move in."

She had the widest eyes. As big and blue as heaven. "Gee, I'm not sure—"

Emily dropped her spoon. "You don't like log houses?"

So much worry rang in the air. But Miss Curtis, to her credit, softened like new butter. "I love log houses. They're so neat and cozy. And they smell good, like fresh pine."

"Pa built our house all by himself." Emily wiped her

mouth on the back of her sleeve. "And I have a room all my own."

"What a nice pa you have." Pauline cast him a quick, appreciative gaze.

And he liked it. Satisfied, that's what he was. Pleased she was here, just like she promised. Pleased that his troubles were over.

"I've been waiting for you forever," Emily sighed.

"Really?" Pauline's mouth twisted. Even, white teeth dug into that pink, luscious lip and he couldn't tear his gaze away.

Just looking at her made him relax. She was beautiful. She liked log cabins. And best of all, the kindness in her smile was genuine, the attention she paid to his daughter as honest as daylight.

Still, she was from a much finer lifestyle than he expected, finer than he could provide. "How do you like Montana Territory so far?"

"I love it." Sparks lit her eyes, glinting like dawn. "It's beautiful country. And so free."

"There aren't a lot of women in a town like this." He wanted her to know for sure what she was getting into. He didn't want to scare her off, but he couldn't mislead her, either. "A woman from St. Louis might not be happy here. We have no theater, no opera house. Not even a lady's club."

"I suppose a woman from St. Louis just might miss those things." Unaffected, Miss Curtis shrugged one slim shoulder. "But it would make her darn stupid. Look at that sky. And the mountains. What more could a person want?"

"That's just how I feel." Ben loved Montana, too.

"We don't need no clubs and operas around here." Emily's adoring gaze never left Miss Curtis's face. "In the summer we can hunt for gold and in the winter we get snow. We can sled and make snowmen and snow angels."

"Snow angels?" Pauline's voice rose, pleasant as a

birdsong.

"Do you know how to make them?" Emily asked eagerly.

"I sure do. I always mess them up, though. Most of the time I can't get up without falling back on my behind. That really wrecks a snow angel."

"Really badly," Emily agreed.

It was perfect. Ben needed a wife. Miss Curtis needed a home. He could get along with anyone, but waking up to this beautiful woman frying his morning bacon would be pleasant indeed.

What he liked best about her was that she was just a little distant, not radiating that neediness most women did. The one that let a man know the woman wanted love and romance, wanted to cling to him.

Miss Pauline Curtis, despite her clothes, beauty and obvious social standing, looked like a sensible, practical woman. It was there on her straight mouth and in her unflinching eyes.

She didn't look like a woman pining after romance, who was foolish enough to believe that something as fickle as love existed.

Yes, she was more than he hoped for. And she seemed to be everything Emily needed.

Polly was getting low on cash. She ought to be worried about it. But that handsome sheriff and his little girl kept filling her thoughts and troubling her conscience. She shouldn't have used them like that. She hadn't wanted to. If she hadn't succumbed to the harebrained idea to dress up in Pauline's clothes, then she would have her gun in hand. She could have at least had a chance when Bad Bart came looking for her.

Now, she'd only gone and messed everything up. Well, she'd simply have to unmess it. She hadn't made any promises to Ben MacLain. She had tried hard not to mislead little Emily, yet she knew she had. Now all she needed to do was to get some money, buy a horse and leave town—even if her conscience smarted.

Polly waited until she was certain Bart was nowhere in sight before she ventured from her room. The hotel was clean and cozy. The proprietor's son had personally shown her to their best room. The sparkle in his eyes and his charming manner hadn't fooled her.

She knew what he was thinking about, what he wanted. And he wasn't going to get it. She might not have the position and education of women like Pauline Curtis, but she knew enough not to let some eager man separate her from her drawers.

The street was quiet in the late afternoon heat. No trouble, no gunfighters, and most importantly, no sheriff. She felt bad fooling him and his sweet little girl the way she had. How could she make it up to him?

The saloon was dark and hot. Cigar smoke blended with cigarette smoke and the sharp scent of cheap whiskey. Clutching her skirts awkwardly, she pushed through the batwing doors. Her toe caught on the edge of that darn petticoat, and she almost tripped.

A big strong hand curled around her elbow, steadying her. "Hello there, Miss Curtis." A voice deep enough to match that grip rumbled in her ear. "I saw you get off the stage."

She tugged her arm free and looked up at the stranger. "And you are . . ."

"Deputy Watson, ma'am." Solid shoulders straightened.

Oh, hellfire. What was a lawman doing in a saloon this time of day? "Is that whiskey for medicinal purposes, deputy?"

"Some call it that." He toasted her, then drained his shot glass. "What is a proper eastern lady doing in an establishment like this?"

"For medicinal reasons." Really. How was she going to win the money she needed if the town deputy kept making chitchat? "Excuse me, sir."

The lawman made no comment as she swished past him with those awkward skirts. She felt his sharp gaze on her back, hot like flaming arrows, but she ignored it. What else could she do? She ordered a whiskey to buy some time.

As soon as the deputy left, she would join the game going on at the corner table. Then, with money in hand she could buy a horse and be on her way. That's what she wanted, right?

Still, she couldn't help but wonder. What would it be like to live here? The town was clean and cozy, prospering and peaceful. It was the first place where she hadn't been plain old Polly Brown. Why, with these skirts and fine clothes, no one looked down at her. No one treated her as if she wasn't welcome, wasn't good enough, didn't belong.

And it was damn nice. For the first time in a long while, she realized just how lonely she'd been—always on the outside, always on the run, always alone.

She thought of little Emily with her unraveling braids and lace-edged dress. And wondered what it would be like to have a little girl of her own. To have a child full of smiles and merriment. To share ice cream and evenings and, when winter came, snow angels.

CHAPTER THREE

"Winning?"

Polly froze. Her heart hammered in her chest. It couldn't be. It just couldn't—

It was. She looked up. He towered over her, all fury and might. Anger tensed his solid shoulders, clenched his square jaw and radiated in those eyes that were intelligent enough to see right through her.

"Howdy, Sheriff." She couldn't think of one explanation to offer him. Especially since the pile of greenbacks and gold pieces in front of her testified to her skill at the game.

"You look like you know what you're doing." He pulled over a chair, all controlled power, and dropped it with a clatter. "It isn't every woman who can beat One-Eyed Tommy at poker."

"I have a talent."

"Then you admit it?" A muscle in his temple jumped.

"I admit that I won some money. That's not against the law, is it?"

"No, but against my principles."

"You're not the one gambling." *Really*. She tried to tell herself she didn't care what handsome Ben MacLain thought of her, but she did. She truly did.

She could read the disappointment in his eyes like stars in a winter sky. "Am I under arrest?"

"Come with me." His gaze narrowed, shadowing like twilight. His big hand wrapped around her forearm and lifted her from the chair.

He must have finally figured out who she was. Disappointment clawed through her chest, but the sadness she felt was greater. She should have known a brown sparrow couldn't dress up like a peacock. Whatever she wore, she was still plain old Polly beneath the satin and velvet, her father's daughter, no one special. She'd always been someone without a drop of luck.

She managed to stuff her winnings into her reticule before the rock-hard lawman tore her away from the table.

"Hold on, Sheriff," One-Eyed Tommy called out, cocking his well-polished Colt. "The lady ain't leavin' until I get a chance to win back some of my money."

"I don't want any trouble, Tommy." Ben's voice vibrated through every inch of her body.

Polly shivered. She'd never felt so manhandled. His grip on her arm was like steel. He lifted her off the floor with the strength in one arm. He felt as undefeatable as a mountain. She could not escape him and she didn't want to. Ben MacLain was larger than life, all flesh and blood man, and he made her intensely aware of being female. Her body sizzled wherever he touched and in some places he didn't. Goodness, no man had ever affected her this way. Ever.

She would not lose her common sense over a man, especially one about to arrest her. And never a lawman who represented everything she wasn't, could never be.

"But she cheated me," Tommy complained, and two other men at the poker table nodded in agreement.

"I cheated?" Temper sparked to life in her chest, hot and hard. "Why, you lying snake! You were the one cheating. No low-life is gonna accuse me—"

"Miss Curtis?" The sheriff interrupted.

Polly fell silent. In fact, the whole saloon was silent. The cowpokes at the bar, the men around the tables, the serving girls and the bartender all looked at her as if she'd sprouted five heads.

"I've never heard words like that come out of a proper woman's mouth." The sheriff quirked one brow.

"Neither have I." One-Eyed Tommy kicked back his chair. "But there was a fella in here a few hours ago lookin' for a woman who could cuss and gamble."

"Let it be, Tommy." The sheriff stood strong, his words silencing the saloon like a thunderclap. "Put away your gun."

Trouble. Polly sensed it coming like the quiet before a storm, like the click of a trigger before a bullet fired.

"And you," he warned low in her ear, so only she could hear. "You have a lot of explaining to do."

"I know." Her stomach sank. How was she going to make him understand? But more importantly, how could she make up for what she'd done, for how she'd misled Emily?

Troubled, Polly sighed. She had never felt so low. She was going to jail. She would probably be forced to pay for a crime she hadn't committed. Whatever that crime was. She couldn't read her own wanted poster. She didn't have anyone to help her.

Polly Brown was tired of being alone, of fighting her way in an unfair and unforgiving world.

* * *

Ben tried to fight down his anger, but it grew with every step. He hauled her out of the saloon, knowing damn well that by nightfall everyone in town would know his bride was a whiskey-drinking card sharp. A respectable woman, indeed!

"How did you manage all this?" Sunlight burned low over the tops of the buildings and straight into his eyes. But he had never seen more clearly in his life.

"Manage what? Beating that cheating, poker-playing Tommy?"

"No. Faking all those letters. You even had me believing you were a desperate daughter of a bankrupted St. Louis merchant."

"I didn't fake anything." She tilted back her head, scattering rich, sable curls over her shoulders. "You really did correspond with Pauline Curtis."

He pulled open the jailhouse door. "What did you do with her?"

"I didn't do anything. She ran off with Roland, the banker's son." Fear framed her face and shivered in her voice. In a voice not practiced at deceit.

"Damn." He'd written six times for a woman. Even proposed to one. And not one of them made it all the way to Indian Trails without finding true love. Not one.

What was he going to do about Emily? She was counting on a new mother. He needed someone to take care of the house and his daughter. He needed someone to do the damn cooking. And all he had was this, this—

"Explain this." He slapped the wanted poster on the desk in front of her.

She tumbled out of his grip, rubbing her arm. She looked up at him with true terror in her eyes, in eyes as gentle as morning.

The jail was empty. Every move she made echoed. Her skirts whispered. Her shoes tapped. Her sleeves rustled as she reached out and took hold of the parchment with trembling fingers. The paper rattled, trembling along with her.

"Why me?" He bit back anger, and tasted it sharp and bitter in his mouth. "What do you want from me?"

"I don't want anything." Her eyes widened like a doe caught in a hunter's sites. "I only wanted to try on a few dresses. I thought it might be a disguise and fool the man after me."

"Dixon?" he guessed, remembering the black-clad

gunfighter.

She nodded, chin bowed, staring at the wanted poster where an uncomplimentary drawing hardly looked like her, did not reflect the wide cut of her eyes and the softness at her mouth. An angel's face. A wanted woman.

"Dixon came into town yesterday. He stopped by the jail to ask about the female on that poster." Ben strode closer, close enough to see the gleam of red strands accenting her brown hair, to breathe in her sunshine and spice scent. "I told him I didn't want trouble in my town. That I wanted him gone by sundown today."

She ran a slim finger over the big black letters spelling out her crimes. Twin brows frowned over her eyes as she studied the paper.

"Did you pull a job with him, then run off with the gold?"

"What?" Her chin came up, all innocent blue eyes and soft, rounded mouth. Not at all the face of the woman in the drawing. But there was no doubt about it. This was Polly Brown, armed and dangerous.

"You're wanted for robbing the Golden Gulch stage."

She fingered the word 'robbery.'

"Is that where you got the money for your pretty clothes?" Ben thought of those three fancy trunks that had arrived with her on the stage.

She shook her head, scattering her curls over her too-thin shoulders. "I told you. The trunks were Pauline's. She left without them in her hurry to be with the rich banker's son."

"The wanted poster says you always wear men's clothes. That you ride a roan gelding."

"He broke his leg in a gopher hole up near Big Horn Creek." She tucked her luscious bottom lip between her teeth and worried it. "That's why I took the stage. I didn't have enough money to buy another horse."

She looked vulnerable. Still, Ben had to be sure. "Where did you hide the gold?"

"I didn't hide the gold." She lifted her chin, and she looked straight at him.

"Then what happened to it?"

"I don't know. I didn't rob the Golden Gulch stage." Her teeth clenched. Her striking gaze never wavered.

He tapped the paper, the crackling sound loud in the silence. "It says right here that you did."

"Well, it's wrong. I'm no thief." Unshed tears stood in her eyes.

"Then what are you?"

"You don't want to know."

She didn't look sorry for herself, Ben realized. She looked angry. And helpless. And damn it, he didn't want to feel sorry for her. Emotions had no place in a business proposition.

He stepped away, striding toward the only window. The street outside bustled with the end of the day traffic. Merchants closed up their shops. Customers hurried home with last-minute purchases. "I'm a tough man, Miss Brown. I've seen a lot in my twenty-nine years. I can handle the truth."

Her throat worked. Stubborn pride thrust that chin up higher and fisted those small, callused hands. "The truth is, I make my living sometimes as a hired gun. Sometimes I get a bounty here and there. But I don't steal."

Ben watched her hands, listened to the conviction in her voice, and measured her unflinching gaze. He'd seen a lot of liars in his line of work, known a lot of men who did more than steal a shipment of gold.

She wasn't lying. Whatever sort of woman Polly Brown was, she was honest. And she wasn't a thief.

"As I see it, you've got quite a problem." He considered his words carefully and the step he was about to take. He was desperate. He figured Miss Brown might just be in worse straits.

Ben took a gamble and made a decision. "Every lawman in this territory is going to be looking for you.

Plus, you've got that gunslinger Dixon looking for you. He means business."

She dipped her chin. "If I'm in jail, it will be easier for him to kill me, as he's sworn to do."

"Why would he do that?"

She blushed. From the collar of her fine dress all the way to the roots of her hair. "Bart, uh, tried to take certain liberties with me, liberties I didn't appreciate."

"He forced himself on you?"

"He tried to." That softly rounded chin lifted another notch. "But I shot him in the privates, and he's been after me since."

She wasn't lying. Not a chance. Ben saw the fury spark in the depths of her eyes and heard the challenge in her voice. She was tough—but not too tough. Fear wrinkled her brow, and he saw something more there, shining in her eyes, something deeper.

Vulnerability.

No, don't even think it. She was nothing but trouble. Big trouble. With those forever eyes and that angel smile . . .

He sat on the edge of his desk and crossed his arms over his chest. She gazed up at him, such a small, slender scrap of a woman with a wide, worried gaze and that soft pink lip tucked between her teeth.

He watched her turn toward the open jail door. Her mouth thinned as she studied the waiting cell with silent dread.

He took a steady breath. "I've got a problem, too. Emily is expecting a mother. She's been corresponding with Pauline Curtis for the last few months. Pauline made promises about the things that they would be doing together—the doll she was going to make Emily, and the clothes to go with it, and pies and cookies and a quilt for her bed. Emily thinks you are going to give her all those things."

"I didn't know." Polly Brown paled. Her face pinched

tight. "You have such a wonderful little girl. I never meant to pretend to be Pauline. It's just that Bart was standing there." Her lower lip trembled. "Are you going to lock me up now?"

"That depends on you." He stood, looming tall and distant, his intense gaze probing hers.

"On me?"

He quirked one brow. "I'm going to give you a choice, Polly Brown. I can arrest you, toss you in that cell and hand you over for trial. Or, you can keep Pauline Curtis's promise to my daughter and marry me.

"What? You want me to marry you?"

"Why not?" He reached for his ring of keys. They jangled and clanged together as he paced toward the open barred door. "You say you aren't a criminal. You say a man wants you dead."

"It's true."

"Then you're no threat to Emily. You need help with Dixon and the law. I need help with my daughter and my home."

"And I'm supposed to marry you instead of letting you toss me in jail?" She took a step back. Horror furrowed across her forehead and tensed her rail-thin body.

Ben stopped at that. Someone had hurt her. He could see it in the way she automatically turned toward the door, looking for escape, and in her quick, startled breath. "I'm not blackmailing you, if that's what you think."

"Then what are you doing?" So thin that voice, struggling to sound brave.

"Think of it as a business arrangement. A permanent one."

"Permanent?"

"Emily is going to need a mother for a long time."

"But you want a wife, isn't that right? You want to—" Pink swept up her face. "I see what you want from me. Just like any man. You think that because I'm not like other women, that I'm not decent, that I'm loose.'" Tears stood in her eyes, and her voice caught, as if she were trying not to cry.

"That's not what I meant, Polly."

"I don't believe you."

"Do you really think I would want a woman with weak morals around my daughter?"

She looked down and released a shaky breath. "No. I guess not."

"I know an honest person when I see one. You might have let me think you were Pauline Curtis, but your kindness toward Emily was genuine. You made her very happy today."

"I did?" A flicker of warmth crept into her eyes. A shade of hope. "I liked your daughter. I wish—"

"What?"

She shook her head. "Never mind. You said it yourself. Both Dixon and the law are after me. Even if I wanted to, I couldn't—"

"What?"

She wrung her hands. "Couldn't accept what you're proposing."

"Why not? I can fix anything." He held out his hand, palm up, waiting.

She studied it, uncertain. "You can get rid of those charges?"

"Sure. I can run Dixon out of town. But what I really want is a woman who will be kind to Emily, who will love her and won't break her heart. My daughter has waited for each woman who promised to come. Each time she was forgotten and I had to try to console her and promise it would be better next time."

He caught Polly's slender hand when she refused to offer it to him. She felt like new silk and smelled like a forest on a spring day. In her blue gaze, he saw an angel's gentleness. "Emily has waited for that stage for the last time. Her heart is set on you."

"Only because she thinks I'm someone else." Her

fingers wiggled against his, but he didn't let her go. This time when she lifted her gaze to his, there was no sign of fear. "She wouldn't want me, if she knew."

"You were the one who came, who showed up and made her smile." His throat caught He hurt all the way down to his chest. "People make mistakes and sometimes, if they are good people, they can make the best of a second chance."

"Does that mean you aren't going to arrest me?"

"Or force you into anything you don't want to do." He wasn't Bart Dixon. He wasn't a man who could take anything from a woman that wasn't offered. "Our marriage can be an arrangement, not a marriage in fact. You can have your bedroom, and I will have mine."

"Why me?" She laid her hand to her chest. "Why would you give me a second chance? Look what I've done to you. You must think—" She paused. "I don't know what you think."

"I've been around. I've seen all kinds of people, done all sorts of deeds, learned a lot." His voice deepened, low and soft like midnight. "You have a good heart, Polly Brown. That's something not even you can fake, and it's what Emily needs in a mother."

"I don't know anything about children." It didn't seem real he could be asking her this, saying such kind words that almost made her believe in happiness and forever, in things she could never let herself believe in. "I'm not wife and mother material, Sheriff. I didn't grow up in a nice house with flowers around it. I don't know much about being a wife."

"Are you willing to learn?"

He was serious. So strong and honest and kind, looking down at her as if she could give him something he wanted, fix his most troubling problems. A mother to Emily. Heavens, she couldn't do it. And yet, the thought of having a home, her very own home, and that sweet little girl who could give her a future tempted her, made her hope.

A future. That meant no more running, no more sleeping wherever she could find a place to lay her head, no more lonely nights. A home, a place to belong, and most of all a child to love, sweet Emily who liked ice cream and snow angels.

Polly's knees shook, but she knew what she had to do. "No deal, Sheriff. I will never be your wife."

CHAPTER FOUR

Ben couldn't believe what he was hearing. "You mean you'd rather go to jail than be a mother to my little girl?"

"I would love—" She stopped and bit her lip. Her eyes darkened and her brow furrowed. It was not defiance or rebellion, but apology that drew a frown to her soft lips. "I can never marry anyone."

"Why not? Are you already married?" He took a step closer.

She shook her head.

"Engaged?"

"No."

"Hoping for a better man to come along?"

Her chin lifted. She was pure fight and hard woman, and not nearly delicate enough for his tastes. "I couldn't—"

He gestured behind her. "Well, there's the jail cell. It's your choice."

He didn't like blackmailing her, but he had a little girl who'd been counting on a mother to braid her hair and play with her, to love her in the way only a woman could.

"I'd rather stand behind those bars and let Dixon find

me then to give up my hard-earned freedom to the likes of you. On the outside, you're all respectability. But you'd threaten me with jail or marriage. For a woman, there ain't a whole lot of difference."

"Is that so? Well, I guarantee there are no bars on my windows and no lock on my door. You can step outside and see the sky and those beautiful mountains as often as you want. In the summers you can go gold hunting with my daughter and in the winters make snow angels. That's a better prison than jail, in my opinion."

Her chin wobbled. She held herself as tough as any man with her shoulders straight, jaw set, and spine as rigid as iron. He wanted a city-bred woman for Emily, someone with refined grace and elegance who would be a good influence on her.

Yet all he had was Polly Brown.

"I can't do it." She met his gaze, level and unflinching, and with a shade of regret. "Even if you offer me the moon. I can't be any man's wife."

"Why not?"

She looked away, the muscles in her jaw working. She stared hard out the window that offered a generous view of that brilliant blue sky and those breathtaking mountains she loved so much, and the front street with its cozy bustle of townsfolk.

"I don't trust a low-down, blackmailing sheriff." She handed him her reticule with the loaded Colts inside, as if welcoming her fate.

He tugged the iron door open and waited for her to walk into her cell. He closed the barred doors and couldn't stop the hard punch of regret in his chest.

He wasn't going to give up. Too much was at stake. He heard the door catch and watched the terror darken Polly's eyes. She was afraid of small places, of losing her freedom.

She made him think of a doe scenting a hunter. He walked away, guilt eating at him. But he wouldn't back down.

He was afraid that neither would Polly Brown.

As the evening lengthened, Polly's anger grew. That sheriff had no right trying to blackmail her. She sympathized with his little girl needing a mother, but that didn't make it right. It wasn't right to dangle a woman's dreams in front of her nose, when those dreams didn't even exist.

Goodness gracious, she would never forget the misery of living with her father. He was a man who liked control. What a man expected from a wife or a daughter was slavery, pure and simple.

No, it was better standing in this lonely jail cell than tossing away her freedom. No matter how much she might want the life Ben was offering her.

Her heart warmed remembering how little Emily had met her at the stage. *I've been waiting for you forever*—those were her exact words. Polly closed her eyes, holding the memory close. She loved children. But to raise them right, children needed a father. And that was the problem—a big problem.

She was never going to marry any man. There wasn't one trustworthy or kind enough in the whole of Montana Territory, maybe even in the entire West.

And yet, the sheriff had the warmest eyes she'd ever seen. The sound of his voice made her feel as if rich, warm whiskey were sluicing over her body. He was a man who loved his daughter and didn't want to see her disappointed.

Ben MacLain was a man who'd figured out he could tempt her with her own foolish dreams.

Polly rubbed her aching brow and sat down on the cot.

The jail cell was small and dark. Even on this hot night of late summer, it felt cold. Maybe it was the steel that caged her in. Maybe it was the stone walls without windows. Either way she shivered, trapped like a bird without sight of the sky.

Still, she had a clean bed, a comfortable pillow, and a wool blanket the sheriff had given her. This was more than she had some nights. She couldn't truly complain. And if her stomach rumbled, why, she'd been hungry plenty enough times to ignore it.

Yep, she'd done the right thing. She might want to belong to a real family, but that didn't mean accepting a perfect stranger's proposal was smart. Especially not a stranger who held the power to have her arrested any time he wanted.

Again and again, her thoughts returned to Emily. She had talked so much. Goodness. What was she doing now?

Probably watching her father try to fix up supper in their cozy log home. Polly remembered the sweetness of sitting with them today, of Emily's constant questions.

The lonesome ache in her chest grew. How she wanted a home and a little girl of her own.

If only she could trust the father.

She heard a door rattle and hinges squeak open. Bootsteps rasped on the wood floor. Someone dared to step foot inside the jail after hours, and she couldn't see who. She sure hoped it wasn't Dixon. Her fingers itched for the comfort of her friendly revolvers.

Those boots were getting closer.

Cold sweat prickled across the back of her neck. Then she heard the rattle of enamelware, and Ben MacLain rounded the corner. My, he was a handsome devil. A shank of dark hair cascaded over his brow. High cheekbones gave his face a strong appearance.

"Had enough of that jail cell?"

"Marriage. Prison." She sat back down on the edge of the narrow cot so he couldn't notice her trembling knees. "Like I said—they're one and the same."

"Don't have to be."

How sincere he seemed. He balanced a tray in his hands. It wasn't the food or the scent of chicken and dumplings that kept her attention, but the steady gleam of his eyes, dark and honest and filled with integrity.

Integrity? Now where did that notion come from? This

was the sheriff who'd put her in this cell.

"I'm not offering you the real thing, Polly. Just an arrangement. A long-term, permanent commitment to my daughter. It's that simple and that important. And if you can't do it, then I'll send for the marshal to come get you."

"Why, you're nothing but a blackmailer, plain, and simple." Indignation burned like a hot ball in her stomach, but it was better than this fear. She hated being trapped in this cell.

What if she never got out? What if she had to say goodbye to Montana sunsets and wide-open spaces for the rest of her life? "You think you're so fine, MacLain, but you're like every other lawman I've met. You use your badge for personal gain."

"I'm using it for Emily."

Even with the bars separating them, she could see the love for his daughter glimmering like a rare and precious light in his eyes. It was the love of a father, something she'd never known or imagined before this.

"I'll use my badge. I'll do whatever it takes. I can't break Emily's heart."

"You need a housekeeper—"

"Emily needs someone to love her. But then, maybe I was wrong about you. Maybe you don't know what it's like to be a child yearning for a mother." He fit a key into the lock.

"Maybe I know something about it."

He turned the key. "She talks of horse rides and gold panning and a new doll and the woman who will give her all her love. Emily thinks that someone ought to be you."

"Not me." Polly smoothed her hand over a small wrinkle in the skirt.

"Yes, you."

His gaze pinned her like an arrow. She saw the steady confidence as he swung the door open. The oiled hinges whispered. His boots knelled on the stone floor. "Do you really want to stay in here?"

"No."

"Then you don't have to. We can help each other out."

"But I won't agree to marriage." Her throat constricted. Her mouth went dry. She remembered how hard those years had been keeping house for her father and his outlaws. Sometimes, the others would have a wife or a woman with them, and it was always the same—violence, submission, unhappiness. She'd escaped her father's influence, and she'd struggled hard to keep her independence. "I can't—"

"What's scaring you?" Ben moved closer. His hand lighted on her shoulder.

She stared down at that hand, big and sun-browned, his fingers blunt and thick, but not meaty or rough-looking. No, his hand was refined and strong. Heat from that touch penetrated the fine fabric of her secondhand dress, and her pulse gave a hard kick.

"Tell me why." Sincerity shone in his eyes.

"No." She didn't know what to do with that. She'd never met a man she could trust. "Go ahead and bring in the food tray, but I don't want to—" She paused. "I don't trust you, Sheriff."

He withdrew his hand. The light faded from his eyes. "Fine."

He retrieved the tray with a cold anger and left it on the bed beside her. "Dixon is still in town. I'll do my best to make sure he doesn't find you here, but that's all I'll do."

Polly stared down at the steaming tray and then up at Ben's retreating back. Steel bars separated her from the world. *I guarantee there are no bars on my windows and no lock on my door.*

"Ben," she called between the cold bars.

He hesitated in the threshold that gazed out onto the twilight street. Then he smiled. Sure, he was glad. He knew he'd won.

"If I agree to keep your house, then there's gonna be some rules."

"What rules?"

She watched him pivot around. The graceful male strength of him was silhouetted by the thick twilight. With slow ease, he shut the door and ambled through the shadowed jailhouse. He approached her like a hunter with a rifle. Every strike of his boot against the stone floor rang with confidence.

Yikes, she never should have called him back. She hated being afraid, but she was terrified now. Marriage. Could she do it?

"Tell me your conditions." His eyes were dark, and his chin set. With those strong shoulders and muscled arms, he looked intimidating.

"I don't want to be treated like your servant."

"Servant? You'll be my wife. You'll have to take care of the house."

"Then I'll be your housekeeper. I might be a bad one, but I'll give it my best shot. I'll take care of your little girl, and we can pan for gold and—"

"No." His voice boomed like a cannon.

"You said you kept trying to hire a girl, but they kept getting married on the way here. I promise I'll stay—as long as you don't hurt me. I'll do my best for Emily—"

"I said, no. Emily wants a mother and that's what she's going to get. I love my little girl, and losing her mother was very hard on her. She's got it in her head that she wants a mother, and that woman is you. So, Miss Brown, you can stay in this jail or do as I ask. It's that simple."

Anger seethed from him. It resounded against the stone walls. It shivered in the chambers of her heart She curled her fingers around the cold bars. Dang it! He wasn't going to give her those dreams. He just wanted a woman to do his housework.

Somehow, she found a way to say it. "Fine. I'll be your wife."

She thought it would make him happy, but he didn't say a word. Not one single word. The jail vibrated with his silence and this awful thing she was agreeing to.

What had she done? Defeat hung on her shoulders like hundred-pound anvils. She leaned her forehead against the cool steel and fought the urge to weep. "Keep this in mind. If you try to harm me—"

"What do I look like? A man who hurts women?"

"You're a man who's blackmailing one." She met his gaze and refused to flinch. "Prove to me marriage to you isn't as bad as standing behind these bars."

"And then what?"

"I'll marry you. I give you my word, and it's as good as any man's. I'll stay and do my best by Emily, as long as you never raise a hand to me."

That would be what, all of a week, she figured. Maybe two.

"It's a deal," the sheriff ground out. "You're doing the right thing."

Well, anything was better than spending the night in this cell. Polly bit back grateful tears as the door swung open.

She wasn't free. She feared she would never be truly free again.

It was dark when Ben and his deputy strode through the batwing doors of Indian Trail's only saloon. Ben's hands landed on his hips, and he was ready to draw. The tinny sound of piano music died. The conversations lulled. Everyone turned to face them except for the lone man at the bar.

Ben strode past the poker games and the serving women. He kicked away the empty stool next to the gunslinger and stood in its place, towering over the scruffy troublemaker. "You didn't heed my warnings, Dixon."

"Yeah, well, it's a free country. A man has the right to quench his thirst." Dixon had beady eyes, hard and mean.

"If I could have found your face on one of my wanted notices, you'd be in my jail right now."

"Sorry to disappoint ya, sheriff. I'm lookin' for a

woman."

"Aren't we all?" He laid a few silver dollars on the bar, enough to cover the ruffian's tab. "This is a respectable town, and we mean to keep it that way. My deputy and I will be happy to escort you out past the town limits, but it would be better for you if you left on your own."

Dixon's hand went for his revolver.

Ben was so fast, he already had his gun in hand, cocked and ready. "I don't want this to get rough, but I'm not afraid of it."

The gunslinger's eyes widened. "That's the fastest draw I've ever seen on a lawman."

"Get off the chair, Dixon."

The gunslinger knocked back the last of his whiskey. "Can't find the gal I'm lookin' for anyway. Thought she may have been the one gamblin' right here in this saloon, but I hear she was yer fiancee."

"That's right, Dixon. She's not the woman you're after. Miss Curtis is from St. Louis." Ben met the gunslinger's gaze, never flinching. "Be on your way."

"I don't take kindly to a small-town sheriff givin' me orders." Dixon slammed the glass onto the bar. "Or tryin' to pull the wool over my eyes. Somethin' tells me your betrothed and Polly Brown could be one and the same."

"If you want to stay out of jail for the night, then you'd best keep your mouth shut. Thinking is dangerous for a man like you." Ben pressed the nose of his Colt hard against the man's throat. "Now, do as I say and get off this bar stool."

Dixon's gaze flashed, lethal and cold. "Sure, sheriff. You've got me tremblin' in my boots."

Ben grabbed the man by the collar with his free hand and hauled him off the stool and across the saloon. Dixon's jaw went slack. The gun slid from his hand. Ben slung him through the double doors. He launched him at the hitching post where half a dozen horses stood dozing.

Dixon hit stomach-first into the bar. He coughed,

holding onto the wood, trying to catch his breath.

"I don't want to see you in my town again." Ben holstered his gun. "This is a peaceful place, and I mean to keep it that way."

"Say what you want, but I know the truth. You're protecting her." Dixon's threat didn't diminish. "I'm not finished, Sheriff. I'll get even with Polly one way or another."

"Then you'll have to deal with me."

The gunslinger paled, but he didn't back down. Dixon limped over to his horse and swung up. He rode away in the darkness, heading toward the lonely trail out of town.

"I'll make sure he keeps going." Ben gestured for his deputy to follow him. "I need you to watch the hotel. Make sure my fiancee stays put. If she tries to sneak off, throw her in jail."

"In jail? But—"

"Lock her up, Woody." Without saying more, Ben loosened the reins from the hitching post and mounted his gelding. The palomino started off without complaint.

He saw her light in the hotel, the corner room on the second floor. The curtains were drawn and that was all he could see. She'd been beautiful in that fine gown and vulnerable behind the bars of his jail. What was she doing, living a life like that?

It troubled him as the lights of town faded away and he could make out the small shadow of Dixon on the trail far ahead. Was he doing the right thing?

Polly had said it herself. She wasn't wife and mother material. And yet, he'd seen her eyes light at Emily's attention. He'd seen the dreams there, tentative but real.

He rode the trail a long time, to make sure the gunslinger didn't double back. No matter what happened, Dixon would never get his hands on Polly. Ben had given the woman his word. He believed in second chances, and he hoped to hell and back that Polly wouldn't let him down. Only time would tell.

CHAPTER FIVE

Polly pushed open the hotel's front door to the gentle morning light and saw Ben MacLain leaning against a post watching the sunrise, sipping his morning coffee.

"Going somewhere?" His gaze slid from the subtle shades of pink and lavender at the horizon to the satchel in her hand. "I thought we had an agreement."

"We do. Are you going to throw me back in jail? Decided you'd rather have the bounty on my head instead of someone to take care of your daughter?"

He raised one brow. "Depends on what's inside that satchel."

"This?" She lifted it a notch, suddenly realizing what he was so surly about. "You think I'm trying to skip out of town?"

"It looks that way."

"In a dress?" She brushed at the pink calico skirt that wrapped around her legs like a noose. "I can't ride, I can't run. I doubt if I could even catch a fish in this thing. Trust me. If I were going to run, I'd be wearing my Levi's."

His eyes narrowed as he studied her. "What's in the satchel?"

"My trousers." That wasn't the right answer, she could see that immediately. He was a big man, as powerful as a bear despite his civilized appearance. His jaw ground. His eyes snapped. He reached out and tore the bag from her grip before she could try to stop him.

He set his mug of coffee on the porch rail and snapped open the brass clasp. The fancy bag gaped open as he pawed through it. "Trousers, boots, a man's shirt, a gold pan. Fish hooks."

"See?" At least he could tell she wasn't going to break her promise. "I'm all prepared. I thought—"

"You admit it?" His mouth twisted. He slammed her possessions back into the bag and thrust it at her. "I guess I know what kind of woman you are. Do I need to haul out my Colt, or will you go peaceably?"

"I've already agreed to stay." He drew himself up full height, and she had to tip her head back to look at him. Dark hair tumbled over his brow and into his eyes. He looked as untamed as a Montana prairie and twice as dangerous. "Is that why you're here? To make sure I keep my word."

"Looks like it isn't much of a word."

She tried to take possession of her satchel, but he wouldn't let go. "This is why I don't want to get married. Look at the way you're treating me."

"You lied to me."

"You wouldn't recognize the truth if it bit you in the rear."

He curled his big fingers around the mug and cupped it in his powerful hand, a hand that was deceptively calm.

The hair prickled on the back of her neck. His other hand was brushing the handle of his holstered revolver.

"I don't want any trouble. I hate to lock you up—"

"You're taking me back to jail?" She didn't understand. "So, this is the way it's going to be. You're going to dangle those darn charges over my head every time I want to go fishing."

"Fishing?"

"Do I have to ask your permission for everything? It was like that with Pa. If I wanted to go to the river to fetch water or out to hunt for supper, I had to ask. I'm not a child. Or haven't you noticed?"

"Oh, I noticed. And no, I'm not going to trust a woman who's packed for a quick trip out of town."

"Are you always this thick-skulled? I wanted to go fishing or gold panning." Fury battered her like fists, and she felt like flinging the darn satchel at his big, self-important head. He may be the most handsome man she'd ever laid eyes on, but he was just as controlling as the rest of his gender.

"You really are going to go fishing?" His hand didn't move from his revolver.

"What did you think? I thought Emily would like—" Then she saw the truth in his eyes. He didn't believe her. He still didn't believe her. "I'm no liar, Ben MacLain."

She swung the satchel and caught him in the belly. The edge of the bag smacked his shooting hand. She marched down the steps and out into the peaceful morning.

Dust swirled with each pat of her shoes. Larks and finches glided by, enjoying the fresh morning air. She heard a horse whinny in the livery as she passed. Ripe apples scented the wind.

"If you're heading out of town, you're going the wrong way." He caught up with her, rubbing his wrist.

"I'm not heading out of town."

"Then where are you going?"

"To rob the bank. Gee, what do you think?" She kept walking. She was too angry to enjoy the morning. The sights and sounds of the new day were some of her favorites, but now they were tainted. Every step she took, he was there, at her side, her very own personal sheriff determined to enforce his own kind of justice.

Jail or marriage. Maybe she'd made the wrong choice.

If she were smart, she would run for freedom while she

still had a chance.

The road turned and the tall, majestic evergreens gave way to a small clearing.

"We're here. Now, let's get one thing straight." Ben's hand encircled hers like an iron band.

His skin was male-hot, and she could feel the calluses in a rough ridge across his palm. She looked up into his hard, suspicious eyes and then to the house just up ahead. "That's your log cabin?"

"It beats a jail cell. Are you complaining?" He crooked one brow. "It's not as fancy as the hotel—"

"It's perfect."

And it was. Honey-colored logs were neatly chinked and laid. The roof looked newly shingled. A center door stood in the middle of the house and wide windows flanked it. A porch roof would keep the snow off the steps in winter, and the second-story sported tall dormer windows facing the rugged peaks of the Rockies. Tall pines spread their gentle boughs skyward, guarding the house. Colorful wildflowers danced in the front yard, in tune with the morning breezes.

The front door slammed open and a little girl dressed in blue calico burst into sight. "Polly! Polly, you came."

"Right on time, too. Just like I said."

Emily's fingers curled around hers, taking her from Ben's grip. "Come on. Hurry. You have to come in. I've been waiting for you all morning."

"All morning?" Tenderness for his daughter sparkled in Ben's measuring eyes. "Why, the sun isn't even up all the way."

But Ben's tenderness didn't last when he looked at Polly. He wasn't cold, but she knew he looked past the pretty calico dress she'd chosen this morning and saw the gunslinger beneath. He didn't look at her the same way as when she'd climbed off the stage.

And that stung.

"Yeah, but it feels like I've been waiting forever."

Emily threw open the screen door with a bang.

"Me, too." Polly followed her through the door. "This has been the longest morning of my life."

Ben frowned, the hardness returning when he looked at her. He was a no-nonsense sheriff and used to being in charge. She sighed. How could she walk away now?

Emily's hand held hers with unbreakable force. The girl dragged her into the parlor. "See our house? I dusted the furniture and everything. I'll be real good. I promise. Want to see what I did?"

Polly couldn't help it. "Show me."

"In here." Emily led the way past pine walls and a gray stone fireplace and big windows that let in the sun.

They wove around furniture finer than she'd ever seen in her life. Emily dragged her through a doorway.

A polished table sat in the room's center. Three places had been set, each knife and fork and spoon in perfect alignment. "Why Emily, you set the table."

"I did. I can do lots of things. You'll stay, right?" A world of worry shone in her eyes, and Emily's grip on her hand tightened. So much need.

Polly knew exactly how it felt for a little girl to lose her mother and to want another desperately. Someone with a gentle voice and loving touches, who could soothe away fears and right every wrong. "You did a perfect job. I couldn't have done better. What do you want for breakfast? I can fix anything you like."

"Pancakes. Pa makes them all the time cuz they're my favorite. Ain't that right, Pa?"

"That's right. It's the only thing I can cook." Ben leaned his shoulder against the threshold that separated the parlor from the dining room. His black shirt emphasized his wide shoulders and broad chest and made him seem invincible.

Was he just standing there, or blocking the only escape?

"The kitchen's behind you and to your left." His gaze

narrowed. "Leave your satchel with me."

"Let me guess. You're not a trusting man." She tossed him the bag.

He caught it easily with one hand. "I just don't trust you."

"So, is this the way of things? Are you going to watch over me all day long, making sure I don't break my word and head for Canada?" She tried to turn away, but he stopped her.

"Trust is something that's earned."

"That goes two ways."

Let him think what he wanted. She knew the truth. He looked at her and saw a gunfighter. He saw someone he thought lived outside the law.

She turned on watery knees and marched into the kitchen. She hardly noticed the pleasant room as she skidded to a stop in front of the stove. She was shaking, feeling both anger at Ben and anger at her father. She'd never wanted to be an outlaw's daughter, but she'd done the best she could.

"Don't you like Pa?" Emily whispered as she ambled into the kitchen.

"I'm just a little mad at him right now." Polly was more than mad, but she didn't want Emily to know it.

"You aren't going to leave, are you?" The girl's chin shot up, and she took a step back. "You said in your letter that you wanted me."

It wasn't pleading. It wasn't accusation. There weren't even tears. And that's what hit Polly the hardest.

"It's okay if you don't want me." Emily's chin hiked higher. Her jaw tensed. "Pa said if you came, you might not like us or we might not like you. That we had to wait to see for absolutely sure."

It was there in her eyes, veiled but there, the disappointment. She was trying so hard to be grown-up.

Polly's hand shook as she reached for the match tin. She fingered a wooden match and knelt in front of the stove. "I don't have anywhere else to go. If it's all right with you, I'd rather stay here."

Emily's chin lowered a notch. "That would be all right with me."

"Good."

Sadness for this child ached in her chest. Polly knew what it was like to be without a mother. She still missed the quiet woman with the gentle voice. She sensed that same kind of person was what Emily needed.

She wasn't quiet and she wasn't gentle. She knew nothing but what she'd learned from her father—how to shoot a gun, how to track down a man, how to cook over a campfire. She didn't know what a child like Emily needed.

The girl skipped to a stop. "I can help."

Polly shook out the match's flame as the fire inside the stove's belly caught. "You know where the pantry is?"

Emily whirled in a froth of blue and dashed to a small door at the end of the row of cabinets. Polly stood and followed her.

Ben's step sounded behind her and his hand caught her elbow. He freed her revolver from her pocket. "I don't want you to carry a loaded gun."

"But I—"

"You're not a bounty hunter anymore."

"I need that gun." It was the only way she had to protect herself.

The hard line of his mouth eased. "If you're going to be my wife, like you promised, you don't need to be watching your back. I'm here to do it for you."

"But Dixon could still find me—"

"I chased Dixon out of town last night."

She glanced at the door where Emily had disappeared. The girl was still safely out of hearing range. "He's gone?"

"Just like I promised. I threw him out of the Lazy Horse Saloon last night and followed him out of town, just to make sure he left." He laid a hand on her shoulder, a touch that scorched through the thin layer of cotton straight to the skin beneath. "He could always come back, but you're not alone. I gave you my word, Polly. I'll keep you safe."

And he meant it, this man who held her freedom in his hands.

Emily stumbled out of the pantry. "Are you two still fightin'?"

"We're done, as long as your father is through ordering me around." Polly took one last long look at her gun before she snatched it out of his hand and slipped it back into her pocket

Ben opened his mouth to protest, but when Emily pulled up a chair and knelt on it, ready to help Polly with the meal preparation, he seemed to deflate a little.

"Just don't keep it loaded." He turned, conceding this small defeat.

Polly watched Ben settle down at the table. Sunlight washed through the windows, burnishing him with a soft golden glow as he unfolded the morning's paper. Newsprint crinkled as he began to read. She could just see him through the wide doorway that separated the rooms. He glanced up at her over the top of the paper and studied her.

She turned away, heart strumming. He was still watching her. Dangnabbit! She didn't need an audience while she was trying to figure out the big black hulking contraption she had to prepare breakfast on.

She'd never cooked on a stove before. It was fancy and polished to a shine. While Emily separated the bacon slices, Polly knelt down and added more coal to the fire. Heat radiated from the monstrosity, and sweat beaded her brow.

Goodness, cooking in a house wasn't as pleasant as she'd hoped. With a campfire, she might get smoke in her eyes, but at least there was always a cooling breeze.

Well, this couldn't be all that hard. After all, she'd been

cooking for herself and her father's men for years. She had the coffee ground and measured. She had the potatoes grated and waiting, and the eggs counted out and ready to crack. Emily was wrapping up the bacon in butcher's paper.

"How come you ain't cookin' yet?"

"I like to get organized first." Really, she just didn't want to admit she was nervous. She swiped the dampness from her brow with the sleeve of her dress, then set the coffeepot on the stove.

She felt Ben's gaze, curious and measuring, as she reached for the smaller fry pan. She set it on the stove, and the dollop of hard butter instantly melted.

Emily inched close. "The stove's awful hot."

Polly dumped the potatoes into the pan and gave them a stir. They immediately sizzled. She salted and peppered them as the coffeepot began to rumble. Dark liquid frothed up beneath the lid and hissed on the stove's cooking surface.

Dang! The coffee kept erupting and she couldn't find a hot pad. Finally she spotted a thin dishcloth slung over the basin by the pump and she grabbed it. The heat from the stove nearly blistered her, but she managed to rescue the coffeepot. Thick liquid still hissed and bubbled out from beneath the lid. Uncertain what to do now, she smelled the scorching potatoes.

"Having any trouble in there?" Ben called from the dining room.

Was it her imagination, or was he laughing at her? She hiked her chin higher. "No, don't get up. I'm doing fine."

She swiped at the smoking potatoes with a spatula, but they were stuck to the bottom of the pan. She applied a little more pressure, but the grated slivers of potato had congealed into a solid mass that was beginning to turn black around the edges. Smoke curled upward in dark black wisps.

"Sure you don't need any help?" Ben lowered his

newspaper. "I smell something burning."

"Oh, no. I'm managing just fine." She beat into the center of the smoking potato mass with the edge of her spatula and managed to break it into two chunks. She wedged the metal tool underneath the charring half and flipped it. It sizzled, and the rest of the potatoes began to spark.

Egad! What was wrong with this stove? Polly beat at the flames with her spatula, but that only fanned them. Little fires broke out along the surface of the blackening potatoes. Lord, what did she do? This wasn't a campfire. She couldn't just toss the pan from the heat.

"Polly." She felt a tug on her skirt. "The stove's on fire."

"I see."

Thick black smoke began to rise from the burning potatoes. The pan was too hot to touch. Panicked, she scouted for a hot pad. "Get me a towel."

"There's one." Emily pulled open a drawer.

Polly took the duck towel and tried to grab the skillet off the burner. More black smoke curled upward from the pan and before she could move it from the stove, the flames doubled in height. They leaped upward, and fire stung her hand. She pulled back, heart pounding.

The flames crackled, feeding on the sizzling grease.

"Stay back, Emily. I don't want you getting burned."

Light flashed and danced dangerously. Panic drove her across the kitchen. There wasn't much time before the fire got out of control. She grabbed the pump handle and pushed. Water flew into the pail. Out of the corner of her eye she saw the flames roil upward to scorch the ceiling.

"Hurry, Polly!"

"Stay back." Polly grabbed the bucket and hurled it as hard as she could. Water flew onto the stove, and the fire flickered.

It didn't go out. Flames exploded against the wall, across the floor, and onto the nearby worktable.

Polly snatched Emily out of the way, shielding her from the fire with her body. "Are you hurt? Are you burned?"

Emily shook her head.

Thank heavens. Polly felt weak as she set Emily down.

"What the hell?" Ben burst into the room just as the back wall caught fire.

Polly raced back to the pump. "I'm trying to put the fire out."

"Ever thought of asking for help?" He grabbed a big kettle lid and tossed it over the flames. The fire struggled for life, but smothered into a deep black smoke. "Emily, go outside and wait."

"But Pa—"

"Do as I say. Use the front door. Hurry."

Ben was sending Emily far away from the flames. Good. She wanted the child safe. She'd never intended— Goodness, the fire just kept spreading. She pumped the handle furiously. Water sloshed into the bucket.

"Hurry!" Ben beat at the ceiling fire with a small braid rug he'd scooped off the floor. "Throw that on the wall. Quick, before it starts to burn through."

Polly hurled the water at the flames. Water sizzled. Smoke curled upward. Heat arced outward at her, and the sting of it chased her back several feet. The bright flames on the wall were out, but now thick, choking smoke filled the room. She couldn't see. She couldn't breathe. More bright spots of flame glowed through the thick mantle of smoke. Desperate, she refilled her bucket.

She tossed the water, and more flickering tongues of flame sputtered and died. Ben filled two buckets at the pump. She grabbed a full one, leaving her empty pail, and ran to douse the last of the flames.

Soot and smoke were everywhere. Polly saw Ben's face, dusted with ashes, through the thick black cloud separating them. She could taste his anger, smell it. Without a word, he stalked across the kitchen and threw open the door. She was too afraid to move.

The smoke started to dissipate. She could see Ben clearly and how tensed he held himself, a tall pillar of restrained male fury. A muscle jumped in his jaw. His big hands curled into fists.

Polly turned to stare at the devastation. Black soot marked the beautiful wood of the walls and floor. The acrid scent of smoke tainted the air. Smoke stained the pretty white curtains and the ceiling overhead.

She'd done this. Polly set her chin, determined to take her punishment. It was all over. This respite here, in this cozy home among the pines, was over. She'd proven her lack of worth, just as she'd done with Pa.

Surely, Ben would throw her in jail now.

"You could have burned down my entire house!" Finally, Ben's anger exploded like a gunshot, sharp and booming.

"I know. I guess I had the stove too hot."

"You guess?" Cords stood out in his throat. Muscles turned to stone beneath his black cotton shirt. "Did it ever occur to you to ask for help? To say, 'Ben, the kitchen's on fire. Could you come help me put it out?' "

"I—" She didn't know what to say.

"You could have burned down my house."

"I know." She felt awful. She braced her feet, bowed her head and waited.

Ben vibrated with anger. He'd looked up to see Emily in Polly's arms, several yards from the dangerous fire, and he'd gone crazy. Now the fire was out. "Hold out your hands."

She extended them, palms up, but she didn't look at him. Her pretty dress was stained with ashes and soot. Her face was smeared with grime and smoke.

He could have helped her. He could have shown her how much coal the stove needed. But he hadn't. He'd barked at her this morning, afraid he'd made a mistake in trusting her, and she couldn't lower her pride enough to ask for help.

He curled his fingers around her delicate wrists. Her hands were so slim and stained with soot. He saw no burns or cuts. No blisters or welts.

He released her. "I guess that's what I get for asking a gunslinger to cook my breakfast."

CHAPTER SIX

Bart didn't think he was such a bad guy. He was just misunderstood. As he rode into the nothing little town of Paradise Bluff, proper ladies scurried up off the street. The sheriff poked his head out of the jail to size him up. When he dismounted, old men sitting on a bench in the shade looked nervous and gave him a look that told him to leave.

See? He was misunderstood. He hadn't come to town to cause a single bit of harm. He just wanted to send a telegram, that was all. Sending a telegram was perfectly legal in Montana.

And unless anyone recognized him from one of the three territories where he was a wanted man, there wasn't likely to be trouble.

This time. He had more on his mind than looking for mischief. He had all he could handle right now. That high and mighty Polly Brown, her bulldog sheriff, and her double-crossing brother, Junior. He might be dead, but that no-good thug had stolen from him, and he'd be damned if he would let it go.

Nobody treated Bart Dixon that way, and they would pay for it. Every last one of them.

* * *

Polly couldn't believe the devastation she'd caused. Ben had hauled the half-burned table outside. Emily had wandered in, wide-eyed at the mess. She and Ben had ridden to town for breakfast

It was just as well. Polly's stomach rumbled as she wrung the soapy water out of the mop and rubbed it over the scorched ceiling. The wood was damaged, but the soot was the greatest problem. It had worked its way into the grain of the wood and threatened to stain it. She scrubbed until her shoulders and neck ached, then took the water outside to change it.

She heard a horse coming up the driveway, and was glad she'd taken back her revolver. The Colt was like an old friend, and the most loyal one she'd ever had. When there was danger, it protected her. When she was afraid, it was at her side and always ready. It was her most prized possession for all the times it had chased away trouble and kept her safe.

She peered through the curtains, now sadly sagging and stained. She saw a brown and white pinto mare pulling a shiny black buggy up the road. It halted in the yard. Ben climbed out and swung Emily to the ground. Her skirts caught the wind and swirled. She kept twirling all the way to the back porch.

"Polly, Pa says he's stayin' home today. To help with the mess." Emily's brightness dimmed a little. "You're all mad at me."

"At you? I'm the one who nearly burned down the kitchen." Polly saw Ben lead the mare to the stable, and she took this moment to draw Emily close. "You didn't do anything wrong."

"But I wanted pancakes."

They sat down together on the top porch step. Deer grazed in the meadow, almost hidden against the goldtipped grasses. The hush of a quiet breeze filled the morning, and Polly looked down at her ruined dress. "It's my fault, Emily. I should have admitted I didn't know a thing about that stove."

"You had lots of maids and cooks in St. Louis. Did you have someone to comb your hair every morning, too?"

"Why?"

"Cuz your hair's pretty messy."

Polly sighed. Even before the fire, her hair had been the last of her concerns. Truth was, she could braid, but that was all. She hadn't thought to try to use any of the pretty hair combs she'd seen among Pauline's trunks—her trunks, now. "I usually don't fuss over my hair."

"Pa said my ma had lots of servants, too. He said she set the curtains afire once when she was trying to learn to cook for him."

"So, your father is experienced with kitchen fires."

Emily nodded.

"Your pa looks experienced with everything." She watched him stroll out from the shadowed stable.

The sunlight seemed to worship him. It glinted in his dark hair and brushed his wide shoulders. Her heart rocked against her ribs. For one moment she forgot he didn't like her, didn't trust her and was blackmailing her.

He was the most handsome man she'd ever seen. Dressed in black, he should look severe, but the bold color only made him look powerful. Dark from hat to boot, he strode toward her with an easy gait that drew her gaze to his body and held it there. He looked rock-hard and iron-strong.

"I brought meals for all of us." He didn't look happy when he saw her. "I figure we need a hearty breakfast if we're going to try to save the kitchen."

That was all he said, but it was enough. He walked right past her. Emily went with him.

She heard the clang of enamelware, the clatter of flatware and the sound of coffee pouring. It was all she could do to stand and face Ben MacLain.

He was going to make her pay for what she'd done to

his kitchen. She just knew it.

Breakfast was quiet and strained, but the food was good. Afterwards, Emily went outside to play in the sunshine while Polly mopped. She could see Emily through the kitchen door, chasing butterflies in the meadow.

Ben didn't look up, but worked hard scrubbing the soot out of the wood. It wasn't easy work. Three hours later, the mess was cleaned up, but the burns in the beautiful wood remained. Polly was heartbroken.

When Ben headed out to the stable, Emily came in.

"Did you catch any butterflies?"

"Nah. I just like to run." She tossed back her braids. Grass seeds clung to the front of her dress and a few shocks of grass had snagged onto her hem. "What's in your satchel?"

"My play clothes." Polly set the bucket and mop out in the sun to dry. "I thought you might like to do something fun today."

"Like what?"

"We could go panning for gold or—"

"You learned to pan gold?" Emily clasped her hands together. "Oh, we could have heaps of fun. Can Pa come, too?"

"It doesn't hurt to ask." For the life of her, Polly couldn't imagine tight-jawed Ben MacLain relaxing with her next to a peaceful stream.

"I'll go see." Emily threw her arms around Polly's shoulders.

Those reed-thin arms clasped her tight, and it was a wondrous feeling. Emily darted away too soon, calling out to her father as she raced across the back yard.

Polly knew Ben would join them. He didn't trust her before she'd set his kitchen afire. He wouldn't trust her afterward.

As she headed inside to grab her satchel, she saw the blackened wood, like a horrible wound in the pretty kitchen.

She headed upstairs to find a private place to change.

"Please, Pa? Pretty please?" Emily clasped her hands together. "Why can't we? Polly brought her pan and everything. It would really make her happy. She's really sad she burned down the kitchen."

"I know." Ben's throat tightened. His gaze wandered to the house and to the open back door. He couldn't see Polly inside, but he knew she was there.

"Do you hate her now? Is she gonna have to go back to St. Louis?"

He heard the wobble in her voice, a wobble she wouldn't admit to if he asked her. Over the past year, he'd watched his daughter lose some of her sparkle with every disappointment and every broken dream. Losing her mother had been hard enough, and being on their own was even harder. She'd wanted them to move back East to be with her grandparents after the funeral, but he couldn't. He didn't dare risk leaving Montana Territory.

Emily must never learn of the man he'd once been.

He saw a movement in the upstairs window. Polly. He caught a glimpse of her lustrous brown hair flowing freely down her back, and then she breezed away from the window.

His conscience hurt. He never should have been hard on her this morning. It just wasn't easy for him to admit when he was wrong. And now he knew he'd been wrong about her satchel.

She just reminded him of Neesa—just a little, but it was there. His wife had been delicate and innocent, more girl than woman. For at the time he was still more boy than man. She'd grown up in a wealthy home and had never set foot in a kitchen before she'd married him. Seeing Polly this morning and the grease fire made him remember the woman he'd lost to a stage accident.

She'd left to visit her ailing father, waving goodbye to

little Emily as the coach pulled out of Indian Trails. With the wind in her hair and tears in her eyes, she'd hung out the window. That was the last time he saw her alive.

"Look." Emily squeezed his hand.

Polly trotted down the stairs in a pair of denims and a blue muslin shirt Her curls tangled in the wind, but she didn't seem to mind. She dropped a battered Stetson on her head and, carrying her gold pan in one gloved hand, slowed her gait as she approached.

She looked every inch a female gunslinger. She might be graceful and feminine, but she walked with an uncompromising gait. She didn't lower her gaze. She didn't shy away. She looked more dangerous than he'd ever imagined.

He never should have taken her from that cell. He never should have made her that blasted offer. Doubts plagued him as he watched the wind tousle her hair the way a lover's hand might.

"I hear you might want to go adventuring with Emily and me." She met his gaze. "Let's head out."

Emily tugged on his sleeve. "Do we getta ride, Pa?"

"Sure."

He headed to the stable with Emily and Polly at his heels. Emily started talking about the creek on their land, just out back of the cabin a ways. With the morning's argument between him and Polly forgotten, Emily began to smile again as she talked. She told Polly about the raccoons who lived in the nearby woods and the little finch nest she'd found in a tree.

Polly looked interested as she lifted the second saddle off the sawhorses. She shouldered it easily, and he figured she'd probably been riding all her life. She set it gently on the pinto's back, double-checking the blanket to make it smooth.

He watched the way she moved—gentle and quiet. The pinto appeared soothed by her touch. Polly's long mane of molasses hair shivered over her shoulders and hid half of her face as she reached down to give the cinch a good pull. The fabric of her shirt tightened across her breasts.

His gaze stroked those soft curves. Heat gathered in his groin. He took a ragged breath and looked away, but he noticed the stretch of her hip and thigh as she straightened up.

Desire slammed through him. He didn't want another woman. He hadn't been truly prepared for this, he realized now. From the moment he saw Polly Brown and her satchel this morning, fearing she would try to run, he'd known it. She made him hunger. She made him ache.

What he wanted was a marriage in name only. But with the way his blood heated, he was kidding himself.

For the first time since he'd buried Neesa, he realized she was truly gone from his life. He'd held pieces of her close, but until this morning no other woman had cooked at that stove. And, until now, he had never desired another woman.

He wasn't ready for this. He didn't want this.

Worse, he didn't want these feelings for a gunslinger, a woman on the wrong side of the law.

"I wanna ride with Polly, Pa." Emily flashed him a charming smile. "Can I?"

"You'll stay with me. This time." He scooped her up onto the palomino's withers, in front of the saddle.

Emily's hand caught his shoulder, keeping him from turning away. "You don't much like Polly, do ya?"

Her whisper was quiet, but not quiet enough. He could see Polly stiffen. She looked pale as she studied him over the top of the saddle.

His chest tightened. There was no way Emily was going to lose Polly, the mother she'd been praying for since Christmas, nearly nine months ago.

"She's pretty, don't you think?"

Emily nodded vigorously. "I don't think she can cook."

"I think you're right."

He watched Polly mount up, all graceful womanly

strength. She looked at home up on the pinto. The animal was a little skittish with strangers, and so kept sidestepping. Polly laid her hand on the mare's neck and crooned softly to her.

He didn't know why, but the more he looked at her, the more he didn't like her. He'd been the one to force this arrangement. And he knew it was the best he would be able to do for his daughter.

After so many tries, he didn't think a single woman could survive the long trip through Montana Territory with so many bachelors on the loose.

Polly would just have to do.

"Lead the way." She wasn't easily cowed, that was for sure. She gazed at him now with big eyes the color of dreams and he saw for the first time what those dreams might be.

The wind snapped her hair across her face. When the trail shifted south, the wind rippled those rich mahogany curls behind her. She rode the trail with an ease he'd seen in no other woman. He noticed how her denim-encased thighs gripped the saddle.

"Pa, why are you so mad at Polly?" Emily wound her fingers through Fugitive's creamy mane.

"She nearly set the house on fire."

"You were mad at her before that."

"Well, it's nothing you ought to worry about."

"But if you don't like her, Pa, then she has to go back to St. Louis." Emily swiped at a stray tendril.

He brushed her gossamer curls out of her eyes. "Do you like her?"

"She's got a gold pan." Emily paused. "When you wrote those letters for me, I told her all the things we could do when she got here. We could fish and hunt for gold. And she said she didn't like the woods or being in the dirt. But see, she changed her mind and all for me."

"All for you, huh?"

She nodded vigorously, betraying her tender heart.

"She must really wanna be my ma."

Ben pressed a kiss to her brow and hoped her words could make it true.

Don't let my daughter down, Polly. I can forgive anything but that. But when he felt that telltale tightening around his spine, he knew they were headed for trouble. He didn't know what, but he could feel it.

Someone was watching them.

"Polly. This is the creek where I found that gold nugget." Emily hit the ground running. "It was worth a whole dollar."

"I found a hundred-dollar nugget once." Polly felt the pinto sidestep, and she tightened the reins and gave the animal a comforting pat.

"You learned to pan on the way here?"

"Well, yes. You could say that." Polly swung down, her conscience wincing. "I bought my pan from a miner who'd struck gold on his claim. He said he found such a rich vein, he was selling it to a big company and didn't need his mining things anymore. He claimed this pan had brought him luck."

"Have you been lucky with it so far?"

"Well, I found that hundred-dollar nugget."

Ben's hand curled over hers. "You tell a good story, Polly."

She could read the skeptical slant of his brows. "You don't believe me?"

"The stage line does go through the mining camps." He took the reins from her.

"It's true, can't you see that, Pa?" Emily took the pan Polly offered her and stared at it as if it were gold itself. "I bet we can strike it rich, Polly."

"We might as well give it a good try."

Ben's hand caught hers. "I want you to stay in my sight."

"Afraid I'll take off for the hills?"

"No, bears live in these woods."

She didn't believe him. He led the horses away to water them. He watched her every step as she joined Emily at the creek bank. She felt his gaze like a long hot touch on her face and then on her body as she took off her shoes, waded into the creek and helped Emily pick a spot to pan.

Whenever she looked up, there he was, his gaze unblinking, his attention on her. When the horses were watered, he tethered them in the sunshine where they could graze and drowse. The lazy breeze carried his low voice as he spoke with the animals.

Although she seemed to have her own personal sheriff watching her every move, jail was not a better choice. Polly vowed to remember that. The blue sky stretched overhead, and tall trees spread their leaves toward the sun. Birds sang and insects buzzed. A toad plopped a few feet along the bank to follow the sunshine. The wind tousled her hair and she breathed in the fresh woodsy scent of the forest. The creek gurgled over rocks and brushed cool water against her ankles. No stone cell could feed her heart like this.

With the sunlight on her face, she knelt beside Emily.

"I don't have nothin' but rocks." The girl swiped at her bangs. "So far this pan ain't very lucky."

"Sure it is." Polly took the pan, cool from the stream, and held it to her chest. "Let's pick another spot. How about over there? See how the water slows down around that bend? It's a better spot."

They sloshed together against the current, scaring little tadpoles and tiny fish. A bird landed on a rock and squawked in protest, then took off for a quieter perch. She spotted Ben on the bank, shoulder propped against a tree, still watching her.

She shaded her eyes with her hand, dripping water onto her shirt. "You're still mad about the kitchen fire."

"I'm not mad." His mouth quirked in the corner.

"He's mad," Emily whispered.

"If you'd set my house on fire, I'd be more than a little

mad." Polly flicked water off her fingertips, then shaded her eyes again just in time to watch that hard line at his jaw soften. "You could have done a lot more than yell. I guess you'll just hold it against me for the rest of my life."

"That's not what I'm holding against you."

"Hmm." He didn't look mad, but he felt distant. "You don't want me teaching your daughter to pan for gold."

"Next thing you know, she'll refuse to go to school and head off into the gold fields to file a claim."

"Oh, Pa." Emily leaped out of the creek and grabbed him by the hand. "I wouldn't leave without you."

"You like the idea of owning a gold mine, is that it?" Ben's eyes warmed, and there was no hiding the love he had for his daughter.

What would it be like to know love like that? The emptiness of her childhood stretched behind her, vast and dark. She'd grown up thinking that's all there was in life, but now, watching Emily pull her reluctant father toward the creek, she saw something else.

The stories her mother had told her were true. There was a magical place where little girls were more valued than gold. It wasn't just in those stories Mother read at night, but here in Montana Territory where fathers protected their daughters and took the time to play with them in the creek.

Emily came up with nothing but gravel again. Father and daughter grumbled about their failure together.

"It was just a story," Ben said. "This pan is exactly like every other."

"That's what you think." So, Ben couldn't see the magic. He'd probably grown up like this, with a safe childhood and a comfortable home and endless stability. But she hadn't, and she could see what he did not.

She wrestled the pan out of his hands and worked it into the creek bed. She went by feel, by heart.

When she hefted it from the water a good twenty minutes later, there were two small nuggets winking in the sunlit water in the bottom of the pan.

From his back steps, Ben watched the sun slide behind the Garnet Range, the rugged mountains glowing dark purple as the great ball of light disappeared. The day was over, this first day with Polly in their lives.

He'd felt watched all afternoon, but there'd been no sign of trouble. The loaded Colt was still unsnapped in his holster, loaded and ready if he needed it.

He hadn't imagined the trouble. His intuition had saved his life more times than he could count. It wouldn't fail him now. The feeling had eased, but he remained alert. The sounds of night came with the setting sun. He could hear Polly's voice in the kitchen behind him, playing checkers with Emily. One last game, the girl pleaded.

What should he do about the pretty little gunslinger? He'd made a mistake, that was for sure. He didn't know how much he could trust a gunfighter, but he figured she would at least be able to cook.

Most of all, he'd gambled that she might want to leave her old life behind.

Hell, that wasn't what was bothering him. It had been a tough three years for them, especially for Emily.

He just wanted to make everything right. To give her a mother who would love her. A woman to take care of her. A legal parent in case the past ever caught up with him.

"Pa, Polly's gonna read me a bedtime story. Do you wanna come, too?"

"Sure, pumpkin." He wouldn't miss it for anything. He'd tucked Emily safely into bed every night since she was born.

Polly stood when he entered the room, and put away the last of the checker pieces. She looked at him with wide eyes, as if she expected him to send her back to jail at any moment.

"You took off your gun belt, Sheriff." She quirked one

lean brow. "I can't believe you trust me that much."

"I don't. I can take you in, with or without a gun." He winked.

"We'll have to see about that." She brushed past him, leaving a scent of sunshine and spice.

His pulse kicked at the sight of those worn Levi's hugging her hips and the curve of her bottom like a lover's hand. He followed her up the stairs with his daughter at his side. He tried to remember she was wanted by the law. She was here by the power of his threats and not by her choice. But it didn't matter. His blood heated, and he fought to look everywhere but at Polly.

He failed.

Emily's room was cozy, with a lamp lit on the bedside table.

"Polly, I wanna hear this story." Emily held out her favorite magazine. The cherished story had been read and reread so many times, the paper was worn around the edges.

Polly paled, and her gaze flew to him. Ben felt a hard clutch in his guts. She was going to refuse. She was going to break one of Pauline's promises to Emily.

He stepped forward, ready to protect his daughter from yet another woman's rejection. "I'll—"

"I'd love to read to you," Polly interrupted, and that whiskey smooth voice of hers had his skin tingling. "I truly would. But you know what? I would rather tell you my favorite story. One my own mother used to tell me when I was your age. Would that be all right?"

He waited, the fight draining out of him.

Emily hopped onto her bed, laid back and pulled up the flowered sheet to her waist. Expectation sparkled in her eyes, and she looked so happy. He'd never seen her so happy.

"Once upon a time in a land far away. . . "

Polly's voice turned dreamy and mesmerizing, but it wasn't the story Ben listened to. It was Polly—the woman, who'd surprised him more in one day than anyone had in a long time.

He'd expected the worst from her. He'd learned to expect that from people. But she'd proven she was as good as her word. So he listened to the rise and fall of her voice. She could change a simple fairytale he'd told Emily a thousand times into something magical. He saw the goodness inside her.

It was a goodness of heart that no bounty hunter could keep for long.

Ben had to wonder now if he'd proposed to Polly for Emily or for himself—for the young man he used to be before a hard world stripped his heart bare.

He was glad that hadn't yet happened to Polly Brown.

CHAPTER SEVEN

Polly gazed down from her window. Night enveloped the town. Every evening for a week Ben had his deputy drive her to the hotel. Every evening for a week she'd told stories to Emily, dodging the written tales the girl wanted her to read instead.

Every day neither Ben nor Emily had let her cook anything. Martha was very happy her business hadn't fallen off because of Ben's new bride.

But every night Ben or his deputy kept watch on her hotel, keeping her a prisoner without bars.

She headed down to the hotel's lobby, where the owner looked up from his paperwork and greeted her with a welcoming hello.

"Nice night out. The kitchen's still open if you need a cup of tea, Miss Curtis."

"I'll keep that in mind, Mr. Mitchell." Polly laid her hand over her pocket, the ever-present gun tucked away there. She kept it unloaded when she was around Emily, but here, at night, she wanted the safety of her old friend.

"My missus wanted me to ask you when the wedding is."

"The wedding?" Then she blushed. "We haven't set a

date yet."

"See that you do. Ben's a good man. He's kept this town free of outlaws and troublemakers, and in this part of the Territory that's a tough feat."

The kindly old man gave her a wink, then returned to his work. He had no notion that a notorious outlaw's daughter was standing right in front of him.

She adjusted the brim of her bonnet and headed out into the night. Cool air met her, not cold yet, but the first real hint that autumn was on its way. The night felt solemn; the streets were nearly empty. Polly crossed through the dust and strolled along the vacant boardwalk. Her shoes tapped pleasantly in the darkness. The faint sound of piano music rose on the night breeze, bringing with it the soothing scent of cheap draft.

"Howdy, Ben." She strolled past him, knowing she'd surprised the heck out of him.

The shadows moved. "How did you know I was here?"

"You aren't as stealthy as you think." Polly kept walking. Sure enough, he caught up with her, his boots falling into a deeper rhythm alongside hers. It was strange to be alone with him, without Emily nearby. "Where's your daughter?"

"My deputy's wife sleeps over when I need to work nights."

"Too bad for your deputy."

"He's working, too."

The snappy refrain of a familiar barroom ditty rang in the air. She elbowed open one batwing door. "You might as well come in and have a drink with me, since you're bound by duty to follow every step I take."

"I'm not following you. I'm protecting you."

How deep his voice, rumbling and sexy. She shivered, and then she realized inviting Ben to spend time with her was a bad idea. She may have accepted his domestic offer, but that didn't mean she liked it.

"Protecting me? You're the man who threw me in jail, MacLain." She stepped inside, leaving him to catch the door as it slapped toward his chest.

The busy sounds of the saloon felt like home. The sharp jangle of glass, the din of men arguing and gambling, the tinny tunes of the piano rising above it all, cheerful and friendly. She could practically taste the beer that scented the air.

"After I saw you with Emily, I knew what I did was right." Ben tugged out a chair and dropped into it.

She looked at him a moment, then chose another table. "I like to face the door."

"I should have known." Ben stood, resigned, just as a scantily clad woman sauntered near, bending over to take his order and show him an exceptional amount of cleavage.

To his credit, Ben turned pink from his chin to his hairline. He muttered something, his strong sheriffs demeanor belying the blush on his face. He placed an order and Polly watched, amused. He acted like a man unbowed by anything.

Except the blush still stained his face.

"Did she make you an offer? Maybe you might want to consider blackmailing her with jail." Polly reached into her reticule and pulled out a packet of thin papers. She spread them out on the small table's sticky surface.

"You smoke?"

"Now and then. I practically grew up in saloons. When my father wasn't working, he spent his time drinking and gambling." Polly tapped fragrant tobacco out of its pouch. "Those memories aren't the best, but they are the best ones I have. Sometimes one of the working girls would take pity on me and make sure I was fed and had a safe place to sleep. One even taught me how to play the piano."

"You play?"

"It's been a long time, but yes." She tucked the pouch

back into her reticule and rolled the cigarettes with the tips of her fingers. She handed Ben one.

"What did your father do?" Ben's fingers brushed hers as he took the cigarette. "Something tells me he wasn't a bartender."

"You know he was an outlaw." Polly struck a match. "Roy Brown, leader of the notorious Brown gang."

Ben's jaw tensed. "The man wanted in six territories?"

Polly blew a ring of smoke. "He's a tough man. I ran away from him when I was sixteen. I'd been trying for years, but it was the first time I succeeded."

Ben's face shadowed. He lit his cigarette and wouldn't look at her. "Roy Brown's daughter."

"I thought you knew, since you had that wanted poster in hand."

But he hadn't known, she guessed, and now it changed how he looked at her. She'd gone from beautiful belle to bounty hunter to being a vicious outlaw's offspring. Ben's opinion of her must be so low it was slithering below ground.

The saloon girl swirled by with two drinks on a tray. She leaned over Ben and batted her eyes, offering more than just the draft.

Polly looked at the glass. "What the heck is this?"

"Sarsaparilla." Ben was blushing again.

"Bring me a beer."

"You're my fiancee. I don't want you drinking spirits. You're an upstanding lady." Ben's gaze pleaded with her.

She stared hard at the soft drink. "Bring me a good draft."

The serving woman shrugged, snatched up the glass, and sauntered away with a generous sway of her hips. Ben didn't look, but he was still blushing.

"I've tried hard to be what you want. I've put up with you watching my every move and always expecting the worst. I've worn dresses and played with your daughter and tried to be presentable enough."

"You don't like playing with Emily?" He challenged, suddenly hard as rock.

"That's not what I said." She thanked the waitress for the beer and took a sip. The malty brew smoothed over her tongue and reminded her of better days. "I like Emily. I really—" She stopped before she said words better left unsaid. "I might as well be in jail. If you aren't following me everywhere, then one of your deputies is."

"With good reason."

"You think I'm going to break my word. Because I'm wanted by the law—" she lowered her voice. "You think Roy Brown's daughter can't be trusted."

"That's not what I said."

"I'll have you know every penny I've ever put in my pocket has been earned, not stolen. I hated what my father did and how he hurt people." She shuddered, remembering. "I lived under his rule for the first sixteen years of my life, and I won't live like that again."

"Your father isn't here, Polly."

"No, but you are." She took a puff on her cigarette, taking pleasure in blowing another smoke ring. It was the real reason she smoked, the relaxation and concentration it took to make one perfect circle after another. "Now it's your choice. You either lock me back up in your horrid jail, or you trust me to keep Pauline's promise to Emily."

"You're right. I thought you were going to leave—at first." Ben set down his glass and stared hard into the foaming beer. "It's hard, but I can admit when I'm wrong. I knew it the moment I saw you teaching Emily how to pan for gold in the creek. You were patient with her and you gave her something she hasn't had since her mother died."

"What?"

"Dreams." It was all he could do to keep his hands wrapped around the cool glass. He wanted to brush at those flyaway curls always falling in her face, untamed and unruly and as sexy as sin. "It's like a light has gone on in her world."

"And you're afraid I'm going to leave and take that with me."

"No. I'm afraid someone is going to hurt you." Ben tapped ashes from his cigarette. "Tell me why you're carrying a loaded gun."

"Because it's nighttime and a woman alone isn't safe on the streets."

"You knew I was watching you. You weren't alone."

She blew another smoke ring, her luscious lips curling like an open-mouthed kiss.

Desire thundered through him. Hard and hot and heavy. He didn't want to feel this way. He didn't want to love any woman, not again. He stared hard at his beer, at the table, at her hands stubbing out the cigarette. Strong, finely made hands that would know how to touch a man, how to give pleasure.

He took another drink. "You never take that gun out of your pocket."

"I keep it unloaded around Emily. You're right. A loaded gun shouldn't be near a child." She bit her lip. "Do you think Dixon will be back?"

"I think it's a possibility." Ben turned when he heard the door swing open. He didn't like having his back to the door either. "Maybe he'll heed my warning and stay away, but I have a bad feeling about it."

"So do I." Her chin shot up, trying to look as tough as nails. "I can take care of myself."

"Polly, it's too late. I've already seen your defenses down." He laid his hand on hers, and his pulse jolted at the contact. "I'm not going to fault you for your soft heart, Polly. Or the fear in your eyes. Everyone gets afraid, whether they show it or not."

"I'd rather not show it." Her set chin, her unflinching gaze, and her tensed stance all said she was a woman able to take care of herself.

But the satin ribbon edging her collar was blue, the

same shade as her eyes, and it was hard not to notice the dark fringe of lashes above those eyes, and the delicate cut of high cheekbones and a sensual mouth. Her lips narrowed into a compressed line, but it took no imagination at all to see the vulnerability there.

A vulnerability that touched him, even when he didn't want it to. "I gave you my word, and I mean it I'll protect you."

She didn't believe it. It was there in the dip of her chin and the wince around those forever-blue eyes. She wasn't used to trusting people. She wasn't used to trusting a man. Well, she would learn in time.

He took a final swig of his beer. "We haven't set a wedding date yet."

She stood, tossing down a silver piece on the table. "I won't marry you."

"You said—"

"I don't care what I said. You're treating me like a criminal and it's over, MacLain. I won't be afraid of you anymore." She rushed past him, nearly tripping when her hem wrapped around one ankle.

He left enough coins for the beer and a tip and strode after her. "Polly, I don't want to frighten you."

"You can send me to jail any time you want."

"Have I threatened you with that lately? Since that day at the creek?" He caught up with her as she tripped again on her dress.

"But the threat is there." She lifted the hem up with both hands and charged across the road. "It's you I have a problem with, not our arrangement. I want to take care of Emily. I want to have a safe bed to sleep in every night. But if I wanted to be watched and judged every time I take a breath, I could have let my father find me—"

"Find you?"

"I mean—Oh, heck." She pointed at the hotel's second-story window where a single light glowed against closed curtains. "I didn't leave a lamp burning when I left my room."

Could be Dixon. Could be just a thief. Either way, Ben didn't like either in his town, much less in his fiancée's room. He loped down the boardwalk just ahead of Polly, who was sprinting like a true champion. He shouldered open the back door and tore up the stairs.

"I'll take the front," she called out.

"Wait—"

She was already gone. Damn. He should have seen that one coming, but he was preoccupied. Polly's words tonight had confused him. He hadn't realized how she'd seen events. And even then—

Geez, she was Roy Brown's daughter, an outlaw who'd been caught but never imprisoned for long. He'd killed nearly a dozen lawmen over the course of his career, and more victims than anyone could count. He was believed to be responsible for the theft of nearly half a million dollars over his twenty-year career.

He was also a man Ben used to ride with.

Sick to his stomach, he charged down the hall and hoped to high heaven whoever was in Polly's room wasn't a member of the Brown gang. Her door was cracked open and he kicked it wide, both revolvers already in his hands.

The room was empty. A lamp with its wick turned low flickered on the bedside table and cast enough light to see that the trunks on the floor had been thrown open. Various articles of clothing littered the floor. The bureau's drawers gaped wide.

Polly. If the intruder had escaped down the front stairs, she would be alone with him. Ben wheeled around and raced down the hallway, hoping he wasn't too late.

He barreled down the stairs, but saw no sign of her. The banker and his wife were emerging from the dining room and were putting on their coats, discussing the lovely tea they'd had. Mr. Mitchell never looked up from his paperwork.

Ben tore out the front doors onto the empty street.

There was no sign of her. Anywhere.

* * *

The darn skirt wrapped around her ankles again and she tripped. She fought for her balance, but she fell fast and hit the ground hard. Rocks dug into her skin. Pain shot through her leg and arm. She heard the fast tap of a man running down the road. That sound faded.

She'd lost him.

When she'd seen a man running out of the hotel, she'd taken off after him. If only she'd been able to see his face. Whoever he was, he was a good runner.

She hauled herself off the ground, wincing at the pain in her arm. Her leg stung something fierce, but it was nothing serious. She hauled the gun out of her pocket, thankful it was loaded. She would have tried to shoot her assailant, but she didn't have the time to stop and aim.

Now it was too late. He'd escaped anyway, and she didn't know who he was. But she did know who he wasn't. He wasn't any of her father's men. They wouldn't have run away from her—they would have taken her with them.

She limped toward town, keeping an eye on the road behind her. She was alone, and the man she'd chased didn't return. When she saw the lights of town, relief washed over her. She was starting to get used to this place, it was going to be her home from now on. Home. That gave her a good feeling. She'd always wanted a place to settle down.

The drum of horses startled her. They galloped hard down the road. She slipped out of sight and crouched in the shadows, heart pounding. But her gaze riveted on one of the approaching riders. She would recognize those broad shoulders anywhere.

She jumped to her feet. "Ben."

The gelding reared to a surprised stop.

"Polly! I thought—" Ben looked down the road, then at the riders behind him. "I thought you'd been kidnapped."

"I was trying to chase him down, but I tripped." She ambled up to his horse. "I'm not used to running in a dress. That's why he got away."

"I thought I'd never see you again—that nobody would." He dismounted with one powerful motion. This man as strong as the night stole her breath away when he wrapped her tight in his arms.

She'd never thought being held by a man would feel so wonderful, but it did. She didn't move away. She let his arms settle around her shoulders and his hands burn hot against her back. She nestled her face against the crook between the curve of his shoulder and the column of his neck.

"I'm glad you're safe," his voice buzzed against her ear, pleasant and hot and magnificent.

He smelled like soap and leather and man, and his chest felt as hard as it looked. His heat burned through the dark shirt and she soaked it in, like the comfort he was giving her. Safe and solid, she held onto him tight.

His lips brushed the top of her head. "Let's get you back to the hotel."

She nodded. She couldn't think of a single argument. All she wanted to do was be held like this forever—to be safe and protected against Ben's solid chest

"You didn't see his face. Are you sure?"

Polly nodded as she shook the wrinkles out of another fallen gown. She knelt on the carpeted floor, the hotel room mostly dark except for the lone lamp. Low flames caressed her face, highlighting the temper in her eyes. "For the sixth time, that's what I said."

"You have a past you want to leave behind, I understand that, but you must tell me the truth—"

"You don't understand a thing." Polly laid the dress carefully in the trunk, then plucked another off the heap on the floor. "You're a hard-nosed, do-gooder who has never had a hungry belly or ever been forced into a life that made you ashamed."

"Don't be too sure."

"You live in the most beautiful house I've ever seen." She flicked the dress hard. "You have a good job and respect from the people in this town. What do you know about my life?"

"I know there's a bounty on your head and a man who wants you dead."

"That's not all that I am."

"I know." His chest tightened and he couldn't look away from the woman on the floor, who was the biggest paradox he'd ever met. "I know that when you tell Emily a story, she looks more like the little girl she was before her mother died. That's what I know about you."

Polly held onto the remnants of her anger stubbornly, her jaw tightly clenched. "Do you really think that? Or are you just trying to get me to drop my defenses so you can interrogate me again?"

"Do you ever drop your defenses?"

"Not for you." She smoothed the gown's collar before setting it inside the trunk. "If it weren't for you, I'd be trying to track that thief right now instead of worrying whether or not he'll come back."

"I sent my deputies out to do the job. Halston is one of the best trackers in these parts." Ben didn't tell her about the fear that had been cold in his mouth when he'd gathered up his men, rousting some from their beds, and ordered a search for his fiancée. He hadn't told anyone Polly was Roy Brown's daughter.

Hell, Roy Brown's daughter. He scrubbed his hands over his face. "Was anything stolen?"

"Just a piece of jewelry and some money from the bureau drawer. About ten bucks." Polly plucked up another garment, folded it, then set it in the trunk. "I don't think he was looking to take anything."

"He was looking for something."

"Maybe he was looking for me." She kept folding as if

nothing were wrong, but he could see the lines of tension around her mouth and eyes. "Normally I just move on, and that takes care of the situation."

"You get men following you around regularly?"

She nodded. "Of course, I thought that sort of thing might stop if I looked like a respectable lady. Maybe it's just the way some men are. They see a woman alone and they figure they can be as bold as they want."

"Or as sneaky?"

She swallowed, and her hand slid to her skirt pocket. Her fingers brushed at the gun through the fabric, and he wondered how many times she'd had to save herself because she had no one else to protect her.

"Maybe this was about Dixon. Or about the price on your head." Ben stepped toward her. "Your wanted poster hasn't been out long. A week or so. It was still in the top pile on my desk. That's how I happened to see it the day you came to town."

Polly clasped the trunk shut. "I don't know who would recognize me. I kept low and avoided towns, except for having to take the stage. I miss my horse."

She stood, her dress cascading around her thighs and hips until he couldn't look away. She ambled to the window and stood just to the side of it, gazing out at the night. The late summer breezes puffed out the white curtains, and she pulled them aside.

"It's Dixon, I think. He might have been watching the hotel." She leaned her forehead against the glass, and her hair billowed in the breeze. She looked tired. She seemed weary.

He ached for her. He didn't want to. Tonight, he'd held a woman for the first time since his wife's death. It had felt good, too good. He took a shaky breath. He wanted to be alone the rest of his life. His love with Neesa was as good as life got. A man didn't get another chance like that.

"Maybe he was watching from the street and saw my light go out. I went out the front he could have started up the back. I don't have anything anyone would want."

"You have the Golden Gulch gold."

"You know I don't."

"Others might believe it." He laid a hand on her shoulder. She felt as hot as the summer night and as mysterious as the breeze tangling her long, molasses curls. He wanted to know more about her. And he was afraid to. "That's why you're coming home with me tonight."

"What?"

"So I know you're safe."

"You have that wrong, mister." She whirled on him, jaw set, eyes afire, all fight. "I'm not your wife yet."

"But you will be. You gave me your word. And until then, I've got to keep my promise, don't I? I have to keep you safe, just like I said."

"Or there will be no mother for Emily."

"No." His heart knocked against his chest. "Or I'll never have your trust."

"I told you. How can I trust you? You're holding my life in your hands."

He leaned forward. He couldn't help himself. Every inch of his body pounded with a growing lust that he couldn't control. And lust was safe. Lust was good. It was a far cry from love, and that was just fine. Lust would never involve his heart. He never wanted to care so much for a woman again.

"You're going to kiss me, aren't you?" Polly licked her lips, her gaze nervously darting past his shoulder to the door at the other end of the room. "I don't want to be kissed by you."

"Too bad. I want to kiss you." He leaned so close their breaths mingled.

"That isn't a good way to earn my trust."

"Then maybe I'll earn your lust." He couldn't help teasing because Polly, for all her soft edges and kind heart, was a woman who knew how the world worked.

He splayed his hand around her throat and covered her

mouth with his.

CHAPTER EIGHT

The brush of his lips to hers was sweeter than anything Polly had ever known before. His mouth felt as soft as crushed velvet and tasted smoky, like a hot fire. A hint of cinnamon and apple still clung to him, and she gave a little gasp as he moved away.

His eyes were dark like dreams, his mouth still shaped by their kiss. A day's growth darkened the bronze of his skin along his jaw, and she wanted to touch him there. She wanted to know the feel of his hot skin and rough whiskers.

His lips covered hers again—all heat and demand and want. His mouth caressed hers and left tingling pleasure everywhere he touched. She wrapped her arms around his neck and kissed him back. Their lips fit together and moved apart in slow, breath-stopping caresses that left her weak and wanting more.

His teeth caught her lower lip and drew it into his mouth. He sucked gently, and she sighed. She had no idea kissing could feel so good. It made her breath quicken and her pulse surge. She caught his bottom lip between her teeth and sucked. His fingers curled around her nape and cradled her head. His breath came fast and harsh.

Then he broke away. Her mouth longed for him, but he took a step back. His eyes were dark with desire for her, and she felt as skittish as a green colt. But she wasn't afraid. She wanted more. Her lips buzzed, and she felt exhilarated. The night breeze fluttered between them and cooled the surface of her mouth.

How could a man's touch feel so good, his kiss so grand?

"Will you let me take a look at those cuts now?" He brushed one hand down the length of her forearm.

She shivered at his touch. "I told you, I'm fine."

"I want to see for myself." His fingers kept traveling all the way down to her wrist where he turned her arm over to look at the scrapes. "Doesn't look like you need stitches, but I could call the doctor—"

"No doctor." She pulled back her hand with regret. A part of her ached for someone to care for her—truly care. And yet the sensible part of her knew it was never going to happen.

She stepped away and closed the window, drew the drapes. Every movement took her further away from him emotionally, and that was good. "Look, I've got to get some sleep. I plan on a rematch with your stove tomorrow, and—"

"Oh, no. No cooking. That's one duty I'm never going to ask of you again." He grabbed her cloak from the peg by the door. "Put this on. You're coming home with me."

"Now?"

He folded his arms over his chest and looked about as easy to conquer as the Continental Divide. "Right now. There's been a threat against you—"

"I can handle it." She yanked the gun out of her pocket and tossed it on the bed.

"Can you? If Dixon's back, then he's brought help—"

"If it was Dixon, he wouldn't have run." Polly tugged her gun belt out from beneath the bed and unsnapped her second revolver. "I'm not afraid."

"You look afraid to me."

"This is my life, MacLain. This is the way I've lived since my mother died. It isn't safe and it isn't secure, but it's all I have."

"Not anymore. You have me." He hefted a trunk up onto his shoulder. "And you don't have a lock on this door."

"I can fix it—"

"No. You're going to be where I can keep you safe." He caught the edge of the door with his boot and wedged it open. "You don't have a say in this."

"We'll see about that." Polly buckled her belt around her hips, despite the dress's bustle. "Bring that trunk back here. I'm going to request another room."

He faced her. When she expected anger, she saw strength. The kind that wasn't driven by the weakness of fury, but by the solid steadiness of his honor. "There will be no more hotel rooms and no more men thinking you're an easy target. Isn't that what you want?"

She hesitated. Why was it so hard to accept his help? Why couldn't she just demurely agree with him and do as he asked?

Because she knew no man was that honorable. In the end, the only person she could really depend on was herself.

And it was easier, in the long run, to not depend on anyone at all. No disappointments. No broken heart. No hurt.

"Besides, if anyone's going to try to bring you in for that bounty on your head," he winked, "it might as well be me."

"See, I knew you just wanted to keep track of me. You're a lawman through and through. The power's gone to your head."

"Believe me, it would be easier to turn you in for the bounty." He stepped out into the hallway. "My kitchen is never going to be the same."

Oh, he thought he was charming when he teased. But beneath the glimmer of humor snapping in his eyes and the charming slant of his grin, she saw the steady worry he did not give voice to. He'd truly been afraid for her tonight. She remembered how hard he'd held her and how true his kiss. She found a way to step out into the hall, lift her chin, and say the unthinkable. "I'll go home with you, MacLain."

"I'm glad. I won't sleep until I know you're safe."

It wasn't as hard to follow him the rest of the way down the stairs and out into the dark.

A bounce on the mattress next to her rousted Polly awake. She opened her eyes to the first rays of sunlight and Emily crouching over her. "Pa says you're gonna stay with us forever and forever."

"That's what he says, huh?" She crawled up onto her elbows.

"What's in all those trunks? Can I see?"

"Sure." Polly tossed off the sheet and stood. Her nightgown shivered down around her ankles and she stretched. Her hand was scraped and her left leg was stiff where she'd fallen on it but other than that, she felt in good spirits.

It was nice waking up in a real bed in a real home. Sunshine glinted through the only window, and she stepped into its light. Through the boughs of a pine, she could see the rugged peaks of the Rockies, dusted pink and purple with the new day's glow.

"Real silk!" Emily's delight shimmered in the sweet morning air. "Are these real pearls?"

The girl knelt on the floor before one of the trunks. She swept one timid hand across the bodice of a beautiful pink gown. Polly knelt down beside her and rubbed her thumb over the satin smooth gems that marched down the front of the dress. She didn't know if it was real pearl or not. "Would you like to try it on?"

MACLAIN'S WIFE

"Can I?"

Polly reached in and lifted out the gown. The dark pink fabric caught the light and shimmered. Emily tugged her calico dress over her head and got stuck.

"Unbutton first." Polly caught hold of the inside-out button and pushed it through, freeing the girl. "Dresses are tricky with all those clasps and bows. That's why I like my trousers. Here." She held up the beautiful satin. "Step into it and I'll button you in."

"Listen. It rustles." Emily's eyes shone.

Warmth tugged at her heart. Polly lifted the dress by the shoulders and helped her find the armholes.

"Do I look like a princess?"

"You're just as pretty as one." The buttons were smooth beneath her fingertips. "There. Let me look at you."

The dress was far too big, but the color was stunning. Emily's face was still round and soft, but time would bring out cheekbones and the sleek line of her jaw. She had a pixie's face and a darling's heart.

Polly's throat ached, and she unclasped the lid of the second trunk. "You need a hat. Help me pick one out."

"Look at all the bonnets!" Emily dug through a pile of them with great enthusiasm. She chose a beautiful straw bonnet with a sprig of flowers and satin ribbons on the brim that exactly matched the dress.

"Perfect choice." Polly set the too-big hat on Emily's head and caught the ribbons into a bow beneath her chin. It wasn't a big, fat poofy bow, the kind most ladies knew how to make, and Polly regretted that. "Go ahead and keep digging. There are some necklaces in there."

"Goody." Emily dropped to her knees and continued her search. "What's in the other trunk?"

"I don't know. I haven't opened it. The clasp broke, and I never—"

"You don't know what's in there?" Emily shook her head, as if adults were very silly indeed. "Pa's real good at fixin' things."

"So am I." Polly grabbed her reticule, dug around inside and pulled out her pocketknife.

"You gotta knife?"

"Yep. And I know how to use it, too." Polly chose a blade.

"It looks real sharp."

"It is. I sharpened it myself." She hunkered down in front of the trunk.

"I'd better go get Pa."

"Look, I've almost got it." Polly wedged the tip of the blade beneath the bent metal and pushed. The strip of metal began to uncrumple. She forced it back into place, then easily opened the clasp.

Emily stared at her with rounded eyes.

"You thought I was going to cause another disaster, didn't you?" Polly clicked the blade safely into place.

"A lady has to have a lot of skills. She shouldn't depend on a man for everything."

A man's step sounded behind her. "Is that so?"

His voice rumbled through her, as intimate and sensual as last night's kiss, and Polly shivered. She tossed her pocketknife onto the bed. "I know I'm going to regret letting you move me in here."

"Why? You're going to marry me in a few days—"

"A few days?" She planted her hands on her hips.

"Sure. By then you'll see that I'm right and we can just get it over with."

"So, that's how you see marriage?"

"Well, yes." He winked, obviously thinking he was much more charming than he really was. "Marriage or jail, what's the difference."

Polly shook her head. "You're not one bit funny."

"Pa." Emily dashed up to him, holding her dress high above her knees so she wouldn't trip. "You gotta stop arguin' with Polly or she'll go away."

"Polly isn't going anywhere." Ben's eyes shadowed and

he knelt down to wrap his daughter in a gentle hug. "Look how beautiful you are. Polly's letting you try on some of her dresses."

"Yep, and look what I found." Quickly comforted, she darted away. "Books."

"What?" Polly spun around to stare at what lay inside the third trunk. Her heart dropped to the floor. Goodness, it couldn't be. It just couldn't—"

"Lots and lots of books!" Emily dropped to her knees with a thud, the dresses, hats and accessories forgotten as she pulled out one leatherbound volume after another. "I love stories. As soon as I start first grade, I'm gonna learn how to read real good."

Ben strolled in, interested now. His eyes brightened at the leatherbound volumes accumulating in great piles on the floor. "No wonder that darn trunk was so heavy."

"You said in your letters you were gonna bring me lots of books. You promised to read me to sleep every night" Emily gazed up at her as if she were a queen. "You didn't forget."

Polly's heart sank. So much hope burned in Emily's eyes, so much longing for a mother's care. How could she keep her vow to Ben? How could she tell Emily that she couldn't read? That she wasn't the fancy lady Emily had wanted—she was just plain Polly Brown.

"I don't know about you two beauties, but I'm hungry." Ben balanced one book in his palm, but his eyes were traveling down the front of her nightgown.

Polly blushed. "Let me get dressed, and then I'll be right down."

Ben spied Polly slipping into the kitchen. He couldn't help noticing the way her slim hips swayed beneath the cascade of pink gingham that draped her from collar to ankle. The memory of their kiss burned across his lips, and his blood heated at the thought of kissing more than her sensuous mouth.

"I have the buggy hitched and ready to go." He leaned against the doorway just to watch the skirts swish against her legs.

"I thought we might eat at home this morning." She tilted her head to watch his reaction.

"I'm not ready to risk burning down my house."

"It was a one-time mistake." Her pearled teeth bit into her bottom lip. "I know you could have lost your house—"

"You're a bounty hunter, not a cook. I've accepted that." And he had. He wasn't happy about it, but they would figure something out. Maybe Martha would agree to teach Polly a few cooking skills. Either way, he wasn't going to risk another fire. "Step away from the stove, Polly."

"No. I've got to face my new enemy. It's a matter of attitude. I know I can convince it to back down and behave." She tossed a grin at him.

His knees buckled at the dazzling sight. "The stove isn't trying to thwart your every step."

"How do you know?" Her eyes twinkled. "Maybe this Family Sunshine range has decided it doesn't want to share the kitchen with me. I've got to show it who's boss."

"*I'm* the boss, and I say let's go into town to eat."

"You have little faith in me."

"You burned down my kitchen. Not to mention what you did to my laundry."

"What did I do?"

"Have you taken a good look at this shirt? It's gray."

She squinted at it, stepping closer and—thank heavens—away from the stove. "It's a lovely shade of gray."

"It's supposed to be white."

"Oops." She shrugged. "I've never done laundry—"

"Before?"

"On a washboard with all those detergents and bluing and laundry stoves and things."

"Sure. I believe you." Ben was just grateful she hadn't caught the shirt on fire when she'd tried to wash it. "Oh, no you don't. Don't you dare head back to that stove."

He caught her by the arm, and she laughed. He tugged, and she whirled into his arms and against his chest. Breathless, she gazed up at him and in the space of a breath he longed to kiss her. He leaned forward—

"Pa? Polly ain't gonna cook, is she?"

"I was just trying to talk her out of it." Ben tried to put a damper on his frustration level. He ached for the feel of Polly's lips to his.

A knock sounded at the front door. He released her, hating to let her out of his grip. "When I come back, I want both of you in the buggy."

Polly merely tossed him a smile, and he had a bad feeling when he marched out of the room.

He recognized the gray roan through the window and tossed open the door. "Woody. Any news on those tracks?"

"We lost them a few miles east of town." The deputy swept off his hat and worked at the brim with his free hand. "I think I caught another set of tracks heading back through the forest. I think he's doubled back to town."

"Then we start a search. I want him in my jail by nightfall." He wanted Polly safe—and her identity. He intended to keep his vow to his bride-to-be, but he had reasons of his own for wanting her past buried. "I'm about ready to head to town. I'll grab a bite at the diner on the way to the jailhouse."

Woody tipped his hat and mounted up. Ben turned around, smelled smoke, and ran.

The Family Sunshine stove puffed smoke when a gust of wind drove down the stovepipe. The lids rattled. The oven belched. Determined, Polly set the brand-new fry pan she'd bought on the stovetop. This time, the lard took a while to melt.

Good. At least she didn't have the blasted contraption too hot.

"Pa's gonna be real mad if you set the kitchen on fire again."

Polly gazed down into Emily's grave eyes, full of doubt at her cooking abilities. "Hand me the bowl."

"I don't think you oughta do this."

"Trust me." Polly dropped the slices of ham into the frying pan and waited.

Nothing caught fire. The melted lard hardly even sizzled.

So far, so good.

Trying to push away the memories of the day when everything had exploded into flame, Polly thanked Emily for the bowl of eggs and set them on the counter. She took one cool egg in her shaking hand and cracked it on the side of the skillet. She dropped it neatly into the pan and then broke another, and another. Finally, she had them all sizzling slow and happily on the heat.

She grabbed the platter with one hand and held the spatula in the other. As soon as the edges of the whites crisped, she flipped it. She cracked open another egg. She filled the platter, and then rescued the ham. Each slice was a bit charred on the outside, but just a little.

"You did it!"

"Admit it, you had no faith. But I can do more than pan for gold and tell stories." Polly let herself wallow a bit with pride in this accomplishment. The Family Sunshine stove belched another cloud of smoke, as if unhappy to claim defeat. "Hurry, let's set the table, Emily. I think I hear—"

"There's smoke in my kitchen." Ben burst around the corner, fury harsh on his face. He jetted right past her in a quest for the source of the smoke.

"It's just the wind." She set the platter piled high with steaming food on the table.

"Polly cooked and didn't set nothin' on fire, Pa."

He disappeared from her sight, but the knell of his angry boots told her he wasn't about to back down. He stormed into view. "I told you not to light the stove. You could have started another fire—"

"I'm not a child, Ben. Maybe you should figure out the difference between Emily and me before you try to talk me into a wedding date." She spread out the napkins.

Emily stepped into the dining room, wide-eyed, and dropped the flatware on the table with a clatter.

"You know there's no negotiating on the wedding," he burst, his face set, eyes dark, six feet of towering fury. "I don't want—"

"Look, Pa. She made eggs and didn't hardly burn 'em."

Ben's gaze fell to the platter. His throat worked. Some of the rage left his face. "I was worried. You could have been seriously hurt."

"I wasn't. This time I didn't add so much coal, and that helped." Polly brushed past him, shaking a little. Did Ben care about her? Did that explain his sudden fury?

She thought of last night and how he'd held her and convinced her he just wanted to know she was safe. Safe. When had anyone ever worried about that?

A hard ball of ache settled low in her stomach as she crossed through the sun-dappled kitchen.

The Family Sunshine stove let out another cough of smoke.

Polly gathered plates, cups, and the milk jug. She felt Ben's gaze on her with every step she took. "Admit it; you were wrong."

Ben took the heavy crock and set it on the table. His jaw looked tight. "I'm willing to admit I could have been mistaken. I should have given you another chance."

"I'm not so useless after all." The cups hit the table with quiet clunks. "I have a few valuable skills."

"I didn't mean to make you feel as if you had no value." His hand brushed hers as he took the plates. "Tell her, Emily."

"You told me to do anything I could think of to keep Polly away from the stove. You said Ma never learned to cook good either."

"I'm just getting used to the stove." Polly poured three glasses of milk, hoping Ben wouldn't mind that she hadn't made coffee. "Let's start."

"That doesn't smell so good." Emily wrinkled her nose. The hat on her head bobbed.

"Maybe the eggs need salt and pepper. I forgot." Polly looked a little closer. No, they didn't appear all that appetizing with the little greasy edges around the whites. "Well, it just will take more practice. I'll do better next time. That stove is proving to be very tricky."

Ben stared down at the platter of eggs. "Okay, then, let's dig in." He valiantly plopped three eggs onto his plate, along with as many ham slices. "Emily?"

The little girl slid one egg onto her plate. "Are you sure you cooked these right?"

"There's no wrong way to cook an egg." Polly felt her confidence waning, but she'd fried eggs thousands of times. It was practically all her father or his men ate. She pushed the last two eggs onto her plate. They made a sickening plopping sound. Goodness, that didn't sound right at all.

Emily poised her knife over her egg. Curls tumbled over her eyes, and the hat on her head was in peril of sliding right off. There was no mistaking the trepidation crinkling her pixie face.

Ben's knife scraped on the plate. She watched as one egg broke open, and runny, yellow yolk streamed everywhere. He cut into another, and it cracked open, the runny insides sluicing out like mud from a dike.

Hadn't she cooked them long enough? Polly's gaze darted to Emily, whose face wrinkled up and turned a shade of gray.

It couldn't be. Polly bit her lip hard to keep it from wobbling. She might not have caused a fire, but she had ruined the meal. Was Pauline Curtis a good cook? Polly felt the heavy weight of her failure. She had so much to prove.

Ben cleared his throat. "Pass me the salt and pepper, will you?"

"Are you sure?"

Ben nodded.

Her hand trembled. She pushed the shakers across the polished table, not meeting his gaze. "Maybe this time I didn't have the stove hot enough."

"Maybe."

"At least I didn't start a grease fire."

"It just goes to show there's a positive side to everything." Ben set down his fork. "I can't eat this. Not even to keep from hurting your feelings."

"It's okay."

"Your feelings are important." He pressed a kiss to her cheek. "Maybe we'd better head to the diner. There's always tomorrow morning to do battle with the stove—as long as you don't start another fire."

"Are you ever going to let me live that down?"

His eyes sparkled. "No."

"It was a good try." Emily grasped her hand. "I like you anyway, Polly, even if you're the worst cook in the world."

"I like you, too." She could hardly squeeze the words out past the emotion in her throat.

Ben held out his hand to help her from the chair, and she didn't feel like a horrible cook or a complete disappointment.

With the way Ben looked at her and how Emily clung to her hand, Polly felt measured. She placed her hand on Ben's arm and let him walk her out to the buggy.

CHAPTER NINE

"Why, you must be the Miss Curtis who's come to marry our handsome sheriff." The clerk at the mercantile beamed a cheerful grin as she finished counting up Polly's purchases.

"Yes ma'am. Call me Polly." She might not like using someone else's name, but she did like her new life. "I was hoping this would all fit into the back of the buggy."

"If it doesn't, I'll have my son deliver it free of charge." The elderly woman, whom Emily had greeted as Mrs. Roberts, finished adding up the long list of numbers. "You tell the sheriff howdy for me."

"I will." Polly laid out a twenty-dollar gold piece and waited for change.

Emily leaned on one hip, a peppermint stick in her hand. "What's all that wood for?"

"Wait and see." Polly glanced out the windows and saw the busy span of Front Street, full of people and horses and wagons. The business day was just beginning, and Ben was nowhere in sight. He mentioned trying to hunt down the man who'd been in her room last night.

She wished Ben would let it go. He was probably just a thief. If he were Dixon or one of her father's men, they wouldn't have run. A chill chased down her spine and she shivered.

She collected her change and thanked Mrs. Roberts's son for managing to wedge all but the lumber into the space behind the buggy's seat. She had to put down the top, but it was a pleasant morning. She liked the feel of the wind in her hair as she took up the thick leather reins. She snapped them against the pinto's rump, as she'd seen Ben do.

The mare took a step forward, but they didn't seem to move.

"The brake," Emily leaned close to whisper.

"Oops." Polly fiddled with the lever and finally it moved. "I'm not used to driving a vehicle."

"That's not what you told Pa."

"Well, I don't want him to think he's got the bad end of the deal. I happen to like being here with you." She tugged on the brim of the oversized bonnet Emily was still wearing.

"I'm glad you come all this way. Even though you had to give up your servants and maid and drivers and cook." Emily leaned against her arm. "And you haven't caught anything on fire yet."

"See? Things are improving already." Polly gave the reins a snap and the mare took off.

"Whoa!" someone shouted.

A teamster's wagon lumbered dangerously close to Polly's elbow. She saw the driver look over at her with terror in his eyes as he hauled back on his many sets of reins.

"Polly! We're gonna crash!"

"Dangnabbit!" She kept the mare to the right to avoid hitting the loaded wagon, but the buggy jerked when one wheel hub clipped the hitching post. She heard a terrible scraping sound, but a bunch of horses stood tethered up ahead and she didn't want to hit them. She yanked hard on the left rein and sent the mare darting out into a space right in front of the teamster's horses.

"Crazy woman driver," the teamster shouted.

Goodness. This was much different than riding astride. It would take some getting used to.

Polly took the turn off Front Street and onto Pines, but she turned too sharp and the wheel scraped along the edge of the boardwalk. Several bystanders jumped back.

"You're a terrible driver, Polly." Emily crunched the last of her peppermint stick.

"I know."

It was better once she got out of the town traffic. The road was empty and she could relax. Larksong trilled in the air and the leaves of cottonwoods, maples and ash whispered merrily with the breeze. A wild rabbit hopped out into the lane and studied them before diving out of sight.

It was peaceful.

"Why's Pa's deputy always followin' us?"

Polly glanced over her shoulder. She should have known that after finding a man in her room, Ben wouldn't put a stop to his spying ways.

And that was comforting. You're not alone, Polly. You 've got to get used to it. You have me. Ben's vow swept through her mind.

The way he treated her was much different than she'd expected. She'd seen men with women all her life. In the outlaw hideouts and the mountain shanties and in the ramshackle hotels they'd stayed at, Pa and his men had women. Mostly working girls, but now and then there would be a girlfriend or a wife who joined them for a spell. She'd seen a lot of life and knew how the world worked.

But until Ben dragged her into his jail and offered her a choice, she'd never known that a man could truly be different. Some men didn't treat women as if they were servants of little worth. Sure, Ben had been angry when she'd burned up his kitchen, but his anger had been honest and fleeting.

And even after what she'd done, he still treated her as if she mattered. He didn't seem to mind she'd ruined his white shirts or couldn't cook on that fancy stove. Her suspicions were wrong. He wasn't spying on her he was protecting her, just like he said. He did trust her to take care of Emily. He trusted her to keep her word.

Two gunshots shattered the peace. The pinto jumped in a panic, and Polly hauled back on the reins hard, using her voice to calm the animal. Another gunshot exploded on the road behind her. She heard a shout of pain, and a horse whinnied with fear.

Every instinct told her to get Emily away from the danger, but she had to at least turn around. She had to see if she could help.

The deputy lay facedown in the road, not moving. His horse was nosing him, clearly worried. Polly scanned the forest, but the foliage was too thick. A dozen gunmen could be hiding in those shadows and she couldn't spot them.

Get Emily away from this, her instincts warned. But how could she leave an injured and unconscious man in the middle of the road? She knew Ben wasn't at the jailhouse, and it was a good ten minutes to town. The deputy might need a doctor.

If she'd been on horseback, Polly would have had no doubts about turning back. But how could she put a child in the line of fire? Yet how could she let a man die? Emily was safer on the floor of the buggy than the deputy would be if she left him behind.

"Polly, I'm real scared. Milton's hurt."

"I see." She grabbed her reticule, hauled out both revolvers and started to load them. "Don't worry. I know how to use these. I want you to lie down on the floor and don't get up, no matter what happens. Do you understand?"

Wide-eyed, Emily nodded. She slipped off the seat and crouched down on the floor. "I don't wanna leave Milton behind with the bad men."

"Good, cuz we're gonna go rescue him." She laid one revolver in her lap and forced the pinto to turn around and lope back down the road. "Whoever you are out there, don't shoot. I've got a child in this buggy."

No answer.

The vehicle bounced and jolted over the ruts and potholes in the road. Polly didn't take her eyes off the forest. The wind flicked boughs into motion and rustled the tall, seed-heavy grasses along the roadside, camouflaging any human movements. Warning crawled down her spine and her finger brushed the trigger, ready to fire. She could feel someone watching her. Someone who dared to shoot a lawman.

So far, so good. Polly drew the pinto into a skidding stop in front of the deputy. The lawman's horse trumpeted protectively and then jumped out of the way at the last moment. Fortunately the buggy rocked to a sudden stop.

"Milton!" Emily cried out.

"Stay down." Polly pressed Emily gently to the buggy's floor and then jumped out of the vehicle. Watching both sides of the road, keeping her back to the horse, she knelt in the middle of the road.

"Can you hear me, Deputy?" She grabbed his fallen revolver, a brand-new Colt, shiny as a new silver dollar. The nose was hot and the acrid scent of gunpowder filled the air.

She'd heard three gunshots. Likely the deputy spotted trouble in the forest and shot first, without asking questions. And so had the armed villain.

She hoped it wasn't Dixon. This wasn't Dixon's style, though. Polly knew the worst of the West's outlaws by name, so she knew how a man like Dixon thought. They didn't hide behind trees without firing first, and they didn't run when caught snooping through a woman's trunks.

The deputy groaned but didn't wake up. Polly grabbed him by the arm, and her fingers touched blood. It was warm and sticky, and there was a lot of it. This man needed a doctor, and fast. She hauled his arm over her shoulder, taking his greater weight on her back. She stood, knees wobbling. She didn't forget to watch the forest.

The gunman was still there, whoever he was. She could feel his gaze on her. Was he going to pull the trigger? Polly grabbed the deputy's horse and used him to block her from any bullets the man in the forest might send her way.

She knew where he was now; she could feel him. She dumped the deputy's body as gently as she could in the buggy. The gelding nickered, clearly concerned for his master.

The gentle old horse reminded her of the sweet roan she'd had to put down, the horse that had been her constant and only loving companion for thirteen years.

Best not to think of it, or her heart would just crack wide open. A woman had to stay tough to survive in this world. Moving quickly, she ducked into the buggy, which was rocking with the mare's nervous prancing.

Just then, armed men tore out of the forest with gunfire and shouts. Goodness, she thought they were charging right at her. She snapped the reins and shouted, scaring the mare into a full gallop. Panicked, the animal ran full out, dragging the buggy over every bump and rut in the road.

Gunfire peppered the air, and she knew those gunmen—whoever they were—would catch up to the wagon in no time. She had to discourage them. She had to keep Emily and the deputy safe.

"Stay down, Emily, no matter what happens." Polly dropped the leather straps and twisted around on the seat. She gripped the revolvers in both hands, ready to fire.

But the men behind her weren't outlaws. She saw Ben haul an armed and bleeding man out of the shadows. Thank heavens. He'd somehow found her. He must have followed the trail that led him straight to her. The danger had passed. She hauled the buggy to a stop with shaking hands.

"Milton." Emily started to cry. "Is he dead, Polly?"

"Not yet." She yanked off her petticoat and tore it in half. She put pressure on the chest wound until the bleeding slowed.

"Polly, what—" Ben hopped off his horse when he spotted his wounded deputy. "Where's Emily?"

"Here, Pa." The little girl launched through the air and into her father's strong arms.

Polly saw the naked relief on Ben's face, betraying deep love. He held his little girl as if she were the most priceless person in the world, and it brought a lump to her throat. She peeled back the deputy's shirt. When fabric stuck to the wound, she dug out her pocketknife and stripped away the shirt and vest.

"How does it look?"

She dabbed at more blood. "Not good. The bullet missed his heart, but it's still in there or he'd be bleeding from his back, too. How good is the town doc?"

"Damn good."

"Then I'll leave this to him. Let me bandage this better." If the wound had been worse, Polly would have lain the deputy out on the road and done the work herself. She tore the remaining half of the petticoat into long strips and bound the deputy's chest good and tight.

"You're a wonder." Ben tipped his hat to her, pride in his eyes. "You can't cook, but you're handy to have around in a gunfight."

"Funny. I'm beginning to think the same thing about you." Polly grabbed the reins, and they raced to town.

"One-Eyed Tommy took a bullet to his arm. My deputies are getting ready to haul him over to the jail." Ben strode across the clinic's lobby. "The doc says Milton owes his life to you. With the way that wound was bleeding, if you hadn't taken care of him he would have died."

"I have a little practice with gunshot wounds." Polly took Emily by the hand and followed Ben toward the door. "One-Eyed Tommy was the one who was in my room last night."

"Looks that way." Ben tipped his hat down, brim against the sun, and braced his feet wide as he gazed out on the peaceful town.

"And you tracked him all the way to me."

"Yep." Ben didn't move; he just stood there, tall and powerful, as handsome as myth. The way he'd burst out of the forest still stymied her.

"You rescued me," she breathed.

"Well, you'd already rescued yourself."

"But you found the man who threatened me." No one had ever done this much for her. "Tommy must have carried a grudge. I've seen it before. He hated losing to a woman at cards."

"Looks that way. He wanted to get even."

She laid her hand on Ben's arm. "That happens now and again. Usually I just move on to another town and that takes care of the problem."

"There won't be any more moving on." Ben covered her hand with his. "You've made a promise to us."

"And you've kept your promise to me."

"I told you I would."

"Yes, but it's the first time anyone has. At least, for me." She ducked so he couldn't see the tears in her eyes.

"Then it's a good thing you answered my letter, Pauline. "Ben's voice sharpened.

Polly realized Emily was listening, silent as could be. Her heart sank. The girl wanted Pauline Curtis, not a woman bounty hunter for a mother. "I know just what to do. Now that the mystery of who's after me is solved, let's go fishing."

Emily's eyes lit, but she didn't say a word.

"I think I could take the afternoon off. We could make a day of it."

"Or more. Come on, let's go make up some bed rolls, grab our fishing gear and go." Polly wanted to get away. Everything here was so different, so new— these feelings, this life, the way Ben had protected her and how Emily looked up at her as if she were important.

Goodness, she needed something familiar and she needed it now.

"Fishing it is." Ben brushed a light kiss to her cheek. "But I have to warn you, I'm pretty good."

"He is, Polly." Emily caught her hand, and they stepped off the boardwalk together.

"This might come as a shock to both of you, but I'm an accomplished fisherman. Fisherwoman. Whatever."

They laughed, clearly not believing her.

Fine, let them doubt. Polly lifted her face to the sun, breathing in the sweet summer air and giving thanks that it was Tommy and not Dixon who'd been after her.

Maybe she could put her past behind her, just like she'd always dreamed. But she had to talk to Tommy first.

"You're not talking to him." Ben blocked the jailhouse door and glared down at her with the meanest look he could conjure up. "He had a gun trained on you. Milton swears to it. He could have killed you."

"And I want to know why." She fisted her hands and despite the beautiful calico dress detailed in frills and lace, she looked tough enough to push him over. "I have the right. I have a new life to protect. Can't you understand?"

More than he wanted to admit. "I'll question him for you."

"No, I need to do this."

Emily peeked out of the mercantile's front door, carrying her little basket full of purchases to take on their fishing trip. Worry marked her brow as she gazed at them from across the street.

He waved at her to let her know everything was all

right. "Emily doesn't like to see us arguing."

"Fine, then, we'll stop. Just let me by."

"You're one hard-headed woman, Polly. Fortunately for you, I'm starting to like hard-headed women." He eased back from the threshold. "But you're not going in alone."

"Okay. I can live with that." She swept past him with a rustle of fine cotton, leaving a summery spice scent that set his teeth on edge.

"That's quite a bride you've snared." Woody shouldered close, fingering through keys on the metal ring on the wall. "Milton said she got him away from danger. Funny how she would know how to do something like that."

"She's a city girl. I've heard there's lots of violence in the bigger cities." He didn't like deceiving his best deputy, but that was the way of things when you had a secret to keep hidden. "Thanks for all your hard work. We arrived in time to arrest Tommy."

"That was mostly your doing, and you know it." Woody found the key and crossed the room to unlock the cell door. "Tommy's still a little groggy from the laudanum, but he's harmless, for now."

Ben couldn't help laying his hand on Polly's shoulder. He liked the feel of her. He liked being close to her. He let her lead the way into the cell. It was hard holding back, but Polly was right. She had the right to face this man and ask why he'd threatened her.

"You." Tommy spat from the cot where he was stretched out, his arm laid out in a splint. "You did this to me."

"I didn't shoot you." Polly didn't look afraid; she looked confident. Ever since that moment on the road when he'd spotted her in the buggy, he'd seen this side of Polly—and he liked it.

Ben stepped close, so Tommy would know he'd better be on his best behavior. The gambler glanced up at him, and his scowl deepened.

"You stole from me, woman. You made me a mockery in front of my friends. I want my money back."

"Then why didn't you just walk up to me and say so?" Polly tossed her head. "We could have discussed it."

"I thought I'd pay a visit to you in your room—"

"You thought I was asleep. Goodness, you were going to make me pay for beating you fair and square in a poker game. Of all the low-down—"

"You ain't no society lady from back East."

"What makes you say that?" Ben gestured to his holstered gun.

Tommy paled, but the belligerent tilt to his chin remained. "Try to scare me all you want, Sheriff, but this cheatin' saddle tramp is pulling the wool over your eyes. She ain't no city girl."

"You're mistaken." Ben growled the words. "This is Pauline Curtis from St. Louis. I know her father. She's come to marry me and care for Emily. Anyone who says differently might do a lot of time in the territorial prison."

Ben caught her by the elbow. "You have your answers, Polly. Let's go."

She followed him out of the cell. She didn't say anything until they were outside and in the warmth of the sun. She swiped at the tendrils loose from her braids. When she looked up at him, her eyes were filled with heartbreak.

"At least he doesn't know who I really am. That's what matters." She sighed and gazed off at the horizon. "About this time I'm always moving on."

"You like wandering?"

"I've never done anything else." She swallowed. "If Tommy were a smarter man, he might have figured out the truth. I know it would ruin your reputation as a lawman. No one would trust a sheriff married to Roy Brown's daughter."

"I have to admit it troubles me. I don't want to lie to

you." He knuckled back his hat. "The last thing I need is to be married to a notorious outlaw's daughter."

"Then you want me to leave." Her throat worked, and she stared hard at the ground. "I understand. I've caused enough trouble—"

"I thought we had an agreement. A permanent one."

Her head jerked up. "I've caused you nothing but trouble. Emily could have been hurt today."

"She wasn't, because you protected her, plain and simple. Now Tommy is headed to prison, and the three of us are going fishing, just like we promised Emily."

He hauled her into his arms, and she came easily. She felt sweet and amazing folded against his chest.

He pressed a kiss to her hair. She wasn't the woman he'd planned on, but she was the one he wanted. No one could replace Neesa, and he wasn't going to even try.

But it would be nice to have a woman in his bed.

Bart Dixon tossed down another shot of whiskey and cursed those fool idiots who'd kept him waiting too damn long. How hard was it to ride twenty miles? Time was a-wastin', even if Polly Brown was probably warmin' up the sheriffs sheets by now. Maybe she'd already lit out of town.

No, when a woman was pulling a scam, she took her time. She'd still be in that little one-horse stage stop when he got there. Trouble was, Polly was one of the best shots in Montana Territory. He could take her if she was alone, but not if that sheriff was protecting her.

Dixon needed help. He needed his men.

Those Browns had double-crossed him for the last time. They were gonna pay, starting with that wildcat Polly. He ordered another shot and tossed that one down, too. The whiskey burned in his guts and matched the fire of his anger.

He would enjoy making pretty Miss Brown tell him where her brother hid all the gold. She might not enjoy it, but he would.

No one bested Bart Dixon. Especially not a woman.

He heard a commotion outside and knew his men had arrived.

CHAPTER TEN

Knee-deep in the North Fork of the Indian Trails River, Polly jerked her wooden pole to set the hook. "I've got another bite."

"You're sure a good fisher." Emily set down her pole and curled up on a boulder to watch.

"You aren't keeping the line taut enough." Ben's whiskey-rough voice tickled her ear.

"Says the man whose line broke and whose only catch got away." She put a steady pressure on the line and pulled it in. "I know what I'm doing. I'm about to bring in my third trout"

"You're going to lose him if you don't tighten up that line."

Polly shook her head, not at all worried. "Emily, is your father always this way?"

"Pretty much. Sometimes he gets really bossy."

"Hey!" Ben seemed offended, but he laughed.

Polly inched in the line. "Don't worry, Emily. I think I can cure this ailment of your father's."

"You can?"

"Sure. I'm about to take his pride down a notch." She felt the trout try to make another escape, but he was tiring.

She inched out the line.

Polly watched Ben grit his teeth and fist his hands. It was really bothering him that she wasn't listening to his advice. "Do you want to bring it in?"

"No." He sat down on the rock next to Emily. "Go ahead, show me how wrong I am. I bet that fish gets away from you."

"You're on." Polly waited, then began pulling in the line. "I know it's hard to believe, but I'm better than you in some things, MacLain. Your inflated male pride is just going to have to accept it."

"At least I can cook."

"Oh, you think you're funny." The line in her hand strummed and vibrated as the trout fought. She dragged him in a few yards. The white-capped water swirled around the length of her line.

"You can't cook real well, Pa."

"Well, I'm better than Polly."

"Don't worry, Emily." Polly eased the fish closer to the bank. "Your father is about to lose his bet."

The whisper of the water was broken only by the trout's last splash. A hawk called overhead as it completed a lazy circle. Leaves sang with the wind, and it was so peaceful, Polly could taste it

"Victory." She knelt down and let the cool water run over her hands. She lifted the flopping fish by the gills, broke the line, and set the trout in a bucket. "The loser has to clean the catch."

"Wait one minute. I don't remember agreeing—"

"I remember it very clearly."

Grumbling for effect, he grabbed the bucket and fished in his pocket for a knife. "You want to help me, Emily?"

She wrinkled her nose. "No way."

"Emily's going to help *me*." Polly held out her hand. "Come on. We need to gather up some firewood."

"You aren't going to make a fire, are you?" Emily's brow crinkled.

Polly's defenses went up. Goodness, they thought she was incompetent. "I'm a skilled campfire maker, among other things."

"You sure are skilled at fishing, for a city girl." Ben's eyes teased as he brushed past her. "Do I need to go out with you so you don't get lost?"

"No, I may be just a little city-bred woman, but I've got an excellent sense of direction." She couldn't help joking, either. "Do you need me to show you how to clean those fish? You don't look like you know what you're doing. You were wrong about how to catch fish."

"I thought proper women were supposed to be quiet and demure." Ben cocked one brow.

"Well, I'm not *that* proper." She left him chuckling, perched at the rushing river's edge.

She liked Ben MacLain.

"Polly, you fish real good." Emily dropped to her knees to pick a spray of wild asters and daisies. "Did you learn that just for me, too?"

"I'd do anything for you, dear heart." Polly's chest tightened when Emily caught her hand.

"These are for you."

Polly stared down at the bouquet. "No one's ever given me flowers before."

"Is that so?" Ben's voice sounded behind her. "A pretty lady like you must have had more beaus than she could count."

He knelt in the shade beside his daughter and began scooping up a collection of asters, wild roses and daisies. The flowers were small and delicate against his strong, sun-bronzed hand. Her heart beat faster, watching him.

When he stood, he offered her the bouquet. "To the victor of the fishing contest."

She blinked, but he still stood before her, as handsome as sin with tender admiration alight in his eyes. It was the man and not the flowers that left her weak. "You're a gracious loser, MacLain."

"You're one, too. I'll get the campfire started and you—"

"No. I'll do it." She gathered the flowers to her and breathed deep. The sharp scent of daisies, the breezy scent of asters and the gentle wildness of the roses filled her senses. "I know the best way to cook fish."

"Urn, Polly." Emily leaned on one hip, shaking her head slowly from side to side. "I don't think you oughta try cooking."

Ben pressed a kiss to Polly's cheek. "It's a man's job to cook over the campfire."

"You don't think I can do it."

"No, that's not it at all. I want you to sit back and enjoy the supper I'm going to fix."

"You don't trust me. You think I'll burn the food to a crisp." Doubting Thomases, both of them.

"Let's face it. Your cooking efforts so far have been miserable failures."

"It's that darn stove, is all." Really. She'd been cooking over a campfire since she was six years old. "Go clean those fish and stop worrying. I won't set fire to the entire forest."

"Sure. I'm just going to get a few buckets of water ready, just in case."

* * *

"You're making me nervous." She fed the fire with a handful of dried pine needles and watched the flames leap.

Ben jumped back from the circle of stones as if searching for escaped embers that might start a forest fire. "You're making me nervous. Let me take over."

"No. I'm perfectly capable. Look, the flames are already dying down. See how smoked the fish are?"

"They looked burned up." Emily wrinkled her nose, deeply skeptical.

"They'll be just right, you'll see." Polly checked the wild yams she'd gathered that were warming in the coals along the edge of the campfire, topped with butter, sweet lemon grass and wild onion shoots. They were almost done. "Ben, get your hand away from my fish. Do you always have to be in charge?"

"It's a man's duty."

"Duty? Look around. I haven't started a single wildfire." She liked to watch the way his eyes twinkled when she teased him.

"Are you sure about that?"

Her blood heated, and she didn't want it to. "Move aside. I want to see if the trout is done."

"It looks done." His warm breath fanned the back of her neck.

Shivers raced all through her body. "Go get the plates."

"I'm supervising, remember?" His eyes darkened and his gaze traveled along the surface of her bottom lip. "Besides, I like the view right here."

His gaze pinned hers, and her breath caught in her chest. "You wanna eat with your fingers?"

"With your fingers, maybe."

The idea of his mouth closing around her fingertips made her heart skip five beats. Maybe more. "Emily, come drag your father over to the packs and dig out the plates. We're ready to eat."

"Are you sure that fish is done?" Oh, he liked teasing her. He leaned close, their mouths almost touching.

She could see the flecks of black in his eyes and the texture of his bottom lip. She remembered how hot and demanding his mouth had felt on hers.

"C'mon, Pa." Emily took him by the hand and dragged him off toward the edge of the clearing. Her whisper carried on the breeze. "I got candy at the store in case she burns up all our supper."

"Good thinking." Ben's gentle laugh filled Polly's heart. It was a warm sound, a tender one.

She was liking him far too much.

She took a cleaned stick and poked the fillets apart. The

Fire's heat radiated against her face. Smoke tickled her nose and she breathed it in, savoring the scent. It was a friendly smell, one she'd missed while she'd been living in town. This kind of cooking satisfied her, and to heck with the Family Sunshine stove.

She sprinkled a few more crushed stalks of lemon grass and small wild onions into the center of the fish while she waited for Ben and Emily. They approached with great trepidation.

She grabbed a cloth she'd been using as a hot pad and lifted one skewered trout onto Emily's plate. "Try it. It's not burned, I promise."

"You look like you know what you're doing." Ben offered his empty plate and she filled it with the biggest fish.

"Take some of the yams from the coals." She dropped the last fillet onto her plate and then set down by the fire a careful distance from Ben.

"Hot." He dropped two small yams on her plate, moving closer, and then leaned away to serve Emily.

"The moment of truth." His gaze met hers across the merry campfire.

She waited, air lodged in her chest, while he forked a small section of white meat into his mouth. Emily looked terrified, as if he was about to be poisoned.

Then he smiled. He chewed, swallowed, and tossed her a kiss. "I admit I was wrong. I doubted you. But never again. This is the best fish I've ever had!"

He made her feel . . . she didn't know what to call it. Happy. Full up. Brimming over. She'd failed at so much she'd tried to do for him and Emily. But here under the canopy of twilight with stars winking to life, she was in her element She hadn't set the forest on fire or burned their food.

"See? I told you it was that stove." Polly took a bite and sighed with pleasure. Goodness, she'd missed this kind of cooking. The fish was lightly seasoned, smoky and buttery.

The sweet yams tasted rich, wild and full of flavor.

The meal was filled with pleasant talk about the town. Emily recounted with great pride how Polly had saved Milton's life. How she'd known just how to hold a gun, carry the unconscious Milton and treat his wound. And all the while, Ben looked at her as if she were someone of great worth.

Polly sat in the growing darkness, feeling strangely at peace. She felt appreciated. She felt as if she belonged. She'd spent her whole life looking for this.

After every bite of the trout had disappeared, Polly brought out the kinnikinnick berries she'd picked while gathering the firewood.

Emily brought her a small frying pan and watched, with a little more faith now, as Polly dropped the rest of the store-bought butter into the pan. She placed it over the dying fire. Together, they waited until the butter was sizzling.

"Are you sure this is gonna taste good?" Emily stared down at the pouch she held, struggling to believe.

"I'm sure." Polly laid a hand on the girl's shoulder. "Pour in the berries."

"Are ya gonna fry them?" Emily upended the leather pouch, and the bright red berries rolled into the bubbling butter.

"Nope." Polly loved surprises. "Just wait and see."

"You're a skilled woodsmen." Ben's chin brushed her shoulder as he leaned close. "I never guessed."

"You never asked." She laid the lid over the pan, leaving it slightly ajar to let the heat escape. Shaking it gently, she waited for Emily's reaction.

"Popcorn!" The girl clasped her hands together. "My very favorite."

"It's like popcorn, but it tastes like baked apples. You'll like it, I promise."

She felt Ben's hand settle on her low back, holding her close, and his roughly textured cheek settled against hers.

Her blood felt as hot as the fire, and her senses snapped right along with the popping kinnikinnick berries.

What was she going to do about the way he made her feel? She knew she'd better have it figured out by bedtime tonight, since they were spending the night here, beneath the stars.

Despite Ben's promises of separate beds, his thigh pressed against hers and she had no doubt. Friendship wasn't the only thing he had in mind.

"The house is dark. Ain't no one there." McKinny spat tobacco juice and swiped at his chin with his sleeve. "Think we ought to check town?"

"It's ten o'clock at night. What in blazes would they be doin' in town?" Dixon roared. This kind of stupidity was the reason he'd broken up his gang after the Golden Gulch stage fiasco. Once again, he was in charge of a bunch of chicken brains.

When he got his hands on that gold, there would be some changes.

"I donno, boss." McKinny gave his tobacco wad a good chew. "Polly sure does like to play poker. She beat me so bad once, I lost my horse to her."

"Only a fool plays against a woman. They cheat." Dixon was sure of it because that's the only way a woman could beat him. "Besides, she ain't in the saloon, not with that sheriff's kid. I sent Patch in there to scout around. If he'd seen her, we'd have heard about it by now. She's out charmin' that bulldog sheriff."

"Poor sucker." McKinny shook his head. "She's gonna take him for all he's worth."

"And he's worth a lot. I checked into it." Dixon had checked into a lot of things. "Tell Howell to get out a lantern and find some tracks. They had to go somewhere."

In the meantime, Dixon figured he might as well see what was in the house. The door wasn't locked, and he headed upstairs. He saw a little girl's room.

He wasn't interested in that. He checked out the desk

drawers in MacLain's room, but found nothing to blackmail him with. Nothing obvious, anyway.

It was the third room that had him humming. Fancy trunks were filled with all sorts of finery. So, Polly was building herself a whole new life.

Dixon wondered what her father would think of that.

"Boss." McKinny called up the stairs. "Howell found some tracks. Two horses heading up into the mountains. Says they're about five hours old."

"That's them." Dixon could feel it in his bones. "Tell the boys to mount up. We've got to move fast and quiet. I want Polly taken alive and well. You hear me?"

Yeah, that wild hellcat was gonna suffer. Big time. And when it was all over, he was gonna be one hell of a wealthy man.

"Is she asleep?" Polly leaned away from the campfire's dying glow to better see the man striding toward her.

"Dead to the world," he assured her.

Polly could see Emily's bed roll, not five yards away. There was no better way to sleep, cushioned in the soft grasses, brushed by the light of a thousand stars. "I guess we should turn in. It's been a long day."

"Thanks for what you did today."

"Me? I caught some fish."

"You've made Emily happy. You gave her happy memories. She hasn't had much of those since her mother's death." Ben stepped over the rock and sat down beside her. "You were incredible. It's all she could talk about when I was tucking her in—how you can do anything."

"Except cook breakfast on the Family Sunshine stove." Polly grabbed the base of her ponytail and loosened the ribbon. She shook her head, and curls cascaded over her shoulders.

Ben's fingers twined through a lock of her hair. "I've

had a hard time accepting you as the woman to make Emily happy. You weren't my first choice."

"I noticed."

He sighed, a thoughtful sound. "I've been afraid. You understand fear, don't you?"

An ember popped in the low flames, shooting sparks up into the dark night. Bright specks of fire dazzled, flying in the air for one brief second, then they died out, gone forever.

She screwed her eyes shut, trying not to remember. "Yes, I know about fear."

"I was afraid you wouldn't love Emily. What if you left? And then, when you didn't, I was afraid you would get too close."

"Isn't that why you proposed? To have a mother for Emily?"

"Yes, but I would have been happy with a housekeeper for the rest of my life." He stared hard into the flames. "If I could have gotten a domestic to come out here, then that's all the commitment I wanted to make."

"I see." Heat radiated against her, but it wasn't coming from the campfire. Ben released her hair, watching as the curls tumbled across her right breast. She knew he was looking at her breasts and not her plain brown curls. "What man doesn't want a servant to cook and clean for him?"

"That's not what I meant."

"Isn't it? No wonder you're so happy tonight. You found out I can cook." The full and happy feeling in her heart faded, leaving nothing in its place but coldness. "I'm glad I'm going to make you a convenient wife after all."

"You don't understand." His knuckles brushed her cheek.

She felt the tender touch all the way down to her toes. She closed her eyes and breathed in the night air. She wasn't ready for closeness, yet she'd been yearning for it all of her life.

She heard the chirrup of crickets and the call of a silver owl. In the edges of the clearing, deer grazed in the shadows. "What don't I understand?"

"I didn't want another wife. I loved the one I had."

"Oh." She hadn't considered that. She stared down into the glowing coals and watched the orange light tease the darkness.

Love. She could hear it in his voice—and the regret. Love made a person vulnerable. It wasn't something he wanted to do again.

Lucky for him, love was something she didn't want. Closeness, yes. Love? Never. Her independence was too valuable.

"I don't want to replace Neesa." He tipped his head back to watch an owl swoop low. Its broad wings spread in a soundless glide.

The night closed in on them, and she waited. She didn't know what more to say.

Ben didn't break the silence either. He braced his hands on his knees, swallowed completely by shadow. After a while, he spoke. "I just want to be touched again. I miss the closeness."

Her heart ached. Touch. She'd been touched so infrequently in her life until she came to live with him.

Yet he sat alone, so far away, as dark as the night. So much distance stood between them.

"Do you want me to touch you?" she whispered the words because they frightened her and because she couldn't find her voice.

"Yes. I want your touch. I want—" He paused, then slanted his mouth over hers.

Heavens, but he could kiss. He caught her lips in a slow sensuous brush that tore a moan from her throat. Her hands curled around his biceps. Her bones felt ready to melt. He tasted like apples and the night. He made her forget everything but the velvet heat of his mouth and the thrilling sweep of his tongue.

His fingers splayed on either side of her jaw and he tipped her head back, opening her mouth. His tongue swept across her bottom lip and the edges of her teeth. Sensation erupted everywhere he touched. She brushed her tongue to his and began a slow sensual dance of give and take that left her clinging to him, helpless to even stand.

His arms swept around her, holding her up, and she leaned against him. He was all iron-strong muscle and strength, and yet he touched her with a brand of tenderness she'd never known.

He took his time, kissing the curve of her chin and then the line of her jaw. He dropped kisses down the slope of her nose and laved his tongue down the length of her throat.

"Ben."

"Hmm." His lips closed over the hollow at the base of her throat. His tongue darted and teased over her sensitive flesh.

"Ben." She laid her hands on his shoulders and gave him a little shove. "I think I—" She paused to catch her breath. "Hear something—"

He tore his lips from her throat. He was breathing hard, and his gaze flicked over to the picketed horses. "The pinto's nervous."

"Where's my satchel?" Polly willed her feet to move. It was hard stepping away from Ben's wondrous embrace. Her body felt strung tight, her blood like molten lava in her veins.

She knelt and opened the bag. She found her gun belt by feel and strapped it on over her hips.

Ben had a Colt in one hand as he crept through the shadows, listening to the sounds of the night silence. That could only mean one thing: danger.

She pressed bullets into the chambers of her .45s and listened, too.

She heard it first, the whoosh of a horse exhaling in the forest maybe thirty yards south. She gestured to Ben, and his gaze locked on hers over the fading glow of the campfire.

He pointed at Emily, and she knew he wanted her to protect his daughter.

And she would, with her life.

She figured if Dixon had decided to come back, then he wouldn't be alone. Maybe they were surrounded. She realized that Ben thought so, too. That's why he was slipping his rifle from the saddle holster and grabbing his saddlebag with the ammunition inside.

He kept to the shadows, silent and waiting. Polly grabbed the bottom of Emily's bed roll and tugged. The blankets and child slid slowly closer to the base of the stand of lodgepole pines where a few low boughs would keep the girl hidden from sight.

"Look." Polly pointed with her revolver in the direction of the campfire. A shadow moved in the forest beyond, and then it was gone.

"They're trying to surround us."

"I know." Polly glanced behind her. "I can wake Emily and put her up in this tree. She'll be safe, and we can—"

"You aren't going to fight, Polly. You're going to stay right here with Emily." His jaw tensed, and he stared out at the advancing shadows that moved and froze and moved again. "I'm going to pick them off one by one—"

"Too risky. There's too many of them, and the first shot would give away your hiding spot. They would surround you."

Didn't he understand the kind of men they were dealing with? Cold killers. And if it were Dixon—

She shivered, knowing they were at a disadvantage.

"Look, they think we're at the campfire." Ben set the saddlebag on the ground and pushed open the flap. "Do you think you can carry Emily out of here? I can keep them busy—"

"I'm not going to leave you alone." Polly's chest felt ready to tear apart. "This is my battle—"

"Mine, now. You head for home along the river bank and then cut over—"

"Ben, I'm not going anywhere." She laid her hand on his wrist. The touch connected them, forged a common bond she'd never felt with anyone before. "I'm not Pauline Curtis, and I'll never be. I'm Polly Brown, and I can't back away when the right thing to do is stay and fight."

"Then we can leave right now. It's not a good plan, but at least I can reach town and round up my deputies—"

"They would catch up to us. Dixon's men have horses and we're on foot." She spun the chamber of one revolver, then the other. "What's your plan, Ben? Because if you don't have one, I do."

"You're a hell of a woman." He said it like a compliment, and she took it that way. "Roust Emily and get her high up in that tree. She'll be safe from the gunfire up there. Our visitors are about to close in and figure out we're not at the campfire."

"They're a thick-witted bunch, but they are darn good shots."

"We need a defensive position away from Emily." Ben gestured toward a boulder deeper in the trees. "It has a good view of the campsite."

"How many men? Ten?"

"I counted an even dozen." Ben nodded to her. "I'll head over. You take care of Emily. If they spot you, stay with her."

Polly nodded, guns ready to cover him in case Dixon's men spotted him. Ben took off, running low through the tall grasses and keeping to the shadows. The forest seemed to swallow him whole and she couldn't even see him.

Maybe they would be safe after all. Maybe Dixon would find them missing and ride on out.

She shook Emily gently, whispering to her as the wind picked up. Clouds rolled in overhead, blocking off a quarter of the sky. Emily woke with a start, and Polly quieted her and tried to explain.

The girl shivered, afraid, but after a hug and a kiss, she understood. There was no way to escape the men in the forest. She had to hide and stay hid, no matter what happened.

The wind rustled the treetops and masked Emily's awkward climbing. When she nearly slipped, Polly reholstered her .45 and headed up after her. She helped boost the little girl into a solid cradle where three sturdy boughs came together.

Emily sniffed. "The ground is so far down."

"That's good, so the outlaws can't see you."

"What about Pa?"

"He's a good sheriff. You told me so yourself——"

Gunfire shattered the night. The spark of gunpowder came and went like a flash in the darkness, but she could see where the renegades were standing. She drew both guns.

"Keep quiet, Emily. And don't move." She eased the revolvers around the edge of the thick trunk and squeezed off one bullet, and then another.

A man cried out. Another fell.

They called to one another, confused by her position up in the tree. While she'd intended to protect Ben, she'd given away Emily's hiding spot.

"Lean right here." Polly made sure the girl was safely protected by the tree's thick trunk. And as the men began firing and running for cover, there was no way she could risk climbing to the ground.

"Polly! It's me, Dixon." A voice called out above the explosion of gunfire. He swore, barking an order, and the gunfire ceased. "Give yourself up, and I'll let the sheriff and his girl go."

"You're a liar, Dixon." Polly tried to judge by the sound of his voice where he was. "Leaving witnesses isn't your style."

"Then I'll make a damn exception. My men want their share of the gold your cheatin' brother stole from me.

Help us out, and we'll—"

She squeezed the trigger. Fire and thunder tore through the night, and Dixon swore again—louder this time.

"You're gonna pay for that, missy."

Good. She got him. She thumbed back the hammer and watched the darkness for another opportunity. No one was going to hurt Ben or Emily, not while she was around.

Emily clung to Polly's chest, her breath coming in fast little puffs. "Are those bad men gonna kill us?"

"Not if your Pa and I can help it." Polly saw Ben nose up from behind the boulder to fire.

She saw Dixon's man McKinny site him, and she squeezed the trigger. McKinny shouted and his gun fell to the ground. She'd got his shooting arm. She recounted and saw there were six, maybe seven left to go.

More gunfire rang out. Bullets whizzed past her shoulder and dug into the trunk. Emily gave a gasp.

"The tree will stop the bullets." Polly pulled the girl close, and they snuggled together in the bough cradle. She didn't like having Emily in the middle of this, but at least she was safe.

There was no way that outlaw was going to win.

"Are you ready to give up, girly?" Dixon called above Ben's answering gunfire. "I just want the gold."

"I thought you wanted revenge."

"I'm willing to settle for gold."

Another man tumbled to the ground. She and Ben weren't a bad team when they worked together. Now it was much better odds.

She knew she had to leave Emily and try to draw Dixon out for Ben to take him. "Dixon, if I come down, I want your word that you'll let the sheriff and the girl go."

"You have my most solemn vow."

"No." Ben's fury rang through the night like the growl of a wolf. "Polly, don't you dare trust him—"

She saw it all in a flash. An outlaw was sneaking around the edge of a pine. She saw Ben turn, leaving himself unprotected. She tried to twist, but the boughs and the child around her neck made it impossible. Gunfire sounded. She squeezed off a shot, but Ben was already falling.

He hit the ground and didn't get up.

CHAPTER ELEVEN

"No." Polly squeezed the trigger, and the gunmen slid to the ground. He groaned, curling up on the forest floor and didn't move again. "Ben!"

No answer.

Panic beat in her chest. "Emily, I have to climb down and check on your pa."

"What happened?" The girl hadn't seen her father get shot. She tried to crawl out onto the bough, her movements jerky with fear. "Where's Pa?"

Gunfire exploded in the air. Polly dragged Emily back behind the safety of the trunk. "I'll see to him. You stay here."

"No, I—"

"Emily, I have to go." Maybe he was dead or dying. Maybe he needed care and protection.

Emily's sobs silenced, but didn't stop. Polly thought her heart would tear into a thousand pieces climbing down that tree. She hit the ground and eased into the shadows. She moved as fast as she dared, praying for Ben's safety.

"We brought down your sheriff." Dixon's voice echoed in the night. "You're all alone."

Polly slid behind the boulder Ben had been using for cover. "If he dies, I'll never tell you where your gold is."

"I'll find a way to change your mind." Dixon sounded as if he meant it. "Toss down your guns."

"Sure thing." Her hands tightened on the revolver's grips.

Out of the corner of her eye, she saw the gunmen move closer, stealing through the shadows, but they stopped at the edge of the forest.

They knew how good she was with a gun. They weren't taking any chances.

She eased around the rock. Ben's motionless body lay sprawled on his back in the shadows—Ben. She knelt beside him, but she didn't let go of her revolvers. She couldn't. Emily was still up in that tree. Dixon had no soft spot for children, like some outlaws did.

Ben didn't move. Was he dead? She laid a hand on his chest and felt a steady heartbeat.

Ben looked up at her. He held two revolvers cocked and ready. A small bloodstain crept across his upper left arm, but that was all.

"I thought I could draw them out by playing up the injury," he confessed.

"You had me scared to death." She could feel the prickle along her forehead, and she knew she was in a gunman's sites. "Are you ready?"

"I'm a lawman. I'm always ready." He rolled to his feet, firing.

Polly did the same. They hit three of the five men and kept running. Polly felt the burn of a flesh wound along her knee as she dodged behind a tree.

Ben dove for cover behind a jagged rock. He reloaded, keeping watch on the forest, and she did the same.

"Dixon, you're down to two men." Ben's voice thundered like a savage summer storm. "Toss down your weapons, and I won't have to kill you."

"I'm not planning to die today, Sheriff."

Warning prickled down his spine. Ben looked over his shoulder and saw the last of the gunmen slinking around a rise to aim at Polly. He spun around and squeezed the trigger. The outlaw aimed as he tumbled through the air, and fired.

Polly. Was she hit? Ben swung with both barrels cocked, grief and fury hammering hard in his guts—

"I got him." He saw her standing over Dixon, who lay on the ground on his stomach. "Toss me your handcuffs. You'd better check on the wounded."

Ben tossed her a pair of cuffs from his belt. He spotted the neat bullet wound through Dixon's thigh. "I thought you were dead."

"Not with you guarding my back." She snapped the bands of steel around Dixon's wrists. "Thanks, MacLain. There's bounties on him in three territories."

Every time he blinked, he saw her sprawled on the ground, dead from the gunman's bullet. He tried to drive the image out of his mind, but it remained, even when he'd confiscated all the weapons and bound the outlaws. He rescued Emily from the tree, and she was shivering with fear.

"Did you see how Polly saved me?" she whispered, clinging fiercely to his neck.

"I saw." He held her close, wrapping his arms around her. Yes, he hadn't missed how Polly had protected his child.

Not that he got the chance to tell her so. She didn't look at him as she gathered up the outlaws' horses.

She worked with a quick efficiency that would do any lawman justice.

Polly Brown might not be the kind of wife he'd been hoping for. But she was the woman he wanted.

Polly couldn't sleep, even though it was late. She settled down on the back porch step, wrapped her arms around her knees, careful of the bandage, and listened to the sounds of the night. She tried not to think of all that could have gone wrong tonight.

By the time they'd brought Dixon and his men into town and tossed them in jail, midnight had come and gone. There had been the doctor to summon and deputies to wake. Polly had held a sleeping Emily in her arms while Ben did his job.

Now the little girl was tucked warm and safe in her bed, and Ben slept behind his closed door. He could sleep. He had a clear conscience.

She didn't.

A raccoon waddled across the yard to wash his hands and face in the bucket beneath the pump. Another raccoon followed, leading three young pups. With their human-like hands, they gripped the edge of the pail and splashed in the water.

The screen door squeaked open behind her. "I thought I'd find you out here. Want a drink?"

She heard the slosh of an opened bottle of whiskey and nodded. "Wouldn't hurt."

"I couldn't sleep either." He eased down on the porch step next to her.

Every inch of her body shivered at his nearness. He offered the liquor to her, but she gestured for him to go first. He tipped the bottle back and took a long pull. She watched the cords in his neck work. She wanted to reach out and lay her cheek against his chest. She wanted to lose herself in the comfort of his arms.

He handed her the bottle. She welcomed the feel of whiskey across her tongue. She didn't like the taste of strong spirits, but she was still shaking even four hours after the shoot-out. Her stomach burned, and she closed her eyes.

"Tell me about it," he invited.

How wonderful that sounded. To just talk about her feelings and have someone listen, have someone care. "I could have gotten us all killed tonight."

"With your gun skills? Not a chance." His hand glided along the back of her shoulders.

She melted at his touch. "They could have surrounded us. You were distracted—"

"I was kissing you. Rather well, or at least I hope."

She rubbed her hand over her face and watched the raccoons scurry off, the mother chirping to her babies.

He leaned close and plucked the bottle from her grip. "You didn't like my kiss? Is that what's troubling you?"

"I wanted to belong here, in this dream. I really did." The alcohol had hit her blood. She felt warm all over, and her feelings just bubbled out into words. "I hoped Dixon wouldn't come after me. I just wanted to be left alone. I should have known better."

His fingers curled around her arm and he drew her against his side.

She ached to tell him all her fears, but she couldn't. "Dixon thinks I know where my brother buried the gold."

"What gold?" Then he nodded his head, his whiskered jaw brushing pleasantly against her forehead. "Wait, I know. The bars missing from the Golden Gulch stage robbery."

"I heard my brother was hurt bad and dropped out of sight. He died later. Some said he robbed a bank, but others said it could have been a stage. I was in a saloon a ways south of here at the time." Polly let her head bob against Ben's shoulder. "I should have figured it out. My brother was involved with the robbery, and somehow my name got on a wanted poster."

"So Dixon thinks you know where the gold is."

"I hope he's the only one." She pushed away from him. "My past has followed me here and put you and Emily in danger. You both could have been killed tonight, and all because of my silly dreams."

"It was my blackmailing scheme that kept you here." Ben's lips brushed her brow.

Want arced through her, and she fought against it. "I

didn't think I would bring any harm to you."

"You haven't brought any more trouble than I get now and then. Sometimes outlaws decide to move in, and it's my job to discourage them."

"Discourage them? You probably arrest every last one of them. You're a pretty good shot, MacLain."

"So I've been told." His lips nibbled down her cheek.

"You'll want to send me away. I don't blame you." Her breath caught in her throat and emotions balled hard and sharp in her stomach.

He brushed the back of his hand against her jaw. "I told you. This is a permanent arrangement, regardless of your past. Emily needs you. And so do I."

His lips found hers, and he tasted smoky with whiskey and tangy like the night. She melted against him, surrendering to the feel of his teeth plucking at her lower lip and the brush of his tongue to hers. She clung to him, desperate to drive away the turmoil inside her.

"I want you." Ben's words hummed against her mouth, and his breath mingled with hers. "Right here, right now. I want you so much I ache."

She wanted him, too. She tilted her head back, offering him the sensitive curve of her throat as he nibbled and laved. He rained kisses along the edge of her chin and brushed kisses all the way down to her collar.

"Here. Come closer." His hands curled around the backs of her thighs and lifted. She went willingly onto his lap, straddling him with her thighs.

A strange dizzying heat left her reeling. Her stomach dropped end over end as he brought her up against him. She could feel the hard ridge of his erection through his denims and see that the top two buttons were loose at his fly. She could see white cotton stretch around the shape of his hard shaft.

She started to tremble. Part of her wanted to touch him and to let that part of him touch her. But the lessons of a lifetime were too well-learned to throw away now.

When Ben's mouth searched for hers, she buried her face in the cradle made by his neck and shoulder. It wasn't enough, but she held him tight. So very tight. Her body strummed with a strange heat, and she knew that if she let him unbutton her nightgown and taste her breasts, then she would lose every last shred of control.

Control was a thing a woman should never lose.

His kiss caressed along the curve of her neck, the outside of her ear, and back to her hungry mouth. Ben took his time, and his kisses changed from fiery to tender. His touch was sweet enough to bring tears to her eyes. She clung to him, even when he shifted his weight. She buried her face so he wouldn't see her emotions. So he would never know how vulnerable he left her.

He held her until dawn came and made the world fresh and new.

Ben MacLain was a man of his word. Sometimes it was damn hard, but living on the wrong side of the law had taught him a few things. Dishonesty never paid, and broken promises had a way of becoming a habit. So he tried never to do either. He'd promised Polly separate bedrooms, and that's what they were going to have—if she wanted. They didn't have to sleep together. Fine.

That didn't mean they couldn't have sex.

He'd been a long time without the comfort of a woman in his arms. Until Polly, he never thought he'd want that comfort again. In fact, he'd been certain of it. It felt as if he were leaving Neesa behind. But it was time, and he was finally ready. He knew she would understand.

He'd come downstairs this morning to find Polly chopping wood. She made a campfire in the back yard, outside the kitchen door, and was frying up breakfast.

Emily was crouched at her side, chatting up a storm. This morning she wore her cowboy hat and her play holsters. Her eyes shone with unending admiration every time she looked at Polly.

He finished oiling his revolvers and rubbed them down. The smell of oil and gunpowder was cozy, a memory from his childhood. His father had been a gunsmith, and they'd lived in the back of his shop. The smells of his pa's workplace had always found their way into the apartment. Those were good times before Pa was killed in a holdup and there had been no one to take him in but his uncle, a thief and an outlaw.

Sometimes it was nice to have good memories. Like the ones he was making now. He grabbed a clean cloth and polished the steel nose of the revolver. Outside the window, a movement caught his eye. Polly hopped up to grab a handful of kindling, then knelt back down.

Today she wore denims, and they shaped her rear, hips and thighs in fantastic detail. It was breathtaking. When she knelt down to flip the pancakes, he watched. Hell, he couldn't look away. Want pounded through his veins, steady and sharp. Desire for her never waned but seemed to double and triple every time he looked at her.

He could still taste her kiss on his mouth. If he closed his eyes, he could remember the soft pillows of her breasts against his chest. Last night, her weight had been sweet on his thighs when she straddled him. The way her body had pressed against his straining shaft had nearly undone him.

Even now, he pounded with need for her.

He spun the chambers into place and holstered the revolvers. Through the open window, he caught snatches of conversation, Polly's summer wind voice and Emily's musical response. They were going gold panning this morning. It was all his daughter could talk about. They could catch fish for dinner and Polly could show her what berries to pick.

He caught Polly's gaze through the window and she smiled, a little shy. He knew damn well that she was remembering last night's intimacy because it was all he could think about. She ducked away, flipped the pancakes from the skillet and didn't look up at him again.

Polly's life had been tough, there was no doubt about it. But she wasn't cold-hearted. And she knew the way things worked between a man and a woman. He figured she had experience, and he was certain he could change her mind.

"Pa! Come see what Polly made. "Emily dashed into the kitchen, flinging the door open wide. "She didn't even burn it."

"I bet you're both going to like my pancakes." Polly looked happy with her wind-tousled hair and her cheeks pink from the fire's heat. She set the platter of fluffy pancakes and sizzling sausage onto the table. "I think we ought to sell that wicked old stove. Wait— no one would pay good money for a clunker like that. You'll have to give it away."

"It would be handy come winter to heat the kitchen with." Ben buckled on his gun belt. "Those pancakes sure smell good."

She glowed, a subtle brightening of her spirit that made his senses spin.

"And look, Mrs. Roberts's son delivered the wood yesterday while we were away. I can get to the kitchen repairs this afternoon, after Emily and I go panning for gold."

"I'm not even going to ask." He had no doubt she knew how to use every tool he owned. "Do you want any help?"

"Sure. If you can spare time away from your work." She passed him the platter.

The scent had his mouth watering and his stomach growling like a wild thing.

Finally, for the first time since she arrived in town, there were no more threats against her. Ben reached for the butter and hoped their lives were about to settle into a peaceful routine.

"Hey, Ben," Woody called from the doorway. "You

gotta come look at this."

Ben heard the amused chuckle and rubbed at the ache behind his brow. "I'm signing off on the paperwork for the marshals."

"Forget it. Put down that pencil. This is something you gotta see. It's your fiancée."

"Polly?" Ben stood up so fast that his chair banged against the wall behind him. The marshals followed him through the office, hands on their guns, expecting trouble.

Ben knew it wasn't that kind of trouble. He tore out the door and into the hot blast of the late summer day. Through a haze of dust stirred up by the lazy wind, he saw his sturdy pinto mare careening down the center of Front Street, hauling a wobbling buggy behind it.

"She's going to cause a wreck." Woody shook his head.

Ben's stomach plummeted as he watched the mare dart left and nearly take out a horse and rider. Polly apologized, but the rider didn't look too happy. She eased the buggy across two lanes of traffic, barely missing the tailgate of a wagon loaded high with fresh hay. She misjudged the hitching post, and the front wheel hub scraped against the wooden pole with a protesting rasp.

"Whew, we made it." Polly set the brake and greeted him with a beaming smile. "This is only my second time at driving a buggy."

"I'm speechless." Ben swung Emily to the ground. He noticed the lady's hat on her head and the beads around her neck. "You look very lovely, Miss Emily."

"Oh, Pa. Polly and me, we've come to file a real gold claim."

"Did you two beautiful women strike gold?"

"Maybe." Polly held out one suntanned hand.

Her palm fit into his. Her skin was brown from the sun and her fingernails were badly chipped, but it was a beautiful hand. She swept from the buggy in a swish of blue checks, and he couldn't look away from her. The soft hue of her dress brought out the sparkling blue of her eyes.

She smoothed out her skirt that had become rumpled from sitting in the buggy. "I have no idea where the land office is."

"Just around the corner." His heart thundered in his chest, pumping pure lust through every inch of his body—every throbbing inch. "I'd go with you, but I have the marshals ready to take Dixon and his men."

"Will you still be able to make it home this afternoon?" Polly tilted her head back to study him. The brim of her blue bonnet cast a shadow across her face, protecting it from the sun. She looked every inch a lady, but he could not forget the feel of her straddled on his thighs, clinging to his body.

Polly Brown was no lady, and that's the way he liked it.

She smiled up at him, as if she felt the charged attraction between them, too. She pushed the floppy brim out of her eyes. "Was I right about the bounty on Dixon?"

Ben shook hot, lusty thoughts from his head. "Yes. The marshals tell me it's a sizable sum, and there's a reward on each of his men. I told them to make the funds payable to you."

"To me? I didn't take those men down alone. You—"

He pressed a kiss to her shapely lips because he couldn't hold back any longer. "You shot Dixon. It's your right."

"Then I'll put aside half of it for Emily's education."

Emily frowned with great disapproval. "I'd rather have a pony."

But Ben liked the idea, Polly could tell. Her cheek still felt the heat of his kiss. Her body felt taut with the need for more. "We'd better get moving, Emily. We don't want anyone to steal that claim out from underneath us."

"No, sirree." Emily began skipping down the boardwalk. "We're gonna be rich."

"Maybe." She released his hand and walked away, wishing he could go with them—and relieved that he couldn't.

"This is the place." Emily patted the flat of her hand on the wooden door.

Polly stared at the sign overhead. A green striped awning shaded the painted letters from the sun. She recognized the word 'land' and figured Emily was right.

The office was small and dark and contained only one desk, which was empty. A thin, pale man ambled out from a back door. She explained the plot she wanted to claim in great detail.

The clerk took out a bottle of ink and a quill and scratched out letters she couldn't read.

"That'll be twenty dollars."

She set the heavy coin on the desk. Emily stepped forward with a swish of skirts and a jangle of beads to drop her half of the payment on the desk.

"My name goes on it, too," Emily explained. "Polly an' me are partners."

The man looked ready to argue, and Polly decided she was ready to argue with him. She knew Emily was too young to place a claim.

But then the man smiled and asked Emily's age. Polly spoke up and said Emily was twenty-one.

That made them all laugh and filled the silence when the clerk handed her a slip of official-looking parchment to read over and verify.

She studied the letters and strange words. She couldn't find the courage to admit she couldn't read it. "This is fine."

The door squeaked open, and Ben filled the threshold.

"Pa! Come see. Polly and me own a real gold claim. We'll be real prospectors."

"I finished up with the marshals and decided to come see what you two are up to. I hope you filed a claim close to home." He strode across the room, and every confident step brought him closer.

Polly's skin heated. The blood pulsed in her veins.

Then his fingers curled over hers, hot and claiming. Her stomach began falling, end over end.

This man was hers. Now, what was she going to do with him?

Bart Dixon nodded to the scruffy youngster standing on the corner. The pup had joined the gang last winter. Said his name was O'Banyon, didn't have no family and followed them from job to job. Soon they gave him a few jobs scouting firewood, tending the horses, that kind of thing, and he looked like he was gonna fit in real good.

Young O'Banyon knew what to do. Dixon had left a message with the boy, just in case. Dixon didn't expect to spend much time in that hellhole they called a prison, and hard labor wasn't how he wanted to spend the next ten years of his life.

Dixon smiled to himself as the marshal rode him past the boy on the corner and out of town. Poor Polly Brown. She was going to get what she deserved.

Too bad he wouldn't be able to see the look of horror on her face.

"Cut that just a little bit more," she coached as Ben lifted the ax a final time and buried the blade deep into the log. The pine split apart and the bottom edge tumbled free to the ground.

"You sure know how to treat a man to a good time." Ben swiped the sweat from his brow.

"A girl has to try." She knelt down to study the wood. Stripped, the pine log gleamed in the fading afternoon light.

Dark clouds gathered overhead, and a strong breeze gusted through the trees. She hoped the coming storm wouldn't put a stop to her project.

"Mind telling me what you're doing?" He leaned the ax against the side of the house.

"Fixing your kitchen." She clipped the hatchet into the edge of the log and chipped away until a two-foot long piece popped free.

"You know how to work wood?"

"Grab the bag of pegs, would you? I whittled some this morning while Emily napped along the river bank." Polly hurried past him. "I want to check this fit."

She smelled like sawdust, sunshine and the tang of the autumn wind. Her skirts swirled around her ankles as she hopped up the steps and disappeared into the house. He heard the bang of the hatchet and the grate of sandpaper.

He snatched up the leather pouch of small wooden pegs. She made him feel a thousand different things—want and wonder and joy and lust. And they all melded together as he halted in the threshold and saw her perched on a chair fitting a new piece of wood into die scarred pock made by the fire.

"It will look as good as new." Her smile beamed.

But it wasn't her smile he looked at. Her dress clung to her soft breasts as snug as a lover's hands and draped over her hips and thighs so that he could imagine how she looked underneath—smooth, curvy and tempting.

Lust drove him forward. Want had him taking the hatchet from one hand and the hunk of sanded wood from the other. She watched him with huge eyes. He lifted her down and pulled her into his arms. She went willingly against his chest. Her mouth met his with a whisper of a sigh. He kissed her until she melted against him.

Outside their cozy house, lightning flashed and thunder boomed. Rain fell in heavy sheets that pinged off the windows and hammered the ceiling. He pressed Polly against the wall and kissed her hard, demanding all the pleasure he could take from her mouth. She moaned low in her throat, a sound of approval.

Gaining courage, he ran his knuckles down the length of her throat, then covered her breast with his hand. She moaned again, her body stiffening. But he stroked her through the layers of cotton and felt her nipple bead against his thumb.

"Ben?" She rasped out his name, breathless, jaw slack, eyes lidded. "I don't—"

"You don't like this? Doesn't seem that way to me." He tugged at her buttons and the bodice of her dress opened up, revealing a thin camisole so sheer he could see the dark discs of her nipples through it. Three little buttons separated him from her breasts. He ran his fingers in circles around her aroused nipple and watched pleasure twist her face.

"You want it. I want it." He ran his tongue along the outer shell of her ear. "Let's go upstairs. Emily's busy in her room—"

"I can't." She sidestepped, rebuttoning her dress. "I have this wall to finish."

"Look outside." He gestured toward the wide-open door where rain slashed through the threshold, wetting the braided carpet. "We can't cut any more wood out there. Not until the storm passes. We can spend the time making love. You know it will be passionate between us."

"But you said—" She paled. "You promised we'd have separate bedrooms. You wanted a marriage in name only—"

"I want you." He took a ragged breath. "We're going to be man and wife—"

"This is not what I agreed to." Her face twisted, and she spun away. "I can't—"

She dashed out the door and straight into the storm. Rain sluiced over her, and she was drenched in seconds. Her hair darkened and clung to her neck and shoulders. Her dress adhered to her like a second skin, outlining every curve. She was power and fragility, temptation and angel. But he knew now, watching her, how wrong he'd been. She wasn't experienced. She'd never been loved by a man.

He jogged out into the storm. Water pooled everywhere. The sky above gleamed dark and leaden, sheets of cold rain washed over him until he shivered. She stared off at the mountains shrouded with wisps of low clouds.

"Polly?"

She looked so lonely and didn't move toward him. "I need to gather my tools."

She brushed past him, avoiding his gaze.

He shouldn't have waited to marry her. He never should have agreed to give her time. He wanted her in his bed. But more than that, he wanted her as his wife.

"Polly?" Emily stood on the covered porch, her eyes pinched. "You were gonna play dress-up with me after you got done fixin' the kitchen. Are ya done yet?"

"For now." Polly snatched up the woodworking tools she'd found in Ben's shed and carried them to the porch, safely out of the rain. The wind blasted against her wet skin, and she shivered. "Come upstairs while I change."

She felt Ben's gaze on her and was glad to escape. Her breast still burned with a strange, quick sensation and she didn't want to feel it. She didn't want to let anyone this close.

Not even Ben.

"Which one should I pick?"

Polly reached around to button up the last of her dress, straining to catch the buttons in the stitched holes. She took one look at Emily crouched down beside the pile of books. "Whichever one you want."

"Ooh, look." Emily pressed her fingers across an embossed title. "Adella's ma has this book. Is it Little Women? I've wanted to read it ever so much!"

Emily hopped to her feet and held out the book for Polly to see.

Polly recognized the word 'little.' "Looks like it." At least she hoped that was true.

"Goody. Will you read it to me now? Please?"

How could she tell Emily the truth? Polly grabbed the silver-handled comb and drew it through her wet hair.

"Don't you want to save it for tonight so your pa can read it to you?"

Boots knelled on the floor just outside the open door. "I don't think I want to read anything called Little Women."

Ben filled the threshold, dressed in fresh denims and a white shirt. His hair was windblown and tousled. His gaze brushed her from head to toe.

How was she going to marry him now that he wanted a real marriage?

"It's still raining like the devil out there." Wind gusted against the window, and Ben's eyes darkened. "Why don't we all go downstairs together and read this book Emily wants."

"I knew you would, Pa." She took his hand, all enthusiasm and happiness. "Polly, come on."

"Yeah, come on." He held out his hand.

She remembered how that hand had touched her, and where. She recalled the hot, sharp burst of pleasure at her breast as he'd caressed her. Panic wedged like an ax blade beneath her ribs.

Ben's fingers closed over hers and led the way. She felt helpless to refuse. She wanted to be with Ben. She wanted to be with Emily.

In the parlor, Ben lit a lamp and Emily hopped onto the horsehair sofa.

"Do it now, Pa." Emily squirmed, hugging the book to her chest. "You gotta ask her now."

"You don't want your story first?"

"Nope. Just Polly for my ma."

"Okay, then." Ben took Polly's hand. He looked serious and irresistible. "Sit down."

She did. Her heart skipped up into her throat, and she felt it beat there, fast and hollow.

Ben studied her with dark, inscrutable eyes. "Emily and I are very anxious to ask you a question."

"A really important one," Emily added.

MACLAIN'S WIFE

"You saved my life and protected my daughter from gunfire. You've brought light back into our lives, Polly, and we want you to stay with us." He knelt down before her. "Marry us. Marry Emily and me."

Air caught in Polly's chest. She couldn't believe this. He'd already gotten her to agree to marriage, but this—Why, it was a real proposal. Based on caring and trust and friendship.

Emily tugged on Polly's sleeve. "You gotta say yes."

Polly looked from the man kneeling before her to the sweet little girl clinging to her side. "Are you sure? I mean—"

"Please, Polly." Emily's hand gripped hers with a stinging need. "You wrote and said you'd marry us. You promised. You said you would love me forever and ever cuz that's how I love you."

"Oh, Emily." Polly pulled her close and hugged her hard. "No one has ever said such sweet things to me."

It was a business arrangement. She knew that, but her silly heart just welled right up with emotion because she'd never felt wanted before. She'd never felt needed.

But these two people wanted her. They truly did.

Ben pushed a ring on her finger. A Montana sapphire, as blue as the Rockies on a summer's day, sparkled in the lamplight. The gold band gleamed on her finger.

"Well, are you going to say 'yes,' or are am I going to have to haul out my handcuffs?" Ben's eyes sparkled. This was no threat.

Her decision was clear—it came straight from her heart. "Yes, I'll marry you. I'll marry you both."

"Yay!" Emily cheered.

Ben silently folded her into his arms and held her tight against his chest. She went willingly. She laid her ear against his breastbone, and she could hear the fast thud of his heart. He wasn't as calm as he appeared.

He brushed a kiss to her temple and when she looked up, his mouth met hers with a fiery kiss that left her breathless, left her wanting, left her weak.

She would marry Ben. But how was she going to keep from falling in love with him?

CHAPTER TWELVE

"Are you almost ready?" Ben pushed open Polly's bedroom door wearing his black suit and looking like the most handsome man on earth. "You're not even dressed."

"I can't make up my mind." Polly felt half-naked in her chemise, and she blushed as Ben's gaze swept across her bare shoulders and arms.

"Wear that. I think it's tempting as hell."

"Half the town is gathering downstairs. They would probably faint from shock if I married you in my underwear." She turned to lift the gown from the bottom of the trunk. "A groom isn't supposed to see his bride before the wedding."

"Emily's downstairs inspecting the cakes Martha brought over. I thought I'd better come up and see if you're going to climb out the window or not."

"The window's awfully tempting." Polly laid the pink silk gown against the white satin. The fabric rustled as it settled. "I decided on the blue, but Emily reminded me that pink is my favorite color, not blue."

"Emily's helpful, she is." Ben stepped inside and closed the door with a click that echoed in the silent room and bounced against the tension. He could tell Polly was nervous. Hell, so was he. "Let me see the blue."

"I've already folded it up." She studied the two gowns. "The white is more formal."

"This isn't a formal occasion."

"Right. Just a business arrangement to keep me out of jail." Then her eyes widened. "I didn't mean it the way it sounded. I just meant—"

"I know. This isn't a love match." He brushed a kiss to the back of her neck, then placed another on the warm satin skin of her shoulder. "But it doesn't have to be business. Wear the blue."

"But it's not Pauline's favorite color."

"It is yours." Ben brushed at the curls tumbling into her eyes and ached to touch so much more of her. The bed was two feet away. She was already half undressed. It would be simple to wrap her in his arms and kiss her senseless, and lay her back and lift that filmy white slip—

"Thank you." She bit her bottom lip, and her chin wobbled. "I'll wear my favorite color for our wedding."

"I want you, Polly. Not Pauline."

"You don't know what that means to me. I can't cook on your stove and I had to hire Milton's wife to clean the house and pay Mrs. Wu in town to do our laundry."

"But boy, can you cook over a campfire."

He held her close, his erection straining the confines of his Sunday-best trousers. He willed his blood to cool down a degree or two. "Let's get you dressed. We have most of the town waiting for the big event."

She swept away and lifted a sky-blue dress from the trunk. "You'll have to button me up."

"I'm only good at unbuttoning. I guess I'll save that skill until after the wedding."

"Keep dreaming, MacLain." She slipped the frothy gown over her head, and the soft fabric glided over her abdomen and hips. The skirt swished, the ruffled hem just brushing the floor. She fit her arms into the short sleeves and turned to face Ben.

His jaw gaped. "You look perfect in blue."

She blushed. Perfect?

He circled around behind her, and his fingers burned a trail along her back as he started to button her dress. "I am proud to marry such a beauty."

"Now you're sweet-talking me." She wasn't fooled. She had eyes. She'd always known she was far from pretty.

"Get used to it, Polly." His lips grazed the curve of her neck. "When I look at you, I see the most beautiful woman alive."

That's how he made her feel when he took her hand and led her down the stairs. The early autumn sunshine teared her eyes and made it hard to see the guests and the minister. When he spoke his vows, swearing to be true to her through good and bad, in sickness and in health, he made her feel beautiful and loved and cherished.

With Emily at her side and half the town watching, Ben took her in his arms and kissed her so passionately that it left no doubt—she was his wife.

"Congratulations," Mrs. Roberts greeted her with a hug. "Now that you're married, you won't be able to get out of our weekly sewing circle meetings. We'll pressure you into it. You wait and see."

"I'm a terrible seamstress." Polly appreciated Mrs. Roberts's fourth offer to join the sewing group.

"We don't care about that." Mrs. Wu, who owned the town's laundry, congratulated her, too. "I go for the food. Mrs. Watson makes the best cakes this side of Denver."

"No one mentioned cake before."

There were more congratulations, and the supper to be served. Ben oversaw the side of beef barbecuing over a pit, and Emily raced around with the other children, laughing and playing beneath the gently turning leaves.

As night fell, the men lit lanterns and the women popped corn over the fire. The band set up, and soon the stable was vibrating to the fiddler's choice. Snappy music filled the air, mingling with the cadence of the breeze.

Ben placed his hand in hers. "May I have this dance?"

"I can't dance."

"It's easy. You just follow me." He swung her into the crowd of swishing skirts and swirling dancers, and she let him. It felt good to be swept away with his strong shoulders to hold onto. She bumped against several dancers and stepped on Ben's toes three times, but his hand settled firmly into the small of her back as he guided her along.

"This is fun." Her shoes landed on the toe of his boots again. "Well, as long as I keep looking down."

"I think that's the fourth toe you've broken."

"I'm a disaster. At least I dance better than I drive."

"True." He liked the low trill of her laughter. He brushed a kiss to her temple and breathed in her enchanting scent.

The mayor saw him and winked. Ben blushed, vowing to control his amorous feelings until he was alone with his bride. The thought of tempting Polly to his bed made his pulse surge. She would be passion and fire. He curled his fingers around the nape of her neck and felt satin skin and silken curls.

He held her in his arms and let happiness fill his chest. He'd done it, he'd put the last remnants of his past behind him. He'd worked hard to make himself new, for Emily's sake. And he had. No one remembered a scrawny boy who once rode with some of the toughest outlaws in the West. He had a good home, a respectable job and Polly at his side. She was a woman strong enough to protect Emily if the past ever caught up to him.

It hadn't for the last six years, but a man could never be too certain. The music ended and he stopped, but he didn't let go of his wife. Polly, breathless, was flushed and beautiful. Her gown matched the blue in her eyes, and her cheeks were flushed with a light brush of pink.

Lust kicked, and he pulled Polly against his chest and

held her there. It was more than lust that he felt for this woman who'd become his friend, someone he could count on and trust.

"Let's go outside and cool off," he whispered in her ear, leaning close just to feel the silk of her cheek against his.

"Good idea. I think I've pulled a muscle in my calf. It's these shoes. I sure miss my boots."

Crisp air met them at the wide open doors. Behind them the music started up again, a sprightly folk tune that set hands to clapping and feet to stomping. They eased away from the lanterns' glow and into the shadows of the night.

Ben pulled her against him and ravished her mouth. She tilted her head back, opening up to him with tricks of her own. Teeth touched, breaths mingled, and tongues met and caressed. She clung to his chest, his shirt balled in her fists. Already he was hard, and he pulled her against his shaft.

A low moan tore from her throat and she broke away. "Ben, I think—"

"If you can think, then I'm not doing this right." He caught her mouth with his and let his hand shape her breast. She was firm and fit against his palm as if she were made for him. Need kicked hard in his chest. "Can you think now?"

"No, and that's the problem." She stepped back, her breath coming in fast little gasps. "We had an agreement."

"To get married." He traced the shape of her breasts with his fingers. Even through the blue satin she felt woman-warm and heaven-soft.

"And have separate bedrooms." Her hands encircled his wrists.

"But I thought—" He blew out a breath. She looked up at him with eyes as dark as the sky. She wasn't ready. Fine, then he would give her time. His body hungered for her, but he lifted her knuckles to his lips and kissed them gently. "Let's find Emily. It's getting late."

"Ben? Are you mad at me?"

"Just at myself. You mean a lot more to me than I'd bargained on back in that jail."

"Me, too." She leaned her cheek against his chest, and he held her tight. It felt good just to hold her.

She tipped her head back, her rich curls brushing his hands. "I've never let any man this close."

"With the way you grew up, I can't blame you." He'd lived in his share of hideaways with outlaws meaner than an attacking grizzly. He'd seen how the women were treated in those camps, and the rare child dragged along just to do the work. "I'm not like those other men you've known. I'll never hurt you. I'll never give you a reason to leave."

Secrets. They gathered in his chest like a hard, dense fog. They made him cold, and he shivered. Polly's arms crept around him and warmed him. He clung to her, pressing kisses in her hair, listening to the dry rattle of the changing leaves and the call of a coyote yipping high in the hills.

"There's one thing I haven't talked to you about," he admitted, "and it's been troubling me."

"Tell me." She cuddled against him. "I want to help if I can."

His past scared him. He'd buried it deep, and he didn't like to think about it. He'd been reborn as a new man that day he'd shot down a rival gang leader and walked away from a lawless life forever. It wasn't a lie he was keeping from Polly—he was a new man, forged on hard work and the love of a good woman. David Benjamin McLaney was dead and buried. He had the newspaper article to prove it, a body found with the gang leader the sheriff had identified.

But now and then, the nightmares would wake him and the worries would haunt him. "Your father won't be showing up in my town, will he?"

"To pay a family visit? No." She held him harder and he could feel her shiver. "I've been gone four long years. He tried to find me for a long while, but he gave up. I don't want anything to do with that man."

"He's a hard man, tough and mean." He hated that Polly had grown up under the thumb of such a man.

"You know of him?"

He nodded. Instead of answering, he caught her mouth in a kiss. He wound his fingers through her hair. He was still hard and throbbing, his blood as hot as a firestorm. She leaned into him, all heat and soft curves.

But he heard voices approaching and he stepped back. A mother was rounding up her children. He took Polly's hand and they found Emily playing in the straw pile with several other girls. With straw sticking out of her hair and clinging to her dress, she muttered an "oh, Pa," but she came along to the house with only a small grumble.

Ben watched Polly take his little girl upstairs, and his heart stopped. How was he going to get through the night without Polly in his arms? Without her kisses and caresses and the fire of lovemaking?

He took a long, cold drink of water and stood on the porch, watching the night. Then, when the driving sexual need for his wife ebbed, he headed upstairs. The slash of light through an open door drew him. He leaned against the doorframe and watched Polly tuck the blankets up to Emily's chin.

"You gotta read to me."

"It's late," Polly's voice soothed. "You just close your eyes—"

"I'm too tired to sleep."

"It was an exciting day." She sounded as if she meant it, as if she were glad she was now a wife and mother. "Close your eyes anyway, and I'll tell you another story."

"But I wanna know what happens next to Jo and Beth and Meg and Amy." The plea was just short of a whine. Emily was tired. "I love that story."

Emily pressed a leatherbound book into Polly's hands.

The light brushed Polly with golden warmth. He watched the change on her face, the apology slipping away to something else. Something sadder. She traced her fingers over the book's embossed title.

"I can't read this to you, Emily." All the joy and music was gone from her voice. "I'm sorry. I'll tell you a story—"

"That's not the same. Why won't you read to me? In your letters, you promised to read to me every night. You promised."

Polly gazed down into eyes filling with tears. Promises were important to Emily. Very important. She thought of all the other women who promised to come and take care of her, but didn't. She thought of Pauline Curtis on the stage, running off to be with her banker's son, never once regretting all these vows she'd made to the little girl who needed her.

"I can't read." Polly set the book on the nightstand.

Emily studied her for a long moment. Then she let out a breath. "I know you're not Miss Curtis, Polly."

"You do?"

A vigorous nod. "You're like Pa. You're a lawman. You saved me up in that tree, and you weren't even scared of all them bullets."

"I'm no lawman." Polly brushed the stray bangs out of Emily's eyes. "I was a hired gun."

"And a gold panner?"

"That, too. Whatever it took to make a living honestly." She stared down at her unlady-like hands, scarred and suntanned and callused. Hands that didn't know how to sew or cook pancakes on the Family Sunshine range. "I'm afraid I might not be a very good mother, Emily. I can't read, and what I know, I doubt your father wants me to show you."

"You knew how to find gold along the river."

"True, but—"

"And you catched more fish than Pa ever has."

"Yes, but—"

"And you saved Deputy Milton's life and mine." Emily flew out of bed and wrapped her arms hard around Polly's neck. "You're the best ma ever."

Tears burned in her eyes and hurt in her chest. Polly held tight to her daughter—*her* daughter—and didn't ever want to let go. "You're not so bad of a little girl."

"I know." Emily just held her harder. "It's okay if you can't read none, cuz this month school starts. I'll learn how to read real good."

"Of course you will. You're the smartest little girl I've ever known." Polly brushed a kiss to Emily's brow. "Do you want that story now? Or should we call your father in to read from your book?"

"Those stories you've been tellin' me are about you, aren't they?"

"Yeah." She'd run out of fairytales long ago. "Do you want to hear about the greatest danger I've ever been in?"

"Is it scary?"

"Very." Polly leaned back on the pillows. Emily snuggled close. She wrapped her arms around her daughter and began the story of the day she beat Deadeye Cletus and Bobby the Kid in a Wyoming poker game.

Polly shut the door, her heart full. Emily slept with a satisfied smile on her face. She'd liked the story. Polly headed down the hall, not knowing what to do. She was a married woman. Her shoes rang on the wood floor, echoing in the pleasant silence of the house.

She didn't know where Ben was, maybe in bed. She pushed open her bedroom door. No moonlight tumbled through the windows to light her way. She found matches and lit a lamp.

She felt him behind her even before he cleared his throat. Her body prickled with awareness and her skin tingled, eager for his touch. Her traitorous body. Polly pulled the pins from her hair, and the curls she'd put back fell free around her shoulders. "I told Emily the truth."

"I know. I heard." He ambled into the room, his eyes dark and hard to read. "I didn't mean to overhear. I was coming to read Emily her story."

"She'd already figured it out." And because it hurt so much, this new sensation of being loved, Polly tugged at the quilt covering her bed. "I didn't do so well being Pauline Curtis."

"All you can be is yourself." Ben's hands curled around her shoulders, a strong and stroking motion that pulled the tension from her tight muscles. "I'm proud to call you my wife. And the marriage certificate is in your real name."

"I saw." Instinct warned her to break away and force distance between them. "I'm truly out of my father's reach, aren't I?"

"I vowed to protect you, and I will. From any threat." He pressed a kiss to the back of her neck, hot and tempting. "From now on, you're no longer Roy Brown's daughter. You are my wife. My beautiful, amazing wife."

The defenses around her heart rent. She was left with a wide-open vulnerability that scared her more than anything. Of all the outlaws she'd faced and rough men she'd fought off, she'd never known this brand of fear. Of laying open one's self to another.

"I can't keep my promise to you." Ben's kisses trailed around her neck. His hands swept to her stomach and pulled her tight against him. She could feel the hard length of his shaft against the small of her back.

"I want to be in your bed," he murmured.

"I can't—"

"I know." His hands caressed her, gliding the length of her hips to her ribs and back again, soothing and tender, just short of provocative. "We will sleep together. The rest will happen when you're ready."

"I don't think I'll ever be ready." He might as well know the truth. "I'll never let anyone—" She couldn't say the words.

"Then let me hold you." He released the button at her

nape, then pressed a fiery kiss to her skin.

"You're undressing me."

"Well, you need to get into your nightgown." He released another button.

"I can undress myself. I don't need help."

"I noticed you never need help. Not with the stove or the buggy or bringing down an outlaw." He popped open the dress all the way down to her waist. "Maybe it's time you started to depend on me a little."

"I can take care of myself, and I can certainly change out of my dress." She jerked away when his fingers caught the edge of her sleeves. The gown slid the rest of the way down her arms, exposing her camisole. He'd seen her wearing less just this afternoon, but he hadn't been looking at her then with those predator's eyes.

"I helped you with Dixon." He grabbed the folded nightgown that lay on top of her pillow. "That worked out all right. We worked together. We make a good team."

"I see where you're headed, MacLain, and it's not going to work. You aren't going to try to reason me into sharing a bed with you."

"I am going to share a bed with you." He shook out the white garment, his gaze never leaving her face. "Now, take off that camisole."

It was his voice that kept her from arguing, the look in his eyes so tender and deep. His fingers skimmed down the straps of her camisole, hooked around the fabric, and guided the cotton down over her breasts. The cool air breezed across her exposed skin. Her nipples tightened.

He let go, and the dress and camisole slid to her waist. The heat of his hands skimmed down her sides and brushed the fabric to the floor. She fought the urge to run and hide—she'd never been so vulnerable before.

Ben plucked at the tie of her drawers. She caught his wrists, but he kept working. Soon those slid down her thighs, too. She stood naked and trembling before him. She watched his eyes darken and heard the rasp of his breathing. She laid her hand along his jaw and felt heated male skin. A day's growth prickled her fingertips. Her body heated with a spiraling need she couldn't give in to.

He gathered the nightgown and slipped it over her head. The soft flannel felt like heaven against her sensitized body. It fanned across her breasts and hugged her arms and hid her nakedness from his sight.

"Here. Let me tuck you in."

He pulled back the covers, exposing line-fresh sheets, and she found her feet taking her across the floor and to the bed. The fashionable shoes tapped on the wood, then whispered on the carpet. She sat down on the edge of the mattress, and Ben knelt to slip off her shoes.

Sweet heaven, Ben made it just short of sinful. He tugged off her shoes with a tender ease. Then he ran his thumbs down the length of her arches, and his fingers across the top of her feet. He used his knuckles underneath her toes, and when she cried out with pleasure, he stripped off her socks and did it all over again, caressing and teasing, both gentle and rough until her feet tingled and her body felt like melted butter.

"I can do that to you all over, if you want"

There was a wicked grin as he waited for her to want more. Goodness, she was ready to beg for it. Her body thrummed with a heady delight, and she wanted his hands to touch more of her, to bring her that same thrilling pleasure.

"You're trying to seduce me."

"Is it working?"

"Absolutely not." She gasped when his hands banded around her ankles and his thumbs dug into the muscles behind her calves.

"How about now?"

"Worse. Much worse. I'm really not enjoying this at all."

His thumbs pushed and pulled at tired muscles not used to dancing around on high heels. She sank back onto the bed. A moan escaped her lips.

His fingertips kneaded and caressed all the way up her calves. His thumb teased at the sensitive skin behind her knee. Pleasure danced through her nerve endings, but her stomach tightened a little.

When his hands brushed up her thighs, she sat up. Ben's hands stilled. They remained splayed against her outer thighs. He was trembling. She was trembling.

"I've never—" She blushed.

"That's what I figured." He stood and moved his hands from her legs. Her skin felt hot wherever he touched, and she felt achy and needy and strangely disappointed. "Having sex would be like that, but much, much better."

"Maybe for you." She curled up beneath the covers.

Ben's fingers caught the blankets and quilt. She couldn't ever remember being tucked in before, safe and secure, and wished sweet dreams. She rolled on her side away from him, wanting more than his touches.

She heard the rustle of clothes as Ben undressed. She didn't want to think about the way the lamplight would gleam along the contours of his bronzed shoulders or how he would look without trousers. She heard his boots thunk to a rest on the floor. She heard the crystal lamp jingle as he turned down the wick.

Complete darkness fell, and the ropes squeaked as he settled down beside her. His greater weight made the mattress dip. She could hear the pillow crinkle. She opened her eyes to see him beside her, gazing at her face.

He rolled her against him. His arms enfolded her, safe and snug. Her head fit just right under his chin. She could feel his arousal through her thin flannel gown and knew that he was naked in her bed.

He wanted her. Her stomach flip-flopped. Fear drummed in her chest and she couldn't relax. He whispered, "Sweet dreams," in her ear and soon, sleep claimed him.

But she lay for hours in the darkness listening to the

wind rock the trees against the eaves.

Rain came before dawn, tapping at the windows and drumming overhead on the roof. Ben held her tight, as if afraid to let her go. He was strength and comfort, and that's what frightened her.

She'd never had much luck. Whenever something good happened, it never lasted. Being here with Ben was the best thing that had ever happened to her.

It was going to last, wasn't it?

CHAPTER THIRTEEN

Roy Brown thumbed back the hammer and nosed the revolver against the skinny little clerk's jaw. "I told you to read it."

"I need proof you are who you say you are." The pipsqueak swallowed, his Adam's apple working beneath his chicken-skin neck.

"Ain't this proof enough?" He pulled the trigger and moved the Colt just enough for the bullet to burn past the pansy's nose and penetrate the wall. He didn't have much of a tolerance for anyone with a bit of schooling.

"Yep, that'll do it." The coward trembled and snapped open the telegram. "It says 'Roy Brown, care of Miss Delia Howell at the Red Sage Saloon. Your daughter is in Indian Trails, Montana and married to a sheriff.' "

"A sheriff? What sheriff?" Roy released the hammer and jammed the revolver into his holster. That girl was the bane of his existence. Always running off. Always shaming the family.

Hellfire! She'd married a sheriff. Not a respectable outlaw, but a damned peacemaker.

"Ensel, Arlan, get my horse. We ride."

* * *

"**G**ood morning," Ben murmured in her ear.

They were warm and snug, nestled together like a pair of spoons. The bed ropes gave a rasp as he moved just enough to press a kiss to her nape. The dreaminess of sleep still gripped her, and she ached to roll over and kiss him long and hard.

His hand inched up from her waist and cupped her breast. He squeezed, then circled the pad of his thumb across her nipple. Pleasure bolted through her. He did it again, and the sensation doubled.

"We had an agreement, MacLain."

"Yes, but we need a new one." His words were a kiss that traveled across the back of her neck to the curve of her collarbone.

"So, you want to renegotiate our betrothal pact?"

"Right now." His hand gripped the hem of her nightgown, gathered high on her hips and tugged. He drew up the fabric despite the weight of her body on it.

"Ben, I—"

He tugged the garment over her head. A part of her knew she could stop this. Another part wanted to lie with him and feel safe and protected, huddled beneath the warm quilts. His mouth snared the breast he'd teased, the nipple still budded. A new sensation speared her as his tongue drew her into his mouth and suckled. Her hands fisted in the sheets. Her head fell back as her spine arched. She clamped him there, unwilling to let him stop. Heat gathered at her breast where he laved and suckled and nibbled and arced straight through the center of her body, leaving a strange ache between her legs.

Goodness, this wasn't what she expected a man's touch to be like. Hurt, yes. Submission, yes. But not this sparkling pleasure. Ben gave her other breast the same attention, his hand reaching up to knead and play with her dampened nipple. Aching tension gathered deep inside.

"Like that?" Ben's words fanned more sensation across her aroused breast. "How about this?"

Then it was his hands that caressed and excited. Hands that brushed over her ribs to tease the sensitive curves of her breasts and then down to the ridges of her hipbones. His mouth returned to her breasts, alternating between the two, kissing and suckling and devouring.

Goodness. Her toes curled. Her muscles tensed. The tension gathering deep inside became unbearable. Then his hand brushed across her thighs. She moaned, drowning in sensation. Like a bullwhip snapping through her, pleasure rolled over and flickered, leaving bright sparks of sensation.

Ben drew her thighs apart and she was helpless to stop him. All the lessons of her life and the ways she'd seen men treat women faded like snow to sun when his fingers brushed against her there, where she was damp and aching for him. White-hot sparks of lightning-sharp fire splintered her, leaving her weak.

She sat up, heart pounding, fear rising. "Mrs. Brooks is going to be here any minute."

"Mrs. Brooks?"

"The housekeeper I hired." Polly rolled away from him and grabbed the nightgown. How could she look Ben in the eye? She wrapped her nightgown around her naked body like a towel and darted out of bed before he could draw her back.

If he touched her like that again, she didn't think she could stop him. She would lose every trace of common sense. Even if touching and kissing felt wonderful, she could never surrender herself to any man— even if she wanted to. Look how close she'd come, moaning and writhing at Ben's heated touch.

She yanked open a drawer on the bureau, rattling the beveled mirror. In the silvered reflection she saw her own face, flushed from Ben's pleasuring hands.

He rose from the bed, naked and visibly aroused. Very aroused. Her gaze riveted on the thick length of his shaft, jutting upward. Goodness, she blushed, her body heating traitorously.

She busily rummaged around in the drawer, just to keep her hands busy. She hauled out a pair of stockings. Where had her drawers gone?

His hands curled around her waist as he embraced her from behind. His chest pressed against her shoulder blades and his hips met her fanny. She could feel the hard heat of his shaft against the small of her back. Her heart hammered wildly and she had to fight a growing sense of panic—and excitement.

It felt like heaven in his arms.

He pressed a kiss to the outside curve of her neck. "You're not getting dressed. Not until I'm finished with you."

"I think I hear a buggy in the drive. The sun is getting ready to rise—"

"I'm already there." He tugged the nightgown from her body, unwrapping her like a Christmas present.

"Ben, I can't—" She tried to step away.

He held her firm against him. "You've just never done this before, have you?"

"A person doesn't have to jump off a cliff to know it's a long hard fall."

"Making love is not like jumping off a cliff."

"I imagine it's a lot like hitting bottom."

"Not if it's done right." His tongue flicked along the edge of her earlobe.

"Oh, and I suppose that was some sort of a boast." She wanted to shove away from him. She knew she should break away from his warm, thrilling hold that was making her body thrum with excitement.

"Well, I don't want you to think I'd be a dud in bed." Humor glimmered in his eyes dark with desire—and certainty. "Come, let me prove it to you."

She wanted him to. His nakedness scorched her from neck to heel, and his hard shaft against her bare skin felt like a brand. Worse, that fascinating part of him was all she could think about. "Emily will be up and—"

"Then we shouldn't waste any time." His hands covered her breasts and squeezed.

Sensation shot through her, and she gritted her teeth to keep from crying out at the pleasure. The images of her past paraded through her head. The way her father's men had talked about the women they'd used and paid for and seduced. And the vow she would never give that much of herself to a man, no matter how tempting.

"What's the matter?" It was concern in his voice.

"I just don't want to do this. I told you that."

"Your body says otherwise."

"I know."

His hands left her breasts and wrapped around her waist, holding her hard to him. She could feel the beat of his heart and the ridge of his erection, yet he held her. Tenderly and lovingly.

Her heart cracked. How easy it would be to fall in love with this man. She refused to do it. She refused to believe any of this could last forever. She'd run out of luck all her life. Why should it be different now?

And yet she wasn't alone. She knew that. And that's what frightened her.

Ben turned her in his arms and kissed her. Passionate and sweet, brazen and comforting. He was an amazing man. He wasn't anything like the outlaws she'd grown up with, the kind of men who used their strength to harm and hurt, to ridicule and dominate.

"Let's get dressed. We have the whole day to spend together." He pulled a pair of her undies from the bureau drawer. "That gives me all day to convince you of the wonderful lovemaking you're missing."

He watched her cook breakfast over the campfire, his blood still pulsing with desire. He studied her during the meal, his body still aching for her. He helped her do dishes, and every brush against her made his need for her flame.

Mrs. Brooks arrived to dry, shooing them away from her work. Then Adella and her mother showed up to take Emily for the day. The little girls waved goodbye, giggling in the back of the wagon.

He was alone with his wife, his beautiful, enchanting, sexy wife.

She did 't seem to know how tempting she was. Her blue skirts hugged her hips when she hurried down the steps, and her breasts swayed gently with her quick gait. She'd forgotten to put up her hair, and the wind tousled her rich, dark curls.

He stepped out of the stable. "I've got the horses saddled."

"You want to go riding? I could go change—"

"No, it'll be easier to seduce you in that dress than in your trousers."

"You're aren't going to give up on that?" She gazed up at him, one slim brow quirking.

"Not a chance."

She tossed him a half-smile, and he remembered the flash of fear across her face when he'd held her this morning, naked in front of the mirror. She'd been responsive to his caresses, and recalling how ardent and free her pleasure had been made his groin heat up. He was hard and throbbing before he even stepped foot inside the stable.

"The pinto is yours." He came up behind her.

Polly sidestepped. "You saddled her for me."

"Yes, but she's yours from now on."

"Mine?" She tilted her head to one side, and he watched her worry that bottom lip. That luscious sweet lip he wanted to lave and suck and kiss.

He reached out.

She dodged and circled around the horse. "I've missed my roan so much." She didn't meet Ben's gaze as she ran her hand along the mare's neck, and let the animal nuzzle her slim hands. "What's her name?"

"Renegade."

"I like it." She tossed him a smile, and she was no longer skittish, no longer unsure. "She's a fine animal. I should pay you for her. I've got the bounty on Dixon and his men—well, the half I didn't put in savings for Emily. And the gold claim has been paying off."

"So I heard." He circled around the mare. "You like having your own money."

"It keeps a woman from being too dependent—" She jumped as his hands settled at her waist. His shaft straining against the confines of his denims pressed against her fanny.

"I don't want you dependent on me." He pulled her against him and placed his hands on her breasts. "Is that what you're afraid of?"

"I've seen it often enough." She sounded strangled, yet there was no mistaking the low husky note of arousal in her voice.

He let her move away and gather the pinto's reins. With one slim hand on the pommel, she climbed into the saddle. Her skirts bunched over her knees and she smoothed them. He was surprised she didn't want to change, then remembered his comment about making love.

Maybe she was thinking over his offer.

Heat pulsed in his blood, leaving him weak. He mounted up and joined her out in the yard. She was heading toward the river and he followed her lead. He enjoyed the view—the slim cut of her back, her soft fanny settled on the saddle, the lean curve of her thighs as she gripped the horse.

When the trail widened, he drew up alongside her. "Tell me about growing up with one of the most notorious outlaws in the West."

"There isn't much to tell. My mother died when I was Emily's age. I cooked for them. It was better than an orphanage."

"Roy Brown is a harsh man."

She didn't answer. She stared up at the peaks of the towering Rockies. They were so close, she had to tip back her head to see those grand, snow-capped peaks. "It won't be long until snow falls."

"The leaves are still turning."

"It won't be long." The beautiful summer had ended, and Polly's stomach tightened. She was afraid to believe this happiness could last. She'd spent her life on the move, one camp to another, then onto a shanty, then up into her father's mountain hideaway. It had never been permanent, never stable, and never kind.

As Ben's hands snaked around her waist and the other around the bottom of her thigh, something changed in her heart. Maybe it was the crisp mountain air or the tenderness as he lifted her to him. They shared the saddle, pressed together. His arms wrapped around her and his lips brushed her hair, and the fear flitted away like those dying leaves on the wind.

She'd been afraid Ben would beat her. He'd turned out not to be that kind of man. She'd been afraid he wouldn't trust her, but he'd been the one trusting her with his daughter's heart. She'd turned away from his tender touches, but he did not turn away from her.

She thought of his touches this morning. Having sex would be like that, but much, much better. Could she do it? Could she trust Ben that much? How could she not?

She leaned against him, closed her eyes, and vowed not to be afraid to love this great, gentle man.

"So, this is the gold claim?"

"This is it." Polly gazed down at the swatch of bank, river and woodland with pride. "Emily chose that spot right by the first curve, and I've been downstream, working the slower current."

He brought the horse to a stop. "Something tells me Emily's spot has produced the most gold."

"Imagine that." She'd helped Emily find the best spot.

The sweet memories of the afternoons they'd spent together, peacefully playing in the water warmed her. She suspected before this afternoon was gone she would have made new memories of this serene spot.

The waters whispered as they rushed in a lazy cadence down the hillside. Sparrows hid in the thinning limbs of a cottonwood as a bald eagle soared overhead on the crisp wind. The grasses rustled, and a doe peeked out of a thicket of huckleberry bushes to stare at them.

Ben's arms tightened around her waist, perilously close to her breasts. "I thought for our first full day as man and wife you'd like to be here at the claim, where you're the happiest."

"I'm happiest with you and Emily."

"You love the outdoors." His hands closed over her breasts. "We could fish, pan for gold, find a quiet spot in the sun and make love—"

"I bet you don't have a whole lot of interest in fishing or finding gold. It's the lovemaking you brought me up here for." She moaned when his thumbs plucked at her nipples.

"I don't deny it." His kiss brazened along the outside of her neck and lingered against the top button of her collar. "I want to make love to you with the leaves overhead and the crisp grass for a bed. I want you to know a better woman couldn't have been locked up in my jail."

"Lucky me." She didn't stop him when he plucked at the buttons at her bodice and the fabric parted. His hands slid inside to knead her swollen breasts, already aching for him. "We had an agreement and you've broken it."

"I didn't break it alone." He ran his thumbs over her nipples, then dipped low to sweep over her ribs and as far down as her dress would allow.

She cried out with pleasure. "Seems to me we need to fight this out."

"Fight?" His hands loosened the ties at her waist. "I don't want to fight. I want—"

"I know what you want." She plucked the pack of cards from her pocket and held them high. "Five card stud. The winner of the best of three games gets to decide if we make this marriage a real one or not."

"Is that a challenge?"

"Absolutely."

Ben snatched the pack from her fingers. "Prepare to be conquered by the best card player in five counties."

She laughed at the confidence in his eyes. Oh, poor respectable Ben MacLain. He probably figured she was as inept at cards as she was at cooking on his stove.

He was dead wrong. And he was going to learn the hard way. She would humiliate him. Then she would make him love her beneath the hot touch of the sun.

With the autumn breezes stirring the blanket spread out in the watery sunshine, Ben tapped the cards from the box and into his nimble hand. "It's showdown time. Are you ready?"

"Ready to win." Polly leaned forward. "Are you sure you want to risk losing to a woman?"

"I haven't been defeated yet."

"And I don't intend to lose." She felt a flutter in her chest when he leaned close and brushed his cheek to hers.

"Don't be afraid," he whispered. "I'll be gentle."

"I intend to be rough."

He arched one brow, as if he liked that idea. His fingers stroked the smooth, blue-backed cards. He handled the cards like an expert, with the ease and agility of a seasoned player.

Polly had to wonder what Ben did for a living before he'd hired on as a small-town sheriff. She could sense a hard and fast game, and her blood sang in her veins. "Deal, Sheriff."

"You seem confident."

"That's because I know I can beat you."

"I'm fairly certain you'll be writhing beneath me on this blanket." He shuffled with amazing skill, stroking the cards with his fingertips, and they fanned together and parted over and over again. Then he tossed out five cards to each of them. "Normally I only play with whoever can challenge me."

She recognized that teasing glint in his eyes. "Challenge you? I'm going to humiliate you. I've played with more at stake than this and won."

"Your pride is about to take a beating." Ben glanced at his cards and his eyes sizzled. He took one card, then lifted a querying brow.

She cupped the cards in her palm and took some pleasure in her royal pair, although she didn't dare let it show on her face. She bit her lip and asked for two cards, just to feed Ben's confidence.

He thought he had a good hand. He was about to be disappointed.

He laid down a pair of queens.

She laid down a pair of kings.

Ben's gaze narrowed, and he measured her up. "It's luck."

"It's called skill." Victory tasted sweet. She gathered up the cards with a sweep of her hand. "My deal."

It was her turn to show him she knew a thing or two about shuffling. Surprise darkened his eyes as she handled the cards, then dealt with quick, professional flicks of her wrist. She may be playing to win, but she wanted him. More with each passing breath.

This time her hand wasn't as good. She liked that. Now was where the skill came in. She tossed out three low cards and was pleased with the flush beginning to form.

"Give me two cards." Ben's brows furrowed. Maybe he wasn't happy with his hand. Maybe he was bluffing. "Let's up the ante."

"There is no ante."

"Maybe there should be." Wickedness gleamed in his eyes.

"If I win this hand, then I want you on top when we

make love."

"On top?" She dealt him two cards, then took two for herself. "Fine. If your hand beats mine, I'll be on top for as long as you want."

"That must be some hand you've got there."

"Maybe." She bit her lip.

Ben's gaze fell to her mouth. His pupils darkened. Momentarily she forgot about the cards cupped safely in her hand to watch his gaze travel slowly along the curve of her bottom lip, lingering in the center where her sensitive skin began to quiver.

"But if I win," she added, "you stop trying to seduce me."

"No more kisses?"

She shook her head. "And no touching me like you did this morning."

He considered that. "I hope you have a lousy hand, because I'm not going to stop until I win."

"Neither am I." Ooh, she loved teasing him.

He wanted two more cards, and she dealt them to him. She took one. "Do you call?"

"You bet."

The moment of truth. She held her breath and spread out her cards.

"I really hate to take advantage of a woman." Ben tossed his cards to the blanket. His flush was higher than hers. "I'll be looking forward to having you on my lap."

The idea thrilled her. Desire tugged low in her stomach, and she tried to hide her shiver. "You haven't won yet, MacLain."

"We're tied, and it's my deal." He shuffled. "What are you going to do if I win?"

Her chin shot up. "What are you going to do if you lose?"

He'd played hard, but he wasn't about to force the issue. Then again, she was the one who'd challenged him. He glanced at his cards, considering. "I want you."

"I know." She tossed him a wicked little grin.

Blood thudded in his groin. It didn't take a genius to know what she wanted. "I'm ready. I call."

"You can't—"

"I call." He laid down his hand; not much of anything.

She had a full house. The shock on her face was priceless. "You wanted to lose."

"I wanted you to win. You're going to regret turning down my invitation."

"About my being on top?" A slow blush warmed her porcelain skin.

"Exactly. I know it's all I'm going to think of."

"Me, too." Her gaze pinned his and left no doubt. "Especially since I was planning to lose that hand."

"I know." He swept the cards aside, the blanket stretched between them. It would make a perfect bed to make love to her on, with the scent of autumn crisp in the air and the sun to warm them. What came next between them depended on Polly. "You won the match. If you want me to lay you out on this blanket and love you long and hard, then you'll have to seduce me."

"Seduce you?" Her mouth fell open, lush and supple.

His groin thudded. "I can take off my clothes if it will help."

"Like you did with me?"

"Exactly." The memory of her naked and in his arms tormented him. His pulse thundered with pure strident need. He wanted to kiss every inch of her. He wanted—

Her hand shot out and tugged at his buttons. They popped like corn from a hot pan. His shirt fell open and her hand splayed against his chest

Her mouth brushed his. "I guess I'll have to seduce you."

Ben had never been so glad to lose a game.

CHAPTER FOURTEEN

She claimed his mouth with hot demand, and she gave him all she had. Lips brushed and tongues tangled. She wound her fingers into the hair at the base of his neck and plundered.

"Be gentle with me," he begged.

They tumbled laughing to the blanket, and he spread out over her. The weight of his body pinned hers to the ground, and it was a thrilling feeling. She tugged off his shirt as his mouth covered hers again.

On a sigh, she tossed the garment somewhere off the blanket. "It's hard for me to seduce you from here. I can't reach your belt buckle."

"There's a remedy for that." His arms slid around her and they rolled.

She came up on top, her hair spilling over her shoulders. "You were serious about this?"

"Believe it." His hands came up to brush the hair from her face. "What about my belt buckle?"

"I can reach it now." She tugged it loose. "I've never seduced a man before. How am I doing?"

"You're talking too much." He rolled her back over and wedged his knees between her thighs. "I'm going to have to take over now."

He tugged off her dress and ran his hands over the sensitive peaks of her breasts, the curve of her stomach, and between her thighs. Sensation roared over her like an avalanche, forcing her along faster and faster toward an uncertain end.

Ben caught her nipple with his tongue. Somehow, he'd taken off his trousers and his bare thighs pressed hers open wide. That sweet sharp pleasure spiraled through her belly again and gathered low and hard. Every sweep of his tongue, every flicker of his hands across her inner thighs made that pleasure tighten.

Then his fingers eased upward along the sensitive skin of her inner thighs. White-hot sparks ignited wherever his fingers touched. She arched up against his hand. Nothing had ever felt this good. And it was because of Ben—because of the kind of man he was. Noble and honest, strong enough to be tender, giving instead of taking.

His fingers moved over her like magic, brushing over a hot bright place that made the pleasure sharp as a knife. Her hips bucked up against his hand. The sensation sharpened, and she cried out. She felt her muscles tighten. She felt her body open. The tension gathering deep inside her began to coil ever tighter.

Ben settled between her parted thighs. "Are sure you want to do this?"

She opened her eyes, breathless, dazed by his question. Her entire body was strumming with so much want that she ached for him. "It will be like this, won't it?"

"Even better."

"Then I want you, Ben MacLain. How I want you."

A smile was his answer, and then his fingers dipped between her parted thighs and touched her again. The molten pleasure returned, ever hotter and brighter, and she leaned back into the blanket. Her hips arched upward, and the pleasure spiked like pain.

She cried out, but his mouth covered hers, swallowing

her cry. His weight pinned her, and his hard shaft nudged very high against her inner thigh. Goodness, her body felt ready to explode as he moved his hips and his thickness pushed at her. She opened to him, hungry for this new way of loving him. She moaned as he thrust inside her.

"Does it hurt?" he murmured, easing up on his elbows to study her face. Concern crinkled his brow and bracketed his kiss-swollen mouth. "I don't ever want to hurt you."

"It feels strange. It's like you're filling me up."

"I am." His mouth caught hers, and he filled her all the way. He felt so big and thick, she felt stretched to the point of breaking but somehow, when he began a slow deep rhythm, the stretching tightened. Pleasure cut like the sharpest of blades, she clung to his shoulders and held on.

He drove into her, then retreated only to do it again. Her muscles tightened around him. He reached down and drew her thighs up over his hips. She felt him thrust deeper, and the pleasure was too much to bear. She couldn't go on, she couldn't keep doing this.

Then her stomach coiled and twisted, and an incredible sensation spilled through her. Like the edge of an avalanche first breaking away, she tumbled helplessly over the cliff, falling. Pleasure tore through her, carrying her away. Her back arched, her hands dug into Ben's back, and she cried out as the first wave of spearing sensation broke through her. The second wave unraveled that unbearable tightness inside. She clenched hard around him, again and again until her climax faded and she gazed up into Ben's dark eyes.

"We can stop if you don't like that." One corner of his mouth drew up into a slow, sexy grin.

"Yeah, let's never do that again." She laughed as he rolled her over, keeping a firm hand to her bottom so they stayed joined. She came up on top, gazing down at him. "You're still hard."

He kissed her thoroughly. "It's a problem I have whenever I'm around you."

"I've noticed this particular affliction." She sat up, feeling powerful as she gazed down at him. "I might be able to make it go away, but it will take a lot of effort."

"I'm never one to shy away from a little hard work."

"Oh, you think you're funny." She lifted up, traveling the length of his erection, then back down again.

Ben groaned, and his hands settled at her hips. They found the perfect rhythm together. She came fast and hard, and he tensed beneath her, driving up into her. His seed pulsed hot and wet inside her and she wove her fingers between his, realizing how truly joined they were.

This wasn't just sex, like Ben had said. This was a real marriage. A true bond. His kiss was tender as he tucked her beneath him and loved her all over again.

Roy Brown traveled only at night, bein' a wanted man and all. His men scouted ahead, just to make sure no do-good lawmen got the notion to take after them. Lawmen were pests, in his opinion, like flies on a dung heap. The world would be better off without them and the lawyers.

Still, he had his Colts and his trusty Winchester, his men and a saddlebag full of bullets. They raced through the night, stopping to scare a farmer's wife into cookin' a late supper for them, and then headed north to Indian Trails.

Every mile he grew angrier. If he hadn't lost his son to a sheriff's bullet, maybe he'd be in a mood to be more forgiving. As it was, he was about ready to tear that lawman apart for daring to touch his daughter.

Even if the no-good slip of a girl had run off on him again. He didn't care about the girl—he never had— but she was his, and hell if he was gonna let her get away with her fool-headed rebellion.

She wanted a life on the right side of the law. A pretty house with flowers. She was always uppity, as if she were too good for the likes of him. Well, she'd double-crossed him, double-crossed them all. He had her wanted poster tucked into his saddlebags. She knew where Roy Junior had hidden the Golden Gulch gold.

Bitterness rolled in his guts. He pulled a flask out of his jacket and drank long and hard.

Polly leaned back in the pillows. Her body thrummed, both excited and sated. Ben gathered her in his arms, and she cuddled against him, the afterglow of their lovemaking mellow and comfortable. Freezing rain tapped at the window, and Ben drew the sheets up around them. They cuddled, sharing kisses until desire renewed again, and he covered her with his body a second time.

They moved together with a leisurely rhythm, their urgency already spent. His mouth played with hers, his tongue mimicking their bodies as they rocked together, then apart. Heat gathered down low, tightening the muscles that sheathed him.

Release came in a tender explosion, and she clung to him, arching to take all she could of his pulsing shaft. Pleasure, pure and keen, whipcorded through her once and then again, snap after snap of pleasure. The intensity faded, leaving her languid and happy, cradled in Ben's arms.

"Emily is going to be up soon." She pressed a long kiss to his throat, feeling the rapid thud of his pulse and tasting the salt of his skin. "I'd better get up."

"The mornings aren't long enough to love you properly." His gaze caressed her as she crawled out of bed.

She shivered. She wanted more of his touch. These weeks of loving him had passed quickly. Their days were filled with gold panning and adventuring and preparing for school. Their evenings were spent together, snug in the parlor if the weather was cold or outside riding horses if the sun was out.

And the nights . . . Polly melted as she thought of the

pleasure Ben had given her. She didn't know loving a man could be empowering. As much as she gave to him, he gave to her in return. Watching him climb out of bed, naked and tempting, she shivered.

"I've got that sheriff's meeting in Paradise Bluff today." Ben grabbed a clean pair of drawers and denims and pulled them on. "I won't be home until late tonight."

"Then maybe Emily and I will work out at the claim this afternoon. We need to close it up for winter. The river is getting ready to freeze over." She tugged on her favorite flannel shirt, blue to match her eyes, and a pair of lace-edged drawers. She found her favorite wash-worn Levi's in the clean-clothes pile she'd brought in from Mrs. Wu's Laundry.

Ben gave her a long kiss that stirred her up. Then he left to milk the cow and care for the horses. She watched him go with a hitch in her heart—she was falling in love with him.

How could she not? He was everything great and noble in a man. He was tender and courageous, strong and loyal—a man she could place her trust in. He was everything her father was not.

"Good morning, Polly," Emily sang as she tapped down the stairs behind her.

"Good morning, princess." Polly brushed a kiss along the girl's brow. "What do you want for breakfast?"

"French toast." Emily skipped through the kitchen, waving her hairbrush. "With real maple syrup."

"Sounds good to me." Polly pulled out a chair. "Come sit here and I'll braid your hair. It's a rat's nest."

"I didn't comb it last night."

"No kidding." Polly took the brush from Emily's hand and knelt on the floor. She worked out the tangles while Emily talked about school.

Polly listened intently and asked questions. She finished braiding the girl's hair in one thick French braid and added some of Pauline's hair ribbons. "Go upstairs and pick out a dress."

Emily took off at a dead run, and Polly watched, affection sharp in her chest. She grabbed her cloak and the match tin and hurried outside.

A blast of cold air met her. Ice clung everywhere—overhead on the porch eaves and on the rungs of the steps beneath her feet. The bare limbs of the trees were dusted white, and the frozen ground crunched beneath her boots.

She piled dry kindling from the woodshed and built her cooking fire. The flames crackled merrily in the freezing morning, and she headed back to the shed for more wood.

A shadow slipped out from behind the structure, and it wasn't Ben. "Hello, daughter."

"Pa." Polly stumbled. Her father stepped back and let her fall. Her knee struck the sharp edge of a rock, but the pain was nothing compared to the shock of seeing him. She'd changed her name and her life, she'd become Ben's wife. She hadn't seen him for more than six whole years and now, as she took in the number of men with him, she knew this was no social visit.

Her hand flew to her hip, then she remembered. She'd stopped wearing her holster.

"Git up." The toe of Pa's boot struck her in the shoulder. "I've got a score to settle with you, girl."

"What score is that?"

"Running off on me. I still haven't found me a good cook."

"I can't imagine why. You're such an upstanding citizen. A true gentlemen." She climbed to her knees.

"Don't get smart with me." His gloved hand shoved her back down. "You married a sheriff, vermin of the lowest kind. One killed your brother."

"My brother was shot while stealing gold from a stage." She climbed to her knees, ignoring the bite of pain. "I want you and your men out of here—"

"Don't give me orders." Pa's fist shot out and shoved her hard against the back wall of the shed. "Where's the gold."

"What gold?" Pain dulled her thoughts, and she bit her lip to keep from crying out. She would not show her father weakness. Not now. "I have money if that's what you want. You're welcome to it if you'll just go—"

"The Golden Gulch heist. Your brother died for that gold, and I want it." Threat gleamed in her father's eyes as he cocked his revolver.

Polly heard Ben striding across the frozen ground. His boots crunched as he approached, and then his voice rose above the driving wind and tap of falling ice. "Polly? Are you out here?"

A wicked grin contorted Pa's face. "I'll kill him."

"Don't you dare." She lifted her chin, ready for a fight. "You harm him, and I'll never tell you where Roy Junior hid the gold."

It was a lie, but the threat worked. Pa pointed his revolver at the sky and released the hammer. "Git that sheriff out of here, then you and me, we'll talk business."

Ice dripped down her neck, but that wasn't what made her shiver. It was the dozen men circling her, all armed well enough to fight a small army. She pushed past her father, angrier than spit, and caught Ben before he strode around the corner and got himself killed. First thing she vowed to do when she got inside the house was to put on her gun belt.

She grabbed a few pieces of wood and hurried out into the yard.

Ben lifted the pail. "The milk's half-frozen already. I've taken care of the livestock."

"You're wonderful." She grabbed him by the arm and scooted him well away from the woodshed. She could feel Pa's gaze on her back. She could feel the cold deadly steel of a gun.

"Is something wrong?" His eyes narrowed and his gaze darted behind her to the woodshed, as if he could sense the danger, too.

"Did you get a good look at that sheriff?" Roy's right-hand man, Ensel, jammed his pair of Colts back into his holster.

"I saw." Roy cursed at the cold and at his dead son for fumbling the Golden Gulch heist. If he'd done his job right, then they would all be in warm and sunny Arizona Territory visiting a pretty little thing he knew in Apache Junction.

He swiped at the ice that was sliding down the back of his neck. "MacLaney. I'd recognize that damn traitor anywhere."

Ensel knocked the ice from the brim of his hat. "He turned us in to the marshals."

That had been a dark time for the Brown Gang. Roy had lost his brother to a knife fight in the territorial prison. He lost his youngest son to pneumonia after they'd broken free. That had been nearly seven years ago, but he hadn't forgotten.

Or forgiven.

This just gets better and better. Roy knocked aside a few sticks of wood and sat down in the woodshed. He'd get his cook back, the missing gold, and revenge on the one man his brother had trusted more than anyone.

Who would have figured it? His Polly happened to wind up marrying the man who'd as good as put them in jail. Jonathan Benjamin MacLaney might be posing as a mighty sheriff, but he was a wanted man with a long-standing bounty on his head.

"Ensel, take five men and ride hard to town for the deputies. I think they need to know about a fugitive in their midst."

Polly silently fumed through the meal. She sent Ben and Emily on their way, hand on her guns as she watched them leave. Ben hesitated, the wonderful husband that he was, concerned that something was wrong. She assured him she was fine, gave him a kiss, and watched the buggy drive out of sight.

At least they were out of Pa's reach. She could hear Pa's men in the back of the house. They had nerve thinking they could just walk back into her life and push her around the way they used to.

She marched to the kitchen and saw half a dozen outlaws stooped over the table, eating the breakfast leftovers right off the plates like dogs.

"I sure have missed your cookin'," Pa said from Ben's chair at the table. "How about fryin' me up some eggs and ham? It'll put me in a real good mood."

"I don't care about your damn mood. Get your filthy boots out of my clean kitchen. Now." She grabbed the broom and gave the first man she saw a hard snap with the handle. Arlan jumped back, a little afraid of her.

"Listen up, Polly." The chair scraped against the floor as Pa stood.

"No, you listen up. You're going to get out of my house and you're going to show me some respect."

Pa's mouth twisted. "Or you won't show us where the gold is."

"That's right." Polly cracked the broom handle against Nelson's shins to get him moving, and he let out a holler.

"Maybe you'll tell us where the gold is," Pa's hands fisted. "Or I'll turn your husband over to the marshals."

"Ben?" Polly blinked. "I'm married to the town sheriff."

"You're also married to a fugitive. Who's high and mighty now, missy? You wound up marrying an outlaw just like your old man." Pa's laughter had a lethal edge to it. "That would be him now, come to rescue you. Did you tell him I was here?"

"He would never have ridden away if I had." Polly charged to the window and heard a horse's steel shoes against the gathering ice. "You hurt him, and you'll never find the gold."

Pa's hand curled around the back of her neck,

dangerous and threatening and harsh enough to bruise. "Jonathan Benjamin MacLaney and Ben MacLain are one in the same—the bastard who turned in your own family."

Jon MacLaney. Recognition struck her like a punch to her guts. She twisted from her father's grip, trying to push out the name of the man who led the renegade gang her father sometimes joined up to ride with. It couldn't be. Ben was honest and upstanding and noble—everything an outlaw could never be.

"You're lying to me." Fury blinded her and she forgot about her guns, forgot about the dangerous men she faced. Her hand fisted and her knuckles connected with Pa's face. "You will not take this from me. You took my mother, you took my childhood. And I'll die before I let you hurt my real family."

Steel hands banded around her forearms. She cried out at the pain, but the rage inside her chest was stronger. She wrestled loose and stepped back.

And noticed six men holding loaded revolvers not at her, but at the man in the threshold behind her.

Ben. He stood like a hero with his chin up, his strong jaw set, his shoulders braced. He held a gun in each steady hand. "Let her go, boys."

Her heart soared. Her father was wrong. Ben was no fugitive. "Pa, I'll go with you. I'll show you where the gold is." Even if she didn't know. "C'mon, let's go-"

"Not so fast, Polly." Pa stepped forward, his gaze never leaving Ben's drawn revolvers. "Hello MacLaney. Nice house you've got here. Did you buy it with the money the government gave you for turning us in?"

"I was merely cooperating." Ben moved out of the threshold. "Polly, go saddle up your pinto. I want you out of here."

"Ben?" She took a wobbly step. "Pa called you 'MacLaney' and you answered."

"That's right." Ben gestured again. "Your father and I have some business to settle. Go outside, and ride to town for the deputies."

"I'm afraid it's too late." Victory rang sharp in Pa's voice. "The deputies are on their way. This time I'll be ridin' free while you rot in that hellhole they call a prison. Polly, come here."

"Never."

"Polly, head outside." Ben took a step forward.

Pa's arm curled around her neck and yanked her hard to his chest. She stumbled, and one gun flew out of her hand. It skidded away, and Arlan grabbed the other from her grip. She was too stunned to fight. She could only look at Ben.

He was a fugitive, just like her father.

She couldn't fight She couldn't speak. A movement outside the window caught her eye. She saw the deputies closing in around the back of the house.

They were coming for Ben, not for her father.

Pa dragged her through the house and she was too heartbroken to fight.

CHAPTER FIFTEEN

"I hate to do this, Ben." Woody closed the cell door. "I have a message into the marshals to verify the warrant."

"Let me out of here, damn it." Ben wrapped his fingers around the steel bars. "That bastard has Polly—"

"I got the tracker and half the deputies out searching for the Brown gang."

"That's not good enough. I need outta here now." He shook the bars with frustration. "Hell, Woody, you know me. You know I'm not going to escape. She's my wife, damn it."

"You're not the sheriff, Ben." Woody stared down at the warrant he held, the paper yellowed with age, shook his head and walked away.

"Are you just going to sit back and do nothing? Damn!" Ben dropped onto the cot and rubbed his face in his hands. Fear drummed hot and fast in his veins. He closed his eyes against images of what a man like Roy Brown could do to Polly.

As long as he lived he would never forget the look of heartbreak on Polly's face. She'd been so hurt she hadn't even fought her father. She'd just let him drag her off.

She'd believed in him. She'd believed in his honor, in his goodness. In the man he'd made her see.

Ashamed, he didn't even argue when the marshals arrived from Paradise Bluff, windblown and half frozen from their fast trek.

"It's been two months shy of seven years, MacLaney." Marshal Powers strode up to the bars. "Two more months, and the governor's pardon would have worked. You hid your past well; I have to hand it to you. I don't like it, but I have to take you to Judge Parker. Then it's jail."

"I don't care about my pardon." Ben launched off the cot. "I want to go after my wife."

"So I've heard." The marshal unlocked the cell door. "A deputy met us on the road to town. Your tracker has found their trail and needs some reinforcement."

"Is she all right? Is she still with them?" The door swung open and he bounded out of the cell. "I'll hunt those bastards down if it's the last thing I do."

"Grab your jacket and get ready to ride. You're the best shot in five counties, MacLain. I wouldn't want to take a gang as mean as the Browns without the best gunmen at my side. Can I trust you not to run?"

"I gave up running seven years ago." Ben pounded through the office and tossed open the door. "All I care about is my wife."

"Then let's get moving." The marshal gestured at his men.

Woody handed Ben his gun belt. "It will be good to ride with you one last time."

Trust. These men trusted him. There was a time in his life when he would have chosen freedom, but a lot had changed in seven years. He had changed. He accepted his gun belt from Woody and followed his friends out into the cold.

The pinto had thrown a shoe. Pa swore up a storm and threatened to shoot the blasted animal, but Polly would no longer be terrorized by his threats.

She calmed the little mare and tapped on a new shoe right there on the trail. The falling ice had turned to a bitterly cold rain, and the wind drove it straight through her clothes. She'd forgotten how miserable riding in this weather could be.

Living in Ben's house had spoiled her. She'd gotten used to the cozy rooms warmed by the stoves, and the snug roof and walls that kept the cold out. But her life there had been an illusion—the pretty things and comfortable life hadn't protected her.

She rested the mare's hoof in her lap and hammered the shoe into place. She heard her pa's grumbling criticism and refused to listen to it. She laid her cheek against Renegade's rain-wet coat, and the mare gave her an affectionate nudge in the back.

She missed her roan, but this pinto was growing on her. She set the hoof down, checking the shoe. The mare pranced, a little uneasy when Ensel approached.

A wad of tobacco shot to the ground near her feet. "Roy wants you ready to ride. Could be one of the deputy's scouts in the woods. Don't know for sure. Cain't waste time finding out. We'll lose 'em over the mountain pass. A storm's coming in."

"Help me put out the fire." She dropped her tools in the pack. "Don't just stand there, get to work."

"What happened to you? You got bossy." He kicked mud over part of the fire.

"I grew up." She swung the heavy pack over her shoulder. "Why did Pa come back for me?"

"He got one of them wires from Dixon."

"Great. I didn't know Dixon knew my father." She laid the heavy bag on the packhorse's back. "I should have guessed it."

"You should just tell Roy where the gold is." Ensel put out the last spark, then jammed his hands into his slicker. "He's gonna hurt you if you don't tell him. You're my cousin, and I've known you all my life. I don't want Roy to hurt you."

"I don't know where the gold is." She grabbed the pinto's reins.

"Shoot, Polly, Roy's gonna have your head."

She mounted up. "I'm a stepmother now. I have to make sure Pa is far away from Indian Trails and is going to stay away. Will you help me?"

"Do what? Lie to your pa?" Ensel shook his head, scattering rain from the brim of his drooping hat "I cain't do that."

"Remember the time I saved your life? When we were ten and both of our pa's were out on a job? You shot yourself with your new revolver and I stitched you up?"

"I remember. I'da bled to death without you." Ensel stared hard at the misty horizon.

Pa splashed through the puddles toward them. "You two quit gabbin'. We've got lawmen on our butts. Mount up. Ensel, you stupid ass, don't just stand there in the rain. Get those packhorses tied up."

Polly watched Ensel's jaw tighten.

"Missy." Pa's bruising fingers yanked at her arm. "I've got enough trouble. Don't you think about making more by trying to run off."

"Don't worry. I'm not going anywhere." She would lead Pa away from Emily. As for Ben—

The wound in her chest cracked open a little more and she refused to think of him.

She never wanted to think of him again.

"I'll try to help you." Ensel whispered low enough that his words wouldn't carry on the wind. "You've always been good to me, Polly. I'd thought more than once about lookin' you up, seein' if maybe you'd help me find some honest work. I figure I'd be a good lawman."

"I bet you would." Polly mounted, studying her cousin who'd always been too gentle-natured to ride with Pa. "You help me, and I'll find a way to help you."

"Deal." Ensel didn't look so sad as he led the

packhorse away, head bowed at Pa's sharp scolding.

"I've been following them for the last mile." Milton drew his gelding close and gestured off in the distance. "They're heading for the mountain pass."

"In this storm?" Ben gazed at the angry clouds shrouding the mountain peaks from sight. It was damn cold, and getting colder. Polly didn't have a coat. "Roy figures we won't follow them through a storm. He's wrong."

"It's dangerous." Marshal Powers stared at those clouds. "This rain is likely to turn freezing, and we'll be riding our horses right along the edge of those bluffs. It's a long way down."

"I'm willing to risk it." His life was nothing without Polly. He wanted her back. He wanted her safe.

"I'm glad we can count on you, MacLain." The marshal's gaze met his. "I'll let the judge know—"

"I'm here for my wife, not for me." Ben squinted at the small band of outlaws headed for the pass. "Let's go get her."

They rode swift and silent. Surprise was their only advantage and they wanted to keep it. Ben and the marshal plotted out strategy as they rode. The men agreed—an ambush would be best.

As he cut his palomino through the scrubby forest out of sight of the outlaws, he spotted Polly on the trail below. The brim of a Stetson shielded her face from his sight. She wore an oiled slicker and battered leather gloves. Her head was bowed, but she didn't look beaten. She looked strong and noble and proud.

She was leading her father away from Emily. His chest ached with long-denied emotion—with a love for her he'd refused to let himself feel. He wanted a friend, a lover, a companion, but he hadn't wanted the emotional risk. He'd just fooled himself, that was all.

He loved her.

"Ben." The marshal kept his voice low. "We've got to keep moving."

He spurred Fugitive and cut around a grove of scrubby trees. Whatever would happen to him, he accepted it. He'd broken the law years ago and was paying for it now. But Polly's life was in danger—and he would make damn sure she was safe. No matter what it cost him.

Ben, Milton and two marshals took the lead, leaving the others to wait. Ben spotted a narrowing of the trail and they headed for it. It was as good a place as any to set up an ambush. The rain turned to ice as they took cover.

He backed his horse behind an outcropping of rock and waited, revolvers cocked and ready. Freezing rain hammered the earth, drowning out the telltale sound of approaching horses. He listened, senses sharp. He didn't miss how Marshal Powers kept a close watch on him.

Like the melting ice sluicing down the back of his neck, Ben felt their approach. He was tensed, ready, heart thundering in his veins. He wanted Polly—and he was going to make Roy Brown pay for trying to take her.

Determined, he eased his horse out from behind the massive boulder. Looked like Roy was in the lead. Where was Polly? Ben had to reach her first, before the battle started. All he cared about was her.

Distant gunfire exploded, stealing their advantage. Ben couldn't find Polly. He fired, driving his gelding into the middle of the fray, despite the volley of bullets. He defended himself, squeezing his triggers as he searched. Outlaws tumbled to the ground; a deputy took a shoulder wound and crawled out of the road. Where was Polly? Ben helped defend the lawmen, but his gaze was still searching for his wife.

She was nowhere to be seen.

And neither was Roy Brown.

In the confusion of the outlaws running and the deputies following, Ben swung his palomino around and searched the terrain.

There—a movement up the steep mountainside caught his gaze. The falling ice hid them, but the white and dark patches marking the pinto's rump were distinct against the ice-encrusted granite.

Ben tried, but couldn't see well enough to fire. He gave the palomino a nudge, and the brave horse lunged up the steep embankment, great hooves digging hard for purchase on the slick rock.

The gelding slid back a few steps, then charged over crumbling earth and gathering ice. Ben felt the powerful animal struggling beneath him, but his attention was riveted on the sight of that pinto disappearing in the thick mist.

Then he saw the mare move rump-first into view. The horse scrambled. Her high shrill neigh of alarm set Ben's teeth on edge. He spun the palomino out of the way, but it was too late. Sliding backwards, the mare struck the gelding's shoulder and knocked the animal to his knees. Ben felt Fugitive slide, but all he could see was Polly on the mare's back as the pinto rolled onto her side and Roy Brown's pistol lifting upward.

Fast as lightning, Ben fired. The old man tumbled into the horse's path, his revolver firing wild. Ben launched out of the saddle, but he was too late as the pinto's feet kicked at the sky and her back hit the ground.

"Polly!" Fear energized him. He grabbed the mare by the bit and helped her roll onto her feet, knowing Polly could be crushed, even dead. Pain speared his heart into a thousand pieces, and he hated that he hadn't saved her, hadn't been able to do the impossible and pluck her from the back of the mare.

"Ben." Her voice came like a ghost's through the crackle of ice and hissing wind.

Blood smeared the left side of her face and mud marked the other. Her shirt was torn at the shoulder and her slicker was askew, but she was alive.

She was alive. He wanted to haul her into his arms and hold her tight, to never let her go, to breathe in the scent of rain in her hair and taste the wonder of her lips.

But she walked right on past him. Rocks tumbled down the steep mountainside as she turned all her attention to the mare. "Shh, Renegade. It's all right" Her gloved hand eased along the mare's bleeding neck.

Ben caught the bit ring and helped hold the animal steady. The pinto's eyes were glassy and white-rimmed with fear. Her nostrils puffed wide and she kept sidestepping, even as Polly knelt down to strip off her shirt and bandage one lacerated fetlock.

"How did you—?" He gestured at the mare.

"I learned how to sit a saddle before I could walk." Polly ran her fingers along the mare's leg, looking for serious injury. "I simply slid off her rump when she went down. I got banged up some, but I'll live. I just hope she's okay."

The mare calmed at Polly's touch and flicked her head away from him to look at her mistress. Renegade nickered low, as if needing reassurance.

Polly straightened and wrapped her arms around the mare's neck. "You'd better see to your animal, Ben. He's cut up some."

Fugitive nosed him in the shoulder. The tough horse was all right, for he was a reformed outlaw, too.

"Hey, Ben." It was Marshal Powers gazing up at them, the look of victory strong in his shoulders and confidence in his voice. "I see you took down Roy Brown."

"Didn't have much of a choice." Ben watched Polly's face, but she didn't so much as wince.

He'd killed her father. Surely she had an opinion on that. Her steady hands kept calming the mare, who had looked down the fifty feet to the trail below and panicked.

"Here," he stepped forward, hand out. "Let me help—"

"I don't need your help." She bit out the words low

and even, without a hint of emotion.

"I'll send a deputy up to get the body." Powers looked apologetic as he aimed his revolver straight at Ben's chest. "Come on down. We've got to handcuff you along with the other fugitives."

Ben nodded. He wasn't about to argue. Powers had given him the dignity of fighting for Polly's life, and he appreciated that. He laid a hand on Polly's shoulder. "Let me help you bring the mare down."

"I can do it." She stepped away from his touch. "The marshal's waiting for you, MacLaney."

His chest kicked. He heard her condemnation— and knew he'd earned it. He was what they said, a fugitive from justice, an outlaw wanted for bank robberies in two territories.

Polly turned her back.

He'd lost her, truly lost her. He didn't know how to reach out and try to make amends. In his heart, he knew there was no way he could.

He'd made her fall in love with him, an outlaw like her father.

Polly watched Milton handcuff Ben. He stood tall and strong, unbowed. The wind whipped the collar of his jacket against his neck and chin, and he looked for one brief moment as untamed as any outlaw.

Marshal Powers eased toward her, her father's dead body slung over one broad shoulder. "What arrangements do you want to make for your pa?"

"Ask one of his men." Polly felt her conscience wince, but the man had never truly been a father. She'd learned what a father was from the way Ben loved Emily. Her father had never loved her—he'd never loved anyone. He was like a wild animal, preying on the weak. "I'm no longer his daughter."

"There's a warrant out for you, too." The marshal eased to a stop beside her.

"Did Ben tell you?"

"No, I've had that wanted poster in my office ever since the Golden Gulch stage robbery." Powers looked her square in the eye. "I saw you catch the stage at Paradise Bluff. A lawman worth his salt can take one look at a person and see what's inside."

Polly leaned against the mare's shoulder because her legs were suddenly unsteady. "You saw me and let me go?"

Powers nodded. "Figured if it was all you could do to scrape up money for the stage, you weren't hiding any gold bars in those saddlebags. Likely someone set you up. Maybe your brother."

"He's dead."

"Yes, but maybe he thought he would live. He'd be able to go back and get the gold later and no one would suspect it." Powers nodded to the road below where the deputies stood guard over the outlaws, including Ben. "I've had my suspicions about Ben for awhile. A person can make mistakes, but it's how he fixes them that shows true character."

"He's a hypocrite. He wears a badge over that outlaw's heart." Polly nearly choked on the words, and turned away so this stranger wouldn't know how big of a fool she'd been.

"He's righting his wrongs. He's protecting the bank instead of robbing it. He's keeping the town safe instead of threatening it. It's not a man's past that ought to determine his future, but how he chooses to live each day."

"You must know something about that, Marshal."

Powers merely shrugged, but the twinkle in his eye proved she was right. "Me? No, I'm a federal marshal. I'm no outlaw. Do you need help getting that mare down?"

"I can handle her." Polly knew it would be a battle, but she and the mare would face it together. That's how trust was earned. "Can you do me a favor?"

"Whatever I can."

She looked again at the men down below. Her gaze found Ben without even trying. "My cousin Ensel has always wanted to be a lawman. I could post his bail, if there is one."

"I'll keep that in mind." Powers tipped his hat.

"What about Ben?"

The marshal sighed. "It's a matter for the judge. There's nothing I can do. Sorry."

She watched him carry her father's body down the steep slope.

It was over. She was free of her father. She felt strangely empty. Knowing Ben's gaze was on her, she turned her back and laid her forehead against the mare's warm neck.

"Pa's still at the jail?" Emily asked, brows furrowed with confusion.

"No." Polly pulled the buggy over to the side of the road. It was too distracting to both drive and talk—and this talk was important. "Your Pa is over at the jail in Paradise Bluff—"

"He's working late again." Emily crinkled up her face in disappointment. "I sure miss him when he ain't here for supper."

The late afternoon traffic bustled past them on the far end of Front Street. The gleeful sounds of children freed from the school peppered the air. Polly watched the school teacher step out of the building to clean her erasing cloths. The world was so normal, but not her world.

The words Polly kept meaning to say got all bunched up in her throat. "I miss him, too. What do you want to do?"

"It's all icky out" Emily studied the falling ice that made the world slippery and cold. "I suppose the river's all froze up."

"I suppose it is."

"When's Pa comin' home?" Emily leaned into Polly's arms.

Polly held her stepdaughter tight. "I don't exactly

know."

Emily sighed. "I'm sure glad I have you. I used to have to stay with Woody's wife. She's nice, but she don't have no kids."

Polly's heart ached, and she hugged her little girl closer. How was she going to tell Emily about her father? That he was a wolf in disguise? An outlaw who harmed people just because he could do it?

"What's wrong?" Emily tilted her head back against Polly's arm. "You look like you're gonna cry."

"I never cry." Polly swallowed hard. Her chest ached with pain for Emily—she knew what it was like to be an outlaw's daughter. She knew the shame and the hardship. The deputies had kept Ben's arrest quiet, but that wouldn't last for long. What would happen to Emily then?

That was the real reason Ben had married her, Polly could see that now. He needed someone to take care of Emily—not a housekeeper or a deputy's wife—but someone who loved her in case the law ever caught up with him.

Polly grabbed the reins, still hugging Emily, and gave the mare a gentle slap. Renegade turned out onto the street. Polly heard someone shout in protest. She didn't have the heart to see who she'd nearly run off the road this time and apologize.

"Polly, you forgot to look at the traffic," Emily reminded her.

"I'm never going to get used to this buggy." She didn't want to. She wanted to light out of here and ride until the pain in her heart eased. She wanted to get far away from Indian Trails, where no memories could haunt her.

While she'd been falling in love with him, Ben MacLain had merely been humoring her. In fact, he'd never said the words. Not when he made love to her the first time, or the last. And when he proposed to her, he didn't ask her to marry him but to marry them, him and Emily.

The landscape slid by in a blur.

Emily tugged her sleeve. "Where did you get that?"

"I fell off the horse today." Polly couldn't bear to tell her more.

"Pa always kisses my boo-boos." Emily crawled up onto her knees and pressed her lips to Polly's cheekbone. "Now you're all better."

"I sure am." It wasn't her cut that hurt—it was her heart.

She stopped the mare in the middle of the road and debated what to do. She couldn't run. She couldn't return to their cozy log home and tell Emily what had really happened. Well, that only left one thing to do.

She turned the buggy around and headed the mare toward town. "How would you like to stay with Adella for a while? I'll ask her ma if it's all right."

"Sure." Emily's brows scrunched, obviously happy at the notion of visiting her best friend, but also worried. "Where are you goin'?"

"To get your pa."

CHAPTER SIXTEEN

Ben couldn't sleep. The marshal had put him in a private cell, way in the back, where a small window gave him a view of the last quarter moon and a piece of the sky. Emily would be sound asleep by now. He wondered if Polly had told her a story. He wondered if Emily was disappointed in him or, worse, ashamed.

He knew Polly was. He'd heard it in the cold tone of her voice and saw it in the hard turn of her shoulder. She'd loved him. Now she hated him.

Well, how could he blame her? He'd never given her his heart.

He heard a sound outside the window. A sort of scratching sound. He figured maybe a dog was out there or a wild animal. Then an explosion thundered, and sharp pieces of the wall fired inward. A chunk struck him in the same shoulder he'd banged up earlier when fighting the Brown gang. Before he could jump to his feet, a shadow filled the significant hole in the outside wall.

"Hurry up," Polly ordered. "A light in the sheriffs quarters just came on."

Ben glanced at the rubble around his feet. He peered through the six-foot hole in the stone wall. "How did you do this?"

"It's amazing what a stick of dynamite will do in a pinch." Polly tossed him Fugitive's reins. "Hurry up. I hear voices."

He couldn't believe his eyes. She sat astride the pinto mare in her denims and man's jacket, her Stetson slung low over her eyes. His heart soared. "You came for me."

"I came for Emily." Her voice was cold. "Mount up, the sheriff's front door just opened."

"Not like this." He had nothing to run for. He was tired of hiding. It was time to face his past

"What the heck do you mean?" Polly swung her mare around. "I blew up a jail for you. For Emily."

"She's why I can't run." Ben heard the drum of distant footsteps and the angry shouts of the prisoners who wanted to be released, too. "I've shamed the both of you enough."

"Then what's the point of staying in prison?" Polly tied a knot in the reins, dropped them over the saddle horn and hauled out her revolvers. "Emily needs you."

"She has you, Polly."

"I know, that's why you married me, isn't it?" She didn't mean to sound bitter. It's just that she'd almost believed she was valuable enough to be loved, truly loved. And finding out she wasn't hurt more than she could bear. "Fine, stay there and play by their rules. In case you've forgotten, I'm a fugitive too and I intend to prove my innocence so Emily won't ever have to worry about losing her mother, too."

Darn him for being so thick headed, so . . . noble. He stood there looking at her as if he couldn't force himself to break the law by running. And heck if she didn't believe him.

Foolish, silly heart. She spun the pinto into the shadows because those lawmen were getting too close for comfort. Once again, she'd been wrong. Ben hadn't wanted her, hadn't needed her. Was she ever going to learn? Or was she going to be like her mother and the other women she'd seen over the years—giving their all to men who would never care?

Ben watched Polly retreat. The reins felt heavy in his hands. Fugitive nosed him and nickered low and nervous. The horse sensed the danger. It wasn't the first time his trusty palomino had carried him away from a broken-into jail cell.

Damn her for forcing his hand like this. For taking charge and making him break the law one more time. Either way, the sheriff and marshals stationed in this town weren't going to ask questions and then shoot. Reining in his anger, Ben swung up into the saddle. Together, he and Polly raced off into the night.

His anger bubbled over after they'd put enough rugged wilderness between them and the lawmen to relax a bit. "What was that stunt you pulled back there?"

"You mean that little maneuver I did to evade the posse?"

"No. Using dynamite to bust me out of jail." Damn, she was being difficult on purpose. "You could have gotten us both killed."

"I know how to use dynamite."

"You could have asked before you blew the wall out of my prison cell—"

She lifted her chin, full of fight. "Funny, every other man I've broken out of jail was grateful."

"I didn't want out. I have two more months left on my clemency period. I have an arraignment with the county judge in the morning. I figured I could work this out. Now you've blown it all to hell."

"Well, excuse me. I guess this is just another instance of the respectable Ben MacLain not really needing anyone." She gave Renegade more rein and the mare shot forward.

Ben's mount kept pace. "Me? What about you? You haven't asked for help the entire time I've known you. Not for the range and not for dealing with your ruthless father."

"Pa is dead. He's dealt with."

"I killed him. Are you angry about that?"

She didn't answer. Her jawline tensed. The drum of the pounding horses hooves against the frozen ground and the rush of wind filled the silence, but nothing could erase the cold anger he felt radiating from her.

"You don't even need me now." He hated that. "You're so damn independent you can't even ask for my help."

"I don't need your help." *I need your love.* She bit back the words before they could tumble across her lips. She ached with it, hurt with it. "I can prove my innocence on my own."

"All by yourself?"

"That's right." She didn't need him. She didn't want him. Really, she didn't. "I just want you to take Emily and start a new life somewhere in Idaho Territory or something."

"But she's going to need her mother—"

"Maybe you could buy another one for her," Polly interrupted. Pain sounded sharp in her voice and she hated it. She wanted to keep her foolish, vulnerable feelings hidden.

"I never bought you and I never used you." He reached across the few feet between their horses and caught her reins. He drew both horses to a halt in the middle of the moonlit road.

"You betrayed me. You made me love a man just like Pa."

"That's not what's bothering you." He gentled his voice, though it rang low as thunder, deep as the night. "I'm nothing like your pa. I never was."

Emotions gathered in her chest, coiling tight into a painful, solid ball. "You made me believe—"

"What did I make you believe?" He laid his hand along

the side of her face. "Tell me."

"That I was loved," she blurted out, hating her own weakness. She jerked her reins from his grip and kneed Renegade into a fast gallop.

The law was after them, but she didn't care. If they caught up to her, she would sure as heck evade them again. The winding path she'd taken through the wilderness would confuse them. They would have to wait for morning light to follow her tracks.

She could handle dynamite, lawmen on her tail, and outshoot half the men in this territory, but she didn't know what to do with a broken heart. How to fix it. How to let it be.

She just wanted to get away from the pain.

"You love Emily." Ben caught up to her.

She drove Renegade harder.

Ben stayed right on the mare's flank. "Emily loves you."

"I know. That's why I'm doing this. For Emily. She needs her father."

"But not her mother?"

That ball in her chest began to expand until she could barely breathe. "I'm a bounty hunter. I wore those pretty dresses and drove a beautiful buggy and cared for a priceless little girl for a while, but that was all. It couldn't last."

"It's still there, Polly."

"No." She gasped for breath, then realized she was sobbing. "You're an outlaw, Emily's going to be heartbroken, and I was wrong. I should have kept on going. I could have evaded you if I wanted to, I just—"

Renegade was tiring and she eased the mare back into a trot. It was easier to ride than it was to try to talk about the confused, jumbled emotions hurting like a gunshot to her chest. "I wanted a real family and a man like you to love me."

"A respectable sheriff?"

No, you. She couldn't say the words. He didn't love her. No matter how much she'd given him, he'd never loved her back. Caring and friendship and sex weren't good enough. She was no longer an outlaw's daughter. She was her own woman, and she would not give up her independence for a life without love.

"This is where we part paths, MacLain." She held her chin high, so he wouldn't suspect she was holding back tears. "You take good care of Emily for me. Tell her I'll write."

"You can't read."

"I intend to learn." She intended to do a lot of things. She spun the mare up the small incline and away from Ben MacLain.

"Polly." His voice sounded warm and rich, noble and strong. No outlaw sounded that way.

And he wasn't an outlaw, she knew that. He was everything her father was not, regardless of his past. He was a man who could love his daughter and rebuild a good life despite the mistakes of his youth.

The rising sun stung her eyes.

"You need me, Polly MacLain. Admit it." His voice followed her.

"You'd better get riding, Ben. The law is going to be after us soon enough."

"I'm never going anywhere without you again." He caught her arm, and the touch startled her. She brought her mare to a stop. Ben's hand brushed up her arm. "I'm sorry I didn't tell you about my past. I just wanted it to go away. Just like you wanted yours to."

"That's no excuse."

"I am Ben MacLain. I am a damn good sheriff, I work like hell to be a good father, and I'm failing miserably at being a husband. But I guarantee I'm going to get better as time passes."

Her chin shot up. "Some lucky woman is going to benefit, then."

"Yes, she is." He wasn't fooled. Polly was hurting inside, and this courageous woman who could ride the wilderness and face ruthless outlaws without blinking didn't know how to let herself be loved.

The fault wasn't all his, but he was going to fix it, and fix it now.

"I love you." He laid his hand against her chin when it looked like she was going to turn away. "I love you in a way I never thought possible. You are the reason behind every breath I take and everything I do. I wake up in the morning thinking of you, and you are the last thing on my mind when I close my eyes at night."

"Fancy words for an outlaw." She looked up at him with tears in her eyes, keen and powerful, and he wanted to take her into his arms and hold her until there was no more fear, no more peril, only the frenzied beating of their hearts.

Fugitive swiveled his ears, straining to hear. There was no time to hold her, to convince her of the love he harbored for her. So he led the way through the trees, heading northeast like she'd been doing, toward the rugged peaks of the Garnet Mountains.

Bad Bart Dixon gave thanks to Polly Brown for blasting a hole in the south wall of the Paradise Bluff jail. All the inmates were talking about it. She'd come to rescue her husband, that bulldog sheriff.

Just his luck, too. He'd had nothin' else to do but sit on this cot and think about all the ways he could get his revenge. He'd been in this local jail for too damn long. The judge had indicted him and here he sat, waiting for the marshals to decide to haul him up to the territorial prison.

Dixon had to worry. How long would the rest of his gang wait? They had orders to free him the minute the marshals tried to take him across the mountains.

The longer he sat here rotting, the more likely it was those damn cusses would give up waiting.

Well, freedom called. It was luck that the explosion blasted apart a cracked door hinge on the neighboring cell. The prisoner inside had grabbed the deputy who came dashing in to check, and stolen his guns and keys.

Dixon loved the sound of his jail door swinging free. He ran out of there like greased lightning. Only a single marshal had remained behind to keep peace, and it was simple as pie sneaking 'round the shadows of the building and into the alley.

He grabbed a set of clothes off a backyard line. The trousers were too big and the shirt too small, but beggars couldn't be choosers. He stole a horse from a small stable and lit off toward the hills, intent on Polly's trail.

They rode hard until dawn, and there was no telling if they'd lost the posse. But if they did, Ben knew it wouldn't be for long.

He had to get to Helena and fast, but Polly was taking them too far north. He tried to question her, but she ignored him. That woman had a stubborn shield around her heart. He knew something about shields, after trying to protect his heart from her. They weren't all that effective.

She led him through rough terrain to a shanty in the foothills. They stopped to water and rest the horses, and he made a fire while she changed the bandages on Fugitive and Renegade's legs.

"That's a pretty smoky fire." Polly's boots crunched on the frozen ground, then she knelt down beside him. "I found some dry cedar. It will burn hotter."

"I'm out of practice. It's been a while since I've been on the run." Ben watched as she sprinkled cedar twigs into the small circle of flames.

Her hands were callused from riding and rough from the cold, but they were beautiful to him. He missed the feel of her touch on his skin. His groin tightened. He missed her so much. If only she would look at him.

Her gaze remained riveted to the flames. "I picked up

some food at the mercantile."

"Before or after you picked up the dynamite?"

"Before." She opened a tin can with her pocket-knife. "I didn't figure on feeding two, so don't eat all the beans. We have to share."

"You didn't want me with you."

"I still don't, but I don't have time to argue. It's a free country." She grabbed a small frying pan and dumped the contents of the can into it. "Just don't think I'm in the mood to give you too many free meals."

It was as if a light inside her had died. Her eyes were not as bright, her voice noteless, her mouth without a smile. He wished he knew what to do.

She heated the beans and the saltpork in the same small pan. She broke a biscuit apart and handed him half.

It was tasty enough to a man who hadn't eaten since breakfast. The beans were hot, and that satisfied him. The temperature was well below freezing. He could smell snow on the wind.

"Why are you heading so far north?" Ben watched Polly smother the fire so that there was little smoke.

She set aside the empty bucket. "It's my business."

"I'm not leaving you to do it alone, whatever it is, so you might as well tell me."

A muscle clenched along her jaw. "Emily needs her pa. You ought to be trying to prove your innocence."

"Now you think I'm innocent. It wasn't too long ago you were furious at me for being just like your pa." But he didn't say the words harshly. Polly was hurting, he could see that. He ached to wrap her against his chest and love her until there was no longer a single doubt.

She scowled at him. "No outlaw is innocent."

She was softening, he could tell. "I haven't been an outlaw for years. I'm a small town sheriff. That's who I've become."

She didn't look impressed, but the muscle in her jaw was no longer clenched so tight that it spasmed.

"You're going to try to find the gold, aren't you?" He scraped the fork against his plate, cutting into the tough saltpork. "Have you figured out where it is?"

"I'm guessing, but I think I do." Polly picked at her meal. "Pa truly thought I knew where Roy Junior stashed the gold. Seeing as how I haven't seen my brother in four years and Pa knew it, I can't know where the gold is. Unless Roy Junior hid it someplace only I would know how to find."

Interest perked him up. "Your father's camp isn't far from here."

"One of them." Her gaze lifted to the top of the jagged peaks, purple against the blue of the sky. "Are you ready to mount up?"

"I've never been this far north. When my men and I rode with your father's gang, we met just south of here, at the waterfalls." Ben helped her wash off the plates with creek water he'd fetched earlier. "That's why I'd never met you before you stepped foot in my town."

"It's still your town, is it?" She wiped off the plates with a dishtowel, then packed them away. "We don't have a lot of time to spare. Mount up. We've got some riding to do."

She didn't look at him again, but he could feel it.

She wanted to give in, to let go. She wanted to love him again.

Every minute with him was torture. Polly set her heart against him and refused to even look up as he took over the lead. She didn't want the hot tingle of need that zinged through her blood every time she gazed at the breadth of his shoulders or the thickness of his thighs as he rode the saddle.

Just like she didn't want to remember the way his kisses tasted, or the fact that she missed their lovemaking. She ached for the weight of his body covering hers and the sweet, thrilling sensation of his hard shaft filling her.

Goodness, she had enough distractions with watching for signs of the posse behind them and robbers ahead of them. But her thoughts just kept returning to the memory of the tender way Ben had loved her.

Tender, not rough. She knew in her heart Ben was not the same brand of man her father was, but her head just wouldn't let her forget.

She could not let herself love a man who wouldn't love her back.

"There, take a right where the road forks," she called ahead to Ben. And because the back of her neck prickled for the fifth time that morning, she turned her mare around and studied the lay of the land.

It was all scrubby pines and outcroppings of rocks. Brown bunch grass spotted the dirt with fingers of frost. The morning sounded the way it should—birds called, a hawk soared overhead, and a gopher darted out of its hole, cried in alarm, and watched them pass.

Still, she could feel the danger.

"Faster." She took the lead from Ben, although he was more than capable. She followed the trail from memory. Renegade shied at the two willows that leaned together at a small creek's edge. Polly reassured the animal and sent her nose-first through the break in the willows.

The boughs scraped along her knee and shin. No one had passed this way for a long time. She thought of her brother, dead, and that saddened her. Pa's passing had been a relief, but this was different. She and Junior had grown up together, for better or worse. She dismounted and gazed around the hundred-foot canyon floor she once called home and felt sad for her brother's passing.

"Polly." Ben was there, and he took her into his strong arms. She wanted to stay there, sheltered from the pain of loving, but her pride wouldn't let her.

She tried hard to find the strength to walk away from him. She did it, but she longed for his warmth and his goodness. "We stayed here the summer I was five and

Junior was eight. It was one of the happier times. My mother was still alive. She used to cook the meals for the men right over there."

She knelt down to rub one of the stones that once ringed a great cooking pit with her fingertips. Remembering hurt the same way love hurt.

Ben knelt down beside her. "What makes you think your brother was here? I don't see any sign."

"Junior wouldn't have left any. He was too smart" She gestured toward the carpet of fallen leaves, half decayed and frozen solid by a thick layer of ice. "We were just children then, too young to understand what Pa did for a living. He told us he was like a pirate."

She stood and gestured toward the far corner of the clearing. "My brother and I would play pirate when Pa was gone on one of his jobs. We would make up heroic battles and protect our pretend gold for hours and hours. All summer long, we pretended we had gold in that cave."

"What cave?" Ben felt watched and turned slowly around.

"This one." With her guard down, maybe because of all the memories, Polly crunched across the leaves.

He recognized the tense line of her shoulders and knew Polly had felt it, too. Her hands were loose at her hips, ready to draw.

Ben felt a warning grip his spine, and he turned. He saw the flash of sunlight reflecting off a gun's barrel high on the embankment overhead. Who the hell had followed them here? And how? He didn't take the time to ask; he simply followed his instincts and fired. His gun and Polly's shot simultaneously.

No answering volley. No shout of pain. Nothing.

A bad feeling settled low in Ben's guts. He studied the sheer wall that rose fifty feet straight up. It was too high to see much of anything.

Whoever was up there, gun aimed down at them, had a serious advantage.

"Head for cover!" he shouted to Polly, but she was already on her way to a line of boulders along the far wall. Gunfire peppered the air, coming straight from the top of the embankment. Bullets bit into the ground and the rocks in a direct path toward Polly.

That damn gunman was trying to shoot her. Furious, Ben dashed out from behind a tree as bullets sprayed the ground in front of him. He dove behind the rocks and landed on his knees at Polly's side.

"I can't imagine that's Marshal Powers." She tapped bullets from her gun belt into her hand.

"What other enemies have you made lately?"

"Since I've met you?" She frowned, darkly teasing. "Probably a dozen or more."

The gunfire started up again. It was one gunman, Ben figured, but two guns, maybe a repeating rifle. Bullets plowed into the dirt, sending dust flying, and broke apart sharp pieces of rock. He covered his face against the debris.

"We need an offensive position." He coughed, trying to see through the grit in the air.

"If you see one, let me know." She eased up just enough to send a volley of bullets back at their enemy.

More gunfire answered, from a different place this time.

"Toss down your guns, MacLain." Dixon's voice rasped on the steep embankment overhead. "I've got your pretty wife in my sites. All I have to do is squeeze the trigger."

Dixon. That bastard would enjoy killing Polly. Fury soured Ben's mouth as he threw one set of guns into the open.

Polly lifted one questioning brow, and he knelt down to pull a third colt from his boot

"I've been in this situation before," he confessed.

"Pa would have had another in his back pocket."

Ben produced it. He watched the shadows return to her

eyes, and she looked away. He cleared his throat and shouted loud enough for the outlaw to hear. "What do you want, Dixon?"

"You know what I want. I want the woman. I want the gold."

"That's going be a problem. I'm not handing over my wife." Ben thumbed back the hammers. "I don't have the gold."

"Roy Junior, the back-stabber, ran off with the strongboxes when my men were out fightin' with the law." Dixon's anger got the best of him, and he stopped shooting.

"Is that so?" Ben listened hard, trying to gauge where the outlaw was.

"That's right." Fury vibrated like cannon fire as Dixon continued. "I got nothin', do you hear me? Nothin'. And that no-good snake-in-the-grass ran off with a fortune I earned. I want it back."

"I told you, I don't have the gold."

"Then I want the woman. Junior said she'd know where it was stashed. I'll kill you for her, MacLain." Dixon sent a round of bullets into the rocks. "And if I can't have the gold, then I'm sure as hell gonna make sure you two don't get it."

The angle of the gunfire changed.

Damn. Dixon was trying to circle around behind them. They'd be caught between the tall embankment at their backs and the rocks they were using for cover. He'd be able to pick them off like rabbits in a ditch.

"He means to kill us." Polly's jaw tensed as her gun's barrel tried to pin down the origin point of Dixon's bullets.

"He does." Ben squeezed off a shot.

Polly fired.

Nothing. Just more answering gunfire.

"This isn't working." Ben could see it flash before his eyes—Dixon pinning them down here and killing them one at a time.

Ben hadn't forgotten the outlaw's grudge against Polly.

"Stay here." He ordered his wife, who looked up at him with no small amount of fury. Well, he didn't have time for her stubborn pride. Dixon was up on that hillside, hidden in the trees, and it was only a matter of time until their small supply of ammunition ran out.

Ben wasn't the kind of man who liked to wait.

He charged through the clearing, guns blasting. Answering bullets fanned through the earth behind him, beside him. He kept moving and headed straight for the sheer cliff of that embankment.

He would get Dixon face-to-face instead of being hunted like a holed-up rabbit. He tucked the guns in the small of his back, grabbed hold of a root, stuck the toe of his boot into a crevice and started climbing. He heard gunfire behind him—Polly's gun—and heard a sharp curse of pain overhead.

She cheered. "I winged him."

"Barely took any skin from my arm." The sneer in Dixon's whiskey-rough voice echoed in the tiny canyon. "I've got to thank you, Polly. I wouldn't have escaped that damn prison if you hadn't busted up the jail the way you did. I owe ya, princess."

"Then let me go."

"Not without the gold and a little torture."

Ben heard the sick triumph in the outlaw's voice. Dixon was looking forward to harming and then killing Polly. Ben knew how men like Dixon worked—he used to ride with them. He dug his fingers into the crumbling earth and pulled himself up another foot.

He also heard the sharp snap of limbs breaking. Dixon was on the move and running fast.

"Polly!" he shouted over his shoulder, dangling thirty feet above the canyon floor. "He's coming for you—"

"I hear him." She tried to guess where Dixon was and fired. Missed. She reloaded fast, knowing as Dixon changed position on the rim overhead that Ben would be a target. And so would she.

The repeating rifle bit into the bark of the tree behind her. She hit the ground and scanned the terrain.

There. Sunlight gleamed on steel. She aimed as Dixon burst out of the thick foliage, aiming straight at her.

Before she could pull her trigger, Ben climbed over the rim. His anguished "No!" tore through the air and he hurled himself at Dixon—and into the path of the firing Winchester.

She saw Ben jerk from the impact and drop to the ground. Fury blinded her and she pulled the trigger. Dixon's body flew back against a tree and stayed there, caught lifelessly on a sturdy pine bough.

Ben didn't move. She saw a bright red stain spread across his back, even from a distance.

Don't let him he dead.

CHAPTER SEVENTEEN

There was so much blood. She didn't see him breathing. Polly's hands shook as she checked for a pulse.

"I'm alive, damn it," Ben bit out between clenched teeth. "If I were dead, I wouldn't hurt like this."

Thank God. A cry escaped, and she wrapped her arms around him. She knew she had to tend to his wound, but she just had to hold him, to feel him alive in her arms. As she'd scrambled up the side of the canyon, she feared she would never hold him again.

"Good thing I have a wife with experience tending bullet wounds." He rolled over, his gaze latching onto hers, full of pain.

"Good thing." Polly fought to hold back her fear. She shook with it, but she had to be calm. Ben needed her. She tore open her saddlebags and laid out her supplies. "I have to see the wound."

He nodded and gritted his teeth as her fingers probed. "The bullet went straight through."

"It did." It was a shoulder wound—not a bad one, but a bloody one. She tapped out a needle from its protective sleeve. A spool of thread rolled into her lap.

"I've never seen you sew, Polly." Ben gazed up at her, dazed with pain.

"I told you the only sewing I know how to do is for a bullet wound." She swabbed at the injury.

"I trust you to save my life." He managed only a half smile, but the truth of it shone in his eyes, rumbled in his voice, and filled her heart.

He woke to a haze of pain. He saw a roof overhead, the boards dark and weathered, and felt the heat from a fire. He moved his head, despite the bolt of pain through his shoulder. Polly knelt before the fire, pouring a cup of coffee.

"I could use some of that." He sat up and realized he was in one of the broken-down shanties in the old hideout.

"You, sir, are supposed to be sleeping."

"I'm too tough to let a bullet wound keep me down for long."

"Sure, that's why you've been out for three whole days."

She came to him, and like a balm to his soul, she healed him. The pain in his shoulder didn't matter. Only she did, this incredible woman he never wanted to disappoint again.

The coffee tasted hot and steadying. He drained the cup, then accepted the bowl of soup she'd made. He was hungry—that was a good sign. He felt like hell, but he figured he could ride.

"What do you think you're doing?" She caught his arm, pushing him back down into the bed roll.

"We're fugitives. We can't lie around with a fire going-"

"The posse came close, but they lost our trail. I went back and erased every trace of our tracks I could find."

She kept her hand firmly to his chest. "I might never conquer the Family Sunshine stove, but I can outwit a posse at twelve paces."

"My kind of woman." Ben tried to pull her to his chest,

but she slipped away.

Was she still mad at him, still hurt? Well, trust would take a long time to rebuild, but he would do it. He would spend the rest of his life showing Polly how much he loved her.

"I'm ready to ride." He sat up. Only inches separated them. His gaze fastened on her bottom lip, lush and kissable. He knew just how she would taste—a little wild, a little tame, and infinitely loving.

She whipped away before he could kiss her. He heard the clatter of enamelware as she dropped the bowl. "I'll ride with you to fetch Emily. You'll probably want to start over somewhere else under a different name."

"I'm not running anywhere." He grimaced, fighting the pain, and stood. "I told you, my fugitive days are over."

"Well, I'm not going to explain to Emily why her Pa is behind bars instead of in front of them." Her voice sounded thick. He took a few steps until he could see her tensed profile, visible pain tightening her mouth and furrowing lines at her brow.

Love struck him like the cold edge of a winter storm—bracing and frightening. He shook with it and he welcomed it. He limped over to her and reached out, needing to hold her, needing her in his arms, against his heart.

She dodged him with expert skill. "I washed and stitched up your shirt. The patch isn't too good, but it'll hold until you reach Idaho."

"Polly, forget Idaho. I'm not running. I just need to speak with the governor." He hauled her into his arms, even when she tried to fight. But she didn't fight too hard. She buried her face against his chest and held him tight. He breathed in the scent of her hair— woman and spice— and gave thanks that it was her and not Pauline Curtis who'd stepped foot off that stage.

"Why do you need to see the governor?" She lifted her face to look at him.

He saw the exhaustion bruising the skin beneath her eyes. He saw the lines of worry. She'd taken care of him all by herself, moved him from the canyon's rim down to this shanty, and healed him.

"I have two months until I'm pardoned." He pressed a kiss to her brow. "It's a deal I struck when I learned I was going to be a father. I turned over all the information I knew on the outlaws in this territory. The governor said I had seven years to prove my worth—to make a new life, live quietly, make a contribution to my community. And I'm almost there."

Her mouth twisted. "You should have told me."

"I should have." He pulled her into his arms before she could move away. He didn't want to ever let go of her. "I should have told you a lot of things."

"I have something to show you." She took his hand and led him out into the bitter cold. Inches-thick frost crusted the world.

Ben followed, grimacing every time he accidentally moved the muscles along his left shoulder and back. Polly pulled aside a spray of berry bushes to expose the dark mouth of a small cave.

She gestured at the strong boxes tucked against one wall. "The gold."

* * *

"You're a free man, MacLain." Marshal Powers met him at the steps in the shadow of the distinguished brick building. Cold rain fell and he pulled his hat against the driving winds. "How does it feel?"

"Damn good. I've worked hard to put the past behind me."

"Now you have." The marshal nodded toward the crowded hitching post. The territorial capitol was busy, and the streets were crowded. "Anxious to get out of town?"

"And get back to my daughter." Ben turned at the light

sound of a woman's step behind him. "Excuse me."

Polly wore her denims and a heavy wool jacket. She looked feminine and tough, tender and strong. Her gaze sought his and he saw relief flicker across her beautiful face.

She ambled past him, headed for the hitching post. "So, they let you go."

"I guess they figured that after seven good years, they'll trust me not to return to my outlaw ways." He trailed her, never letting her out of his sight. "That is, unless my wife is a bad influence on me. She's wanted for robbery."

"You're in luck. Marshal Powers saw to it that the charges were dropped." The bitter cold made the leather reins stiff, and she yanked at the stubborn knot with nervous fingers.

"Going somewhere?" He leaned back against the wood post and looked at her. He took pleasure in this woman who was all his.

"I'm going back to Indian Trails." But she didn't seem happy about it. The knot gave, and she gathered the reins. "I need to explain to Emily. And to say goodbye."

"Why goodbye?"

Her face clouded. "Because I don't want to ride off and leave her wondering why I'd broken all my promises to her."

His heart cracked. "Why are you breaking promises?"

"They were never mine to begin with." She swung into the saddle.

Ben caught Renegade's bit, holding her still. "Emily's going to be disappointed."

"So am I." Her chin wobbled, but she was pure steel.

"She loves you, Polly. I know you can't ride away from that."

A muscle twitched in her jaw. "I love her, too. But it's not enough. It's not enough for her or for me."

"Are you saying you don't love me?"

"Something like that."

He released the bit and she backed the horse onto the street. He mounted Fugitive and headed off after her.

"You're crying," he commented when he'd caught up to her.

"Impossible." She tossed her head. "I never cry."

"You saved my life." His voice rumbled low. "You saved me, Polly."

Despite the noise of the streets and the bustle of traffic, she heard every word. And it sparked through her like air to flame.

"I don't have to listen to this." She pressed Renegade into a steady lope.

Ben caught up. "I admit I was wrong. I should have told you that I loved you. I should have opened up my heart and said the words that would have made you believe. Words that would make you stay."

"You don't love me, Ben. You never did." But her chin kept wobbling and those aching, horrible tears kept burning behind her eyes.

"How do you know?"

"I saw it in a thousand different ways—how you touched me and how you loved me. That you never lost your temper when I ruined your laundry or said a thing about the scrapes on your buggy." How it hurt to talk like this. She pressed her mouth shut, trying hard to keep the pain inside.

The traffic thinned as the town street led them into the country. Ben's hand clamped around her thighs. The next thing she knew he was lifting her into his saddle. He eased her between the cradle of his thighs, so snug she could feel him from toe to chin. Her body cried out with want for him. Her heart ached.

"I was afraid to say the words." He pressed a kiss to the back of her neck. "I was afraid to let anyone into my heart. That's a scary thing, loving someone more than your own life."

She nodded. "I know something about that."

"I thought you might." His arms wrapped around her, strong and sure. "I took this bullet for you."

"I saw. You stupidly threw yourself in front of Dixon's gun." She closed her eyes and saw it again, the horrible moment after the gun fired and Ben slumped to the ground. "You took a bullet meant for me."

"I sure did. It hurt like hell, but it's nothing compared to the pain I'd feel if I lost you. I'd do anything for you, even trade my life for yours. Don't you know that by now?"

"I do." And that was the problem. She shook with it, with the horrible agony of letting go of the one thing that had kept her safe all these years.

How could she let go of her independence? How could she let herself need him so much? It felt as if her very life depended upon his love for her, and that left her far too vulnerable.

"I just want you beside me." Ben's words stroked the curve of her jaw. His lips pressed there, to her windburned skin, and spread warmth. "That's all. I want you, Polly Brown."

"Polly MacLain," she corrected.

He pressed another kiss to her face. "Stay and be my wife, Polly MacLain. There is no one I need more than you."

She felt it—the change in the air and in her heart. Snow feathered down with the wind, falling with a gentle ease that gave her hope and gave her peace.

Love wasn't dependence; it was strength. It was choice. She could walk away now, cowardly protecting her heart, fearing that someone as noble and wonderful as Ben could never really love her, plain old Polly Brown.

Except she wasn't plain old Polly Brown anymore. She was Polly MacLain. She was a part owner in a gold claim. She had a beautiful daughter she loved with all her heart. And she had a husband—a man who'd willingly taken a bullet for her.

For her.

Because he loved her.

Their pasts no longer had a hold on either one of them. They were free to live their lives as they chose.

Polly laid her hand on Ben's and twined her fingers through his. She made her choice, one of the heart. "Let's head home."

The sleepy town of Indian Trails never looked so good. A thick mantle of snow clung to trees and roofs and covered the streets. It accumulated on the top of hitching posts, awnings and boardwalks.

As they rode through town, Woody stepped out of the jailhouse to wave in greeting. Mrs. Wu stepped out of her laundry shop, with envelopes to mail in hand, and called out a warm hello.

Emily burst out of Adella's house with a slam of the door. "Polly! Pa! You're back!"

Polly swung down and held out her arms. Her daughter flew against her, and she held the little girl tight. "We had business to take care of, but we're back for keeps now."

"Forever and ever?"

"And even longer than that." Ben knelt down to brush a kiss to his daughter's brow.

"Look at the snow." Emily shivered.

Polly swung off her coat, faster than Ben, who was doing the same, and settled the warm wool around her child's shoulders. "I see. We rode through it all the way across the mountains."

"I'm so glad you came back," Emily confessed as Ben swung her up on Renegade's back.

Ben was there, giving Polly his coat. The wool was warm from his body and smelled like his soap and his scent. She breathed it in, no longer afraid to feel love.

Their house was a welcome sight, shrouded with pristine snow. It was like a picture in a storybook—the falling flakes were a mist cloaking the beautiful castle. Well, their castle was a log cabin, but it was close enough.

Emily slid to the ground, and Polly dismounted after her. Already the child was off, running through the untouched snow.

Ben's hand found hers, and he pressed the length of his body against her. "It's not long until suppertime. And then after we put Emily to bed, I'm going to make love to you until the sun rises."

"I'm going to make you keep that promise." She leaned back against him, savoring the feel of his arms holding her tight. "I love you, Ben."

"I love you more." His kiss tasted like snowflakes and promises. "I'll never let you doubt that again."

"Polly, come look!" Emily shouted. "I made a snow angel."

Some dreams were meant to come true Polly thought, as she joined her daughter in the yard. She spread her arms wide and fell back into the downy snow. She looked up to see Ben at her feet, gazing at her with love in his eyes.

A forever kind of love she would never doubt again.

He fell into the snow beside her. They all three flapped their arms together, making wings and laughter and memories to last the rest of their lives.

# # #

The Wedding Vow

England—during the Reign of King Henry I

"Quickly, now. The road is not far." Gwyneth pushed back the woolen cloak, exposing her face and ears to the bitter night wind.

"But milady, I—"

Determined to ignore more of the girl's complaints, Gwyneth broke through low brush and across rough ground. A steep rise ascended into the darkness. She gathered her skirts and searched with one foot for purchase.

"Milady." Ivy's urgency whispered above the creak of the bare tree limbs overhead as they rubbed together in the heady wind. "A ghost lives. I saw it slither upon the ground behind us. I swear my life upon it!"

"Ghosts do not exist Tell yourself that and it will go away. I promise it."

Whilst Gwyneth loved her young companion dearly, she had more dire concerns. All depended upon her success with the traveling merchant this night. She could not miss him. She could not wait through another new moon to escape to see the king. And escape she would. No matter the cost.

Determination weakened her fear of heights.

Gwyneth settled the bulging sack against her side. Her breath fogged in the bitter night air. Frozen grass crunched beneath her feet as she approached the high embankment. *I can do this. I have little choice.*

The frozen ground supported her weight as she struggled higher. Then a root gave way and she slid a good three feet until her toe caught against a rock. She huffed in exasperation.

By the rood, she had no time for this! If she was not at the designated place by midnight, when the merchant passed (on his way to more clandestine transactions no doubt), he would not wait for her.

Fie! Her foot slipped again. She dangled by one hand. Fearing a long fall, she scrambled for a hold.

"Milady," Ivy hissed, urgency great in that pronounced whisper. "I told myself ghosts don't exist, just like you said."

"Good." Gwyneth cast her gaze up at the sky. The full moon peered between foggy clouds, high at the hill's zenith. 'Twas already midnight! She had to hurry or all would be lost.

"But the ghost that does not exist brushed against my ankle."

"Impossible." Gwyneth grabbed hold of an exposed tree root and pulled herself up and over the embankment. She looked left, then right. No one approached on the dark road.

"Now it circles down below." Ivy grunted as the earth beneath her feet began to slip. "Look and see for yourself."

"I cannot see what does not exist." Gwyneth untied the bundle from around her neck, set it safely on a moss-covered boulder, and dropped to her knees. She clasped Ivy's wrists and pulled the plump girl up onto solid ground.

"Oomph." Ivy righted herself, pulling twigs and clods of dirt from her hair. " 'Tis dangerous. We ought to take the main pathway to the road."

"Nay, 'twould be worse. Thieves and outlaws, is why." These were desperate times. Gwyneth had learned at far too young an age the nature of men and the lawless rules of the land, of how one stronger could take from those not as strong simply because he could. "Look to. Someone approaches."

With any luck, she hadn't missed the merchant

"The ghost! It comes." Ivy grabbed her hand, frantic. "Run, milady. Run for your life."

"Nonsense." Gwyneth had the blood of knights coursing in her veins. She refused to run, just as she refused to admit her fear.

Yet Ivy was frightened. Gwyneth unsheathed her dagger. The sharp blade of the long metal knife glinted in the silvered moonlight. "Ivy, stay and meet the merchant. I will see what has followed us. Probably one of the lambs, no doubt, escaped from its mother."

"Careful," Ivy warned, her voice low and wobbling in apprehension.

"Call to me when he arrives. Loudly, so I hear you." Gwyneth tossed a smile at her friend.

Ivy only frowned, huddling afraid and cold in the center of the lane.

Gwyneth peered over the edge of the embankment She saw a hundred shades of darkness and shadow, the smooth curves of naked limbs. She saw the craggy face of a gray boulder brushed in moonlight, the shiver of grass in the north wind. But no ghosts. Not one.

"There is naught amiss." She sheathed her dagger, certain they were safe.

"He comes." Ivy's response sounded strangled. "Gwyneth?"

"Aye."

THE WEDDING VOW

"Why would a merchant wear chain mail?"

"A merchant would not." Gwyneth turned her back on the embankment to cast her gaze up the road. The faint gleam of moonlight glittered on the thousand links of a metal shirt, the smooth roundness of a helm, the shield of a man hidden behind weapons and armor.

Had they missed the merchant? Gwyneth felt her hope dwindle, ebbing away like blood from an open wound. She knew what this meant. No escape from either the endless days of backbreaking work beneath her uncle's roof or the latent threat from the lord who ruled this land.

Agony tore through her. How could it be? How could she endure it? Worse, how could she have allowed herself to be so late?

"He's a wraith, a demon ghost in warrior shape. Look how he hovers!" Ivy crossed herself and ran like a madwoman down the road.

"Easy, Ivy. Look, he is only a man. His horse is black, 'tis why you cannot see it." Gwyneth tried to calm her friend, but even the danger from a man and not a ghost was great. "Quick, down the embankment. We must hide."

No one must know of their presence here, not even a strange knight who may or may not try to harm them. Gwyneth snatched the bundle from its perch atop the boulder.

"Hold!" The knight's voice boomed like thunder, rumbling and echoing through the night.

A strap on the sack snagged and caught. Gwyneth gave it a tug. She could not leave her precious goods to be discovered. Yet she could not risk being taken— or worse. She released the bundle and ran.

A scream tore through the night. Ivy scrambled back up the embankment, eyes wild, hair and skirts flying. Gwyneth's jaw dropped as the knight, faceless in the shadows, lifted his sword and charged. He meant to kill Ivy!

Astonishment gave way to action. Gwyneth ran and

shoved her young friend to the ground with one quick push. Ivy cried out in surprise, but Gwyneth knew only that she was safe. Jaw set, she caught sight of the murderous knight's sword lifted high, shimmering and lethal.

Too late to grab her dagger.

"Run, Ivy!" Gwyneth closed her eyes and waited for the blow. Better her than sweet Ivy, who had a future to look forward to.

The stallion brushed past her in a rush, and the low, guttural battle cry of the knight tore apart the silence. Gwyneth spun around and saw a dark form impaled on the warrior's sword. Crimson dripped to the ground.

"I would not kill a woman, even you, Gwyneth of Blackthorne."

"How do you know me?"

"I thought you might remember," the knight mused.

"Remember you? I cannot see your face."

He did not answer. He circled his stallion in the shadows of the road and lowered his blade. The dark form slithered to the ground, the dead body of a wolf.

Ivy screamed at the sight and fainted in the center of the road.

"She appears to be overwrought." His voice caressed the words, low like a joke but coupled with concern. "Were there more predators?"

"I do not know." Gwyneth darted around the enormous black stallion. She tried to sneak a glance at the knight's face, still hidden in darkness, and saw naught. Yet she felt his scrutiny like a cold blade against her cheek.

Concern for Ivy overrode her curiosity. Gwyneth knelt beside her friend's prone body and felt a pulse. Strong and steady. It was as she thought Ivy had a terrible fright, 'twas all. She needed only to be roused and all would be well.

"The wolf was a loner. See how silver marks his face? He was old and looked for easy prey."

As did any of the lone knights who traveled these

roads, striking with ruthlessness and the might of their swords. Again, she wondered how this warrior knew her. Or knew of her enough to recognize her in the dark. She was glad of the dagger tucked within the folds of her mantle. Very glad. Gwyneth's fingers trembled as she patted Ivy's face. The girl murmured, giving Gwyneth hope.

"Surely she lives." His chain mail jingled, lending an unnatural sound to the nighttime woods.

"Surely." Gwyneth watched Ivy's eyelids flutter. The maid was awakening. "Ivy, can you hear me? Try to sit up."

The horse strode closer with the faceless knight, cloaked in darkness, upon it. "I shall take you both to the village."

"We are in no need of assistance." Now that Ivy was attempting to sit, Gwyneth could take stock of their situation. A chivalrous knight did not exist, she had learned the hard way. A knight thought only to benefit himself. 'Twas best to avoid the lot of them. "Ride on, knight."

"So little appreciation from a woman nearly killed by a wolf." He leaned one steeled fist on his thigh, broadening the set of his solid shoulders. "Aye, I remember now. Your father's land was seized. I never heard what became of his daughter."

"Who are you?" Surely this nosy man was a rogue. How did he know of her? "Come out of the shadows. I want to see your face."

"'Tis my wish always to oblige a lady." His voice came velvet soft, but she heard the steely authority beneath.

Not a man to trust.

The warhorse sidled closer, silvered by the faintest moonlight. She saw chain mail glittering across a broad chest and down powerful arms. Then the moon dusted his face and she saw at once the strong cut of a square jaw, a straight blade of a nose, and piercing eyes, their color lost to her in the shades of night.

Recognition pounded beneath her breastbone, building with each beat. "Bran, the second son of this land's baron."

Of the land's murdering baron. Her knees wobbled. "Have you come searching for me?"

Her uncle, during a fit of vile temper, would often threaten to hand her over to the baron. To a man who had ended the sweet life she'd known and made her an orphan, then a hated wife.

"Nay, I come to see my kin." Bran the Fair, as they called him, dismounted with a steady confidence, but not with the brashness of many famed knights. "Let me think. 'Twas rumored an aunt had taken you."

"She died last year. I didn't know you would remember a scrawny girl who climbed apple trees." The warmth of the memory came quickly and far too harshly. Gwyneth turned from his handsome face. 'Twas best not to remember those times, what could never be again.

Ivy rubbed her head, returning to a state of calm. Gwyneth spoke in low tones to her friend, the young companion found for her all those long years ago. She felt pleased the girl appeared stronger.

But the knight—he kept watching her. He strode past them, a shining silver man in the night "I know what my family took from you."

"You know naught." She held back the heat of her bitterness.

"I know my father is a cruel, unjust man." Bran knelt to wipe his blade clean in the grass at the roadside, then sheathed it. "You have every right to hate him."

"Hate is too kind for what I feel." She turned her back to him when Ivy moaned. "Here, dear one, try to stand."

Bran towered over her, all substance and will and power. "I am bastard born and no true part of that family." His declaration made her spine tingle and threatened to touch the grief concealed in her heart.

She did not seek alliances, as he did. She only sought seclusion. "You have helped us this night, and I am grateful. Now I must ask you to leave us be."

"But your maid is not yet strong. I will take you both to the village."

She bristled. Help? She would not accept it from anyone spawned by the man who had betrayed her father. From anyone who would give her pity. "We do not need you, Bran the Fair. Be on your way."

" 'Tis not right to leave you here in the road. Be sensible. Come with me. 'Tis a fair walk home."

"I have no home, thanks to your father."

He stepped back, a man of steel and power, but when he spoke, his words were kind. "Hate my father, Gwyneth. But remember I am not responsible for his deeds."

"I hate you just the same."

He watched her turn away and saw her thin, rigid back. She was all skinny arms as she struggled to help her friend walk. The tension held in Gwyneth's body was as easy to see as the stones in the road.

All these years, he hadn't thought of her. He'd had no real reason to. But the memories drifted back, the image of a very young girl's sweetness, of how she'd once chased him in the orchards. Why, she had been able to climb almost as high as he could. He spent one summer over a dozen years ago fostered by Gwyneth's father, once a great knight. Ere the feud, ere he was betrayed.

Aye, it hurt to look at her. Once dressed in riches, now she wore peasant's garb, old and worn and roughly made. But the look of exhaustion she shouldered saddened him more. He guessed that she endured a hard life, and even harder work filled her days.

"Where do you live now?" He shouldn't care, but he had to know. Or he would think of naught else the night through.

"My uncle has remarried since my aunt's passing. I have been allowed to remain." The sadness in her voice betrayed her. She moved efficiently as if still the lord's daughter.

"I see. You live in the village then?"

"Aye. And work there, too." Still, she did not face him. "I thought I bid you to go, Bran the Fair. Leave us."

He saw the tiny bumps of her spine through the cloth, the lean lines of her shoulder blades and the knobs of her elbows. Too skinny. From too much work, or too little food?

The plump young woman stood on wobbly feet and tossed him a dimpled smile. "You slew the wolf. I thought he was a ghost after my soul."

"I always offer what protection I can to pretty maidens," he returned, uncomfortable as always with the killing he did for a living, even if this night it were a beast and not a human.

The maid bobbed a curtsy, blushing. But Gwyneth— why, she was another matter entirely. She arched one brow. Not even the night shadows could hide her distrust of him, yet he could not in good conscience leave her here unaided.

"If I cannot offer a ride to the village, what can I do for you?"

"You can do as I have asked." Gwyneth met his gaze, defiant, her chin set. "Ride on, Bran. Go to your father the murderer. We have no need for a bastard like you."

Anger threatened, but then he heard the fear in her words, the tears hidden beneath a voice false with hatred. She did not hate, as she claimed. Nay, it was a deeper, more broken emotion she hid. A grief so great she could not speak of it

Nor would he. He could not help her. He would do as she asked. Perhaps he would find a way to offer his help at a later time. If she would accept it.

Bran rode on, against his better judgment. With every step of his stallion down the lane, Bran's troubled mind filled with thoughts of her—thoughts of the sad-eyed woman and her stalwart concern for her lowborn maid.

His heart squeezed, as if he harbored feelings for her, for ungrateful Gwyneth of Blackthorne. Yet he remembered the young girl who laughed in the orchards, tripping over her skirts, her voice sweet, like summer sunshine.

He would ask questions about her later, learn what he could. But now . . . his gaze drifted ahead of him, to the road of stone and dirt, then beyond to the forest of trees and fern.

He had grave fears this night His father lay dying. Bran's courage faltered. What awaited him at Blackthorne Keep? He had traveled far to beg for the right to see the old man. Much too far to be tossed aside yet again, the bastard son of a long-forgotten leman.

All the respect he'd earned by his sword had little altered his father's opinion of him. Bran spurred his stallion into a canter. There, along the crest of the hill, loomed the keep, dark and distinctly manmade against the gentle rolling forms of vale and hill.

The wind kicked up from the north, hard as a gale, and yet it was not as cold as the trepidation licking his spine.

ABOUT THE AUTHOR

Jillian Hart makes her home in Washington State, where she has lived most of her life. When Jillian is not writing away on her next book, she can be found reading, going to lunch with friends and spending quiet evenings at home with her family.

Made in the USA
Lexington, KY
17 October 2013